The
Red Line

NIKKI JEWELL

Book Cover by Sweet 15 Designs LLC

First edition 2024

Special Edition Paperback ISBN: 978-1-7382632-2-6

Dear, Mom. Thanks for the lifetime love of reading. I know how much you love a little spice, but please, I'm begging you, don't read this book.

CW & TW

Content Warning

Thanks for choosing The Red Line. Here's a few things you should know going in. There may be some spoilers, so feel free to skip if you've got no triggers.

This is a steamy romance novel and contains explicit open door sexual situations, as well as alcohol consumption, The hockey boys are a little crude and use a fair bit of adult language, so if this offends you than this isn't the book for you. This is intended for a mature over eighteen audience.

Some events or situations may be triggering for some including past trauma that includes the death of a sibling.

I care about my readers well being and mental health.

1. VIOLET – BAD SUNS
2. SATURDAY SUN – VANCE JOY
3. COLORING OUTSIDE THE LINES – MISTERWIVES
4. TALKING BODY – TOVE LO
5. WINDOW – MAGIC GIANT
6. NEW RELIGION – THE HEYDAZE
7. AMERICA'S SWEETHEART – ELLE KING
8. WOMAN – KESHA, THE DAP-KINGS HORNS
9. BAD IDEA RIGHT? – OLIVIA RODRIGO
10. TALK TOO MUCH – COIN
11. I WANT YOU – DREAM WIFE
12. AND SO IT WENT (FEAT. TOM MORELLO) – THE PRETTY RECKLESS
13. LET'S MAKE OUT – DREAM WIFE
14. UNSTOPPABLE – SIA
15. 1950 – KING PRINCESS
16. WHERE DO YOU RUN – THE SCORE
17. DO MY OWN THING – AMERICAN AUTHORS
18. CHASIN' HONEY – WILD PARTY
19. I JUST WANNA SHINE – FITZ AND THE TANTRUMS
20. FALLING LIKE THE STARS – JAMES ARTHUR

CHAPTER ONE

ENNUI AND HOCKEY

JACKS

N othing better than the after party when we snag the win. Dev hip checks me as I shove past him, leaning on the tarnished brass handle to get into Wright's Wingers. The noise level in our favorite hangout spot ratchets from zero to a hundred as soon as I step inside. The bar is jammed with college students looking for any excuse to celebrate. And a hockey win on our home turf is a fantastic reason.

"Jacks! Good game." Someone closes their damp palm around mine for a shake. There's a pat on my back from another rando before I've even pulled away.

I paste on a huge smile while glancing over the guy's shoulder. Looks like we'll be running the gauntlet to get to our unofficially reserved booth in the back corner. My eyes skate over the girls in short, tight dresses that are totally unsuitable for late fall in Michigan. But given the oppressive heat of the place, I kind of wish I was wearing something a little skimpier. The drawback would be all those long fingernails brushing my bare skin as I push through. No thanks. I'll save that for the lady I choose to take home with me. She's welcome to leave behind some scratch marks if she's so inclined.

Dev, Beau, and Seb have all fought their way to our spot and claimed their seats when I slide with a squeak onto the torn red leather bench seat. Aspen sits down across from me a moment later, pulling his girlfriend Jordan onto his lap. She giggles, giving me a view of her curly red hair as she leans down to snag a kiss.

I look away, flipping open the top couple buttons of the dress shirt that's trying to strangle me. Those two are lifers for sure. And yes, Jordan's a fantastic woman, but that's not for me. I've got the rest of my life to settle down.

College should be about seizing every opportunity to experience life. Sure, other than ice time, most of my experiences are in bedrooms. Or bathrooms, kitchens, couches, cars. It's more about the woman than the location. I did the whole boyfriend thing in high school. Haven't met anyone I'm interested in trying that out with again, especially after the way it played out. So, I stick to one-night stands. I prefer a little variety in my life anyway.

Speaking of variety...

"Ladies." A slow smile curls my lips, while I lean back in my seat admiring the brunette and blonde heading our way.

They're both fantastic. Long, lean bodies, short tight black dresses. I could go either way with the almost matched set. The brunette's hair falls around her face in loose waves, while the blonde has hers pulled back in a sleek high ponytail, perfect for wrapping around my fist. Yes. That's the one for me.

"Hey, beautiful."

Her chocolate eyes light up at my greeting and she gives me a wide smile, baring her perfect white teeth. Golden tanned skin is exposed by her tiny dress. It's gotta be from a bottle or a tanning bed. Sunbathing in Michigan in late fall is not a thing.

"Hi, Jackson." My lips slide into a smile that has her leaning in a little closer, sending a wave of perfume my way. The overly sweet candy scent wrinkles my nose.

There's no space left in the booth we're packed into, so she drops onto my lap, and I automatically curve my arm around her torso. Her friend pulls up a chair.

"That was an epic goal, captain. That backhand. Saweet!" Beau says to Aspen as the crack of their palms slamming together rings out above the excited roar of the bar. He swings around to me. "And I guess you can have a teeny, tiny bit of the credit too, almost captain. Your slapshot was acceptable."

"Fuck off. It was an epic goal, and you know it." I let my hand curl into a fist to give his palm a punch instead of the high five he's waiting for. "And all that, even while trying to hold together this chaos." Almost captain, my ass. Thinks he's hilarious. He just wishes he was picked as the alternate this year. Better luck next year when I've graduated.

We're still riding the adrenaline high from our game as we cut in on each other's comments, voices getting louder as we sip away at the pitcher of beer the waitress dropped at our table, compliments of who knows. Someone sent it over for us.

There's an electric vibe in the crowded bar tonight. The buzz of excitement in the room would usually have me hyped, but tonight it feels a little oppressive, like a vice tightening around my chest. After a devastating loss in the finals last year, we're under so much pressure to prove ourselves and get the win in our last run at the championship trophy before we graduate. Not to mention the looming shift into a pro hockey career next year.

Even the guys rehashing every single play we made on the ice are grating a little on me, since we're going to be doing the same thing with the team and coaches tomorrow. Usually, I live for the post game rehash, but tonight I'm feeling a little off.

I've almost forgotten about the girl in my lap when she interrupts our discussion of the one goal Jensy let in. "Jackson, can you get me a drink?" There's a whiny tone to her voice. Am I being a bit of an asshole? Maybe, but she's the one who invited herself over. It's not like I requested her presence.

"Sure. What do you want?"

"Rum and Coke, please."

"You're gonna have to get off if you want me to go to the bar."

A high-pitched titter comes out of her mouth. "Right, yeah. It's just so comfortable here."

I nod, but I'm not sure I agree. I lift her off my lap, rubbing my leg where the bones in her ass were digging into it, and stand up.

The crowd around the bar is three people deep. I flash a smile, but I'm not going to be pushy and use my hockey status to butt in. Not my style.

I shift from one foot to the other in the small space as people crowd in around me. Bare skin slightly sticky with sweat brushes my arm, but I resist the urge to wipe it away. The pretty bartender with the short blond hair finally makes eye contact.

"What'll you have?"

"A Rum and Coke, please." I eye the few sips left in my beer. Better not. "And a water."

Her smile looks genuine as she fills up a plastic cup for me. "I heard it was a good game tonight. You've got a solid team this year." She stops the taps, sliding my drink across the well-worn wooden surface.

"Too bad you couldn't come. It was a good one." The bar is sticky under my elbows as I lean in.

She shrugs. "Yup. Work. I finish at two. If you're still up, send me a text." Her eyes slide down my body as she scribbles her number on a napkin.

"Thanks..." My eyes flick down to the napkin. "Taylor. I'll keep that in mind."

I stuff her number in my back pocket, weaving through the crowd to our table. Blondie is practically on top of Seb when I get back. The small lines around his mouth show a little strain, and he's leaning away from her.

She looks up when I tap her shoulder. "Here's your drink, milady." I dip into a bow, and she laughs.

Seb's shoulders ease up and the tension in his hazel eyes clears as she focuses her attention back on me. Her white-tipped talons close around the drink she requested, while I drain half my water cup in one draw. The icy liquid burns the back of my throat, but I don't mind. Fuck, I'm thirsty after the game. The mediocre beer did nothing for me.

I fall back into conversation with my teammates, sipping at my water. It always comes back to hockey. Beau and Dev are bickering in the corner about some play while blondie traces idle circles on the back of my hand.

Blondie must be getting bored, because she twists around, reaching up to tug on the back of my head and attempting to whisper in my ear. "Let's go back to your place." Her voice is too loud, and her breath is hot on my sticky neck. I look down at her, then back at the guys and weigh my options, stifling a yawn. I'm not really feeling the party tonight, so I give her a nod. May as well have some company if I'm gonna split.

She jumps to her feet, linking her arm through mine. Her eyes are clear, and she didn't even finish half of the drink I grabbed for her, so I'm pretty sure she's not intoxicated.

"Jacksy!!!! You leaving us?" Beau smirks from under the disheveled swoop of hair hanging in his eyes. The heat in here has even done some damage to his perfectly gelled coif of dark blonde hair.

Dev uncrosses his massive biceps to offer a fist bump. His bulk barely fits behind the table in our booth.

"Have fun." Aspen's eyes are telling me to be safe, so I give my captain a nod. He's got the major responsibility of keeping us all in line. I'm just the backup.

I turn to the girl whose name I still haven't gotten. "You wanna say bye to your friend?" Don't girls have some sort of stay safe girl code or something? Usually, they make a big deal of saying loud goodbyes when you take them home.

Her eyes flick to the brunette she came in with who seems to have gotten bored with the hockey team. She's moved over to the next table and has already perched herself on the knee of one of the mountainous football players. Braxton, I think? Football is not my sport of choice, so I'm not that familiar with the team.

"It's fine. She's busy." She waves dismissively at her friend, turning back to focus all her attention on me.

"Okay." I shrug, leading her out through the crowd. You'd think leaving a bar would be a simple task. Not so much.

"Leaving so soon?" A cute redhead pouts at me. Her narrowed eyes send laser beams at the blonde clinging to my arm as if she just won a pageant and I'm the coveted tiara.

Fuck, this is a lot.

The energy of a crowd usually jazzes me up, but tonight I really need to get out of here.

We finally make our way through the mass of people riding high on our win. I pause near the entrance. "Did you bring a coat?"

"Nope." Her glossy pink lips push out and she flicks her eyes to mine as if she's trying to see if her studied move worked. It did, but she's looking at the wrong place. My cock twitches to life, straining my zipper at the thought of those full lips wrapped around it. Maybe this was the right decision. My vibe's been all off tonight, but nothing like a hot and eager woman underneath me to fix that.

The chilly November wind is soothing after the stifling heat as the two of us step through the front door. Wright's is a great spot, but one of its best features? Walking distance to our house. I'm kinda glad we came out tonight, otherwise our place would have been overflowing with all the well wishers. Peace and quiet would be nothing but a hope and a dream with everyone partying at our house.

High winds are whipping the trees into a frenzy. It doesn't bother me, but I feel bad for the guys on the team who grew up in warmer climates. Michigan in winter can suck, but nothing this Ontario boy isn't used to.

Blondie is shivering, bare arms clutched around her torso. "How far is your car?"

"Car? I didn't bring a car. We're walking."

She stumbles on the heels that make her legs look fucking incredible, but probably don't make for easy walking on the cobbled pathway. "I'm not walking."

"The team house isn't far. Twenty minutes, tops."

"Twenty minutes? Um. It's freaking freezing." Her shoulders shudder as if she's trying to punctuate her point, and she glances down at her ridiculous shoes.

I sigh. "Fine. I'll call us a ride." Twenty minutes might be a simple walk for me, but I'm wearing comfortable kicks.

She plasters her shivering body to my side when we get to the sidewalk in front of the bar.

I bite my tongue to keep in the comment about wearing a coat in the winter, instead sliding my thick winter jacket off my shoulders. I may not be looking for a relationship, but I'm not a complete asshole.

The dark cloud on her face brightens up when I help her slip my coat over her arms. She takes a deep inhale, and a quiver of unease stirs in the pit of my stomach. I really hope she's not reading too much into this. It's just a coat, not an engagement ring. At least she's not complaining anymore.

It's never a problem to catch a ride around here, but a chill has set into my bones in the couple of minutes that pass before a white Honda Civic pulls up to the curb.

The tidy white porch stretching across the front of our shared house is a welcome sight as we pull up in front.

The lock clicks open, and I usher her in, shoulders relaxing in the warmth of home. I'm never ashamed to bring girls back to our surprisingly clean and well-decorated place. Probably way too nice for the ragers we occasionally host, but I just live here. Beau's parents are like crazy rich, so they bought the place for him, and did it up all fancy. I'm not complaining.

Blondie makes a beeline for the couch, plopping down and ripping her heels off, but leaving my coat on and snuggling in. My eye twitches.

"You're kind of buried in there. How about I help you take that off?" I'm talking about the coat, but her eyes gleam. They're a hazy brown color, glazing over with lust.

She tucks her bottom lip between her teeth again, looking up at me with wide doe eyes. "Yes please, Jackson." It's grating on me a bit that she keeps using my full name as if we're long-lost friends or something.

"Call me, Jacks, beautiful."

The tension eases a little when I slide my coat off her shoulders, revealing long, lean arms begging for a trail of kisses. Her small hand is soft as I pick it up and press a kiss to her palm, then her delicate wrist and all the way up to her neck.

She's already squirming and moaning by the time I make it to that spot just under her jaw that drives most girls crazy. "Jackson," she moans, pulling me out of the moment.

"Jacks," I grumble.

Her eyes fly open. "Right, sorry. I just thought..." Her words trail off, so I lean in to capture her lush lower lip between my teeth.

She forgets whatever she was about to say, pressing in, returning my nips and licks.

"Fuck!" I yelp as icy hands creep under my shirt, stealing my breath for a moment.

"Sorry," she says.

I still her hands when she tries to pull them away. "It's fine, sweetheart. Just took me by surprise."

I grab the back of my shirt, ripping it off in a swift move that flexes my abs under her touch. The shivery sensation of her chilly hands running over my muscles has goose bumps popping up.

It takes no time to get her miniscule black dress peeled off, and it joins my shirt on the floor. My torso dwarfs hers as I press her back into the couch, sliding a hand up her side, and pausing before I snap her bra open.

"This okay?" She may have come back here with nothing but sex in her eyes, but I'm still going to ask.

"Oh God, Jackson. Yes, take it off. I need your hands."

The sight that greets me takes the edge off the irritation at her using my full name. A pair of fantastic, full tits topped with light pink nipples emerges from the black lace, and I bend down to suck one, then the other, into my mouth.

"These are fucking beautiful." A nice set of tits is my weakness. Big, small. I'm not picky. They're all gorgeous.

"That's what you said last time." It takes a minute for her words to sink in, but when they do, I let her nipple slip from my greedy lips.

"What?"

Her eyes are glossy with need when they land on my confused face.

"You said that last time."

I pull away from her nakedness, sitting up and running a hand through my hair.

"Last time?"

"Yeah. Last month, when we..." she trails off, narrowing her eyes.

"We..." I wait for her to elaborate as alarm bells start clanging in my head.

"Slept together." She sits up so fast I pull back to avoid getting conked in the chin by her head. "You don't...remember me?" The lust is all gone now, chased away by horror.

"Uh. Fuck." I don't sleep with the same girl twice. That's just asking for a stage-five-clinger type situation.

I rack my brain, trying to place her face. It would probably be rude if I asked her for details. A month ago. I shut my eyes, and then. There it is. Those big brown eyes staring at me while her red lipped mouth was wrapped around my cock at one of our house parties. I was kind of drunk that night, celebrating a win, and her hair was different. Darker blonde. The fuzzy details slip into place, but do you think I remember her name? Nope.

"You don't even know my name, do you?"

My stomach twists with that gut punch of fear you get when you walk into class, knowing full well you didn't finish the assignment you're supposed to be handing in.

"Fuck." I say again. Apparently, my brain has forgotten all other words at the moment.

"Oh my God. You're an asshole, you know that, Jackson? I thought you'd invited me over because you remembered me. I thought maybe we had something."

My hand goes up to scrub over my face. She thought we had something? In what universe...? I'm always perfectly clear that I'm only in it for the night, and never make promises I don't intend to keep, and yet here I am.

"I'm sorry..." The sentence dies a slow and painful death on its way out, since I realize I still don't have a freaking clue what her name is. Not even a first letter.

"You're disgusting. I'm out of here."

Her foot catches in between the couch cushions as she's scrambling up, but I grab her elbow to keep her from hitting the questionable carpet headfirst. The place is tidy...for a house full of hockey guys. But with the amount of people passing through at parties, who knows what germs are lurking in the threads of the grey carpet.

She rights herself, shaking free from my hold, yanking her dress up, and fumbling with her shoes and phone.

"Can I at least call you an Uber?" I ask, peeking at her from behind the hand I've got rubbing my temple.

"Fine," she huffs.

Relieved to be able to make it up to her in some small way, I swipe the app open, arranging for a ride from the closest car possible. "Five minutes."

"Good."

She jams those long legs back in the sparkly pink heels and picks up the tiny matching wallet thing she had slung around her wrist. Then does her best to stomp off to the front door to wait for her ride.

I push up off the couch on auto pilot, joining her at the door while staring at the tiny car approaching on my phone screen. Feels like about an hour of awkward silence passes before it arrives.

"It's here. Blue Corolla." I flash the license plate number at her.

"I can't say it's been fun, but my name is Kiera. If you're ever looking for more than one night, look me up."

My mouth drops open as I stare at her. Did she really offer herself up to me? After all that? Man, I don't have a fucking clue when it comes to women.

Her round ass wiggles its way out my front door and into the waiting car. I'm staring after it for way too long before I collapse back on the couch.

I'm not sure how much time I've spent staring at the wall when the door crashes open, jolting me out of my stupor. Loud laughter booms into the formerly quiet space.

"Jacks!!!" Dev crashes in, eying the empty space speculatively.

"Where's your girl? Did you scare her off?" Seb arches a dark brow at me. I've been railing him relentlessly about the new girl in his life that he's pretending isn't a thing, so I'm sure I'll never hear the end of this.

"I do not want to talk about it." My head tips back on the couch without much hope that the nosy bastards will leave it at that.

The cushions sink under the weight of Dev and Seb crashing to the couch on either side of me.

"If you don't share with the class, we're going to assume it's that your dick was too small for her," Dev says.

"Fuck you. You know that's not true." You can't be on a hockey team without seeing all the goods on the regular. Unfortunately.

"Must not have been working then. Poor Jacksy. I'm pretty sure I've got an email in my spam folder that can help you with that." Seb slides a thumb up his phone screen.

"Shut up." I shove at him. I'm glad he seems to have dug himself out of his funk, but does he really need to be such an asshole?

"What do you think, Dev?" Seb peers over me.

"Whiskey dick," Dev replies, running a hand along the top of his closely shorn head, giving me the evil smile that earned him the nickname Lucy, short for Lucifer.

"I wasn't even drinking." I'm going to have to tell these jerks. They won't leave me alone until I do. My eyes find their way to the ceiling. "I'd already slept with her."

Beau's leaning on the wall beside the bookcase, stomach shaking as a laugh spills out. At my expense. "Of course. Jacks never sleeps with the same girl twice. Are you telling me you didn't recognize her?"

I wince. "No." Wow, that sounds even worse than I thought.

"Holy shit. How did you figure it out?" Beau asks.

"She called me out."

"Oh man. Harsh, dude. Even for you."

"I know. I didn't even know her name. I am such an asshole. After she mentioned it, I did vaguely remember her." My hands are scrubbing at my face as if I can wipe away the shame.

"Well, I guess that's it. You've clearly made the rounds through the entire campus. I think you're gonna have to swear off girls for the rest of the year." Seb laughs as he says it, but there's a ring of truth to his words.

"Maybe I should. No more one-night stands." The thought of no more beautiful ladies in my life makes my poor dick sad, but it's probably the right thing to do. This is one of the most important years of my life in terms of locking down an NHL contract. I've got a promise to keep.

"What are you saying? Going to try out the girlfriend experience?" There's something in Seb's expression. An interest. He's got something going on. He used to be my wingman, but I haven't seen him with anyone since he started hanging with that chick, Abby. She's cute, but I almost lost an arm when I told him that, and I need my arms to hold my stick. Both of my sticks.

"Hell no. Not for me, but maybe I'll try lying low for a change." The g-word is a terrifying thought. I prefer to enjoy my ladies for the night and move on. Free and clear. I haven't met one since high school that I'd be willing to risk my heart on.

"Like no girls at all?" The smirk on Beau's face tells me he doesn't believe a word of it.

"Well, maybe not no girls. Don't get too crazy. I'll just be a little choosier."

Dev punches me in the shoulder with a bark of a laugh.

"I'll believe that when I see it, Jacks."

CHAPTER TWO

PRINCESS IS NOT A LIFE GOAL

TASHA

"Okay, ladies. One last lap on my whistle, and then Kat will lead you in your stretches. Hustle. I've got a prize for the winner!"

The shrill blast of my whistle cuts through the air, and the clatter of skates pushing off the smooth surface is music to my ears. I wince when one of the noobs gets tangled up in her skates and goes down hard, but it's all part of the game. If she really wants it, she'll have to get used to taking some knocks.

I love leading the Derby Foundations sessions. Watching brand new skaters find their wheels and gain confidence is such a thrill. It takes me back to when I was struggling to fit in, and I said fuck it and found my own way.

"There are a couple with solid potential in this sesh," Cherry says, crossing her padded arms and rocking back on her wheels.

"Right? Essie has outstanding balance, and Tam's got style already." I nod to the blonde and brunette leading the pack. The dark-haired girl pulls ahead a couple more feet as they hit the finish line, throwing her arms up in the air with a victory wiggle. Perfect derby attitude already.

She catches the Milky Way I toss her without losing her balance, rolling over to the end of the rink to join her fellow skaters in their cool down. They're gathered in front of the colorful mural that stretches across the end of our practice space. The skaters painted on the wall are so lifelike I sometimes expect them to roll right out of the scene. I'm forever impressed with Cherry's artistic abilities.

"Are you sharing your stash?" Jo shoves me. "Do I get one?"

I roll my eyes at her, dropping my hands to cover my waist pack. Maybe I'm a little protective of my chocolate. "I buy extra for the foundations kids."

"Kids." Emma snorts. "Pretty sure Essie is in the final year of her PhD."

"All the power to her. They're still my kids when I'm teaching them to skate."

"That doesn't answer my question," Jo says.

"Fine. Only cause I love you." The wrappers crinkle under my fingers as I grab a few mini bars from the graffiti print fanny pack I wear when we're teaching.

They're gone so fast I'm convinced my friends must be a pack of starving wolves, not allegedly civilized university students.

Emma's short stature and cute, blond pigtails are a little deceptive. She's scarfed down her chocolate and tossed the wrapper, while I'm still nibbling at mine, savoring the sweet chocolaty goodness. "How'd your date go last night?"

I lift a questioning brow. "I'm pretty sure you're confused as to what a date is all about. Has it been that long for you, Em?" We were all at Niche last night when I found myself a guy to bring home. Dating is not something I do.

"I'd consider that your version of a date."

"If you say so. Well, it was trash. He did not know how to please a woman, so I finished the job myself after I left. Maybe I should quit trying at all. The last three guys I brought home were uninspiring at best."

Cherry holds up a finger. "Wild idea." I'm shaking my head at her before she even finishes the sentence, knowing where this is going. "You could, maybe, I dunno, try getting to know a guy first."

"Um. Not a chance. You know that's not my thing. Relationships. Commitment. No thanks. I know how those things end up." Trapped in a marriage that slowly consumes your happiness like rust eating away at a car.

Cherry wraps her arms around Jo's shoulders, giving her a squeeze. "Go on. Tell us how these things end?" There's a challenge in her brown eyes.

Jo cracks her knuckles, and I wince. The sound is like knives scraping along my ear canal. But I think the menacing glare she's sending my way is worse.

"I didn't mean you two. You're like the perfect couple. I have no doubt you'll be skating around the retirement home in sixty years, terrorizing the other residents while you bicker about whether to get a cat or a dog."

Emma clears her throat. "What about me?"

They really know how to corner me. She found the love of her life this year and he's fantastic. Ace treats her like the lady she sometimes pretends to be. I'm not sure how she was even able to date someone named Ace to begin with, though. I couldn't have done it.

"Fine. You've all found love and are now trying to drag me into your weird relationship cult situation. I'm so, so happy for you, but it's still not happening, and Emma, you need to stop bringing random guys with you to set me up. You know I'm only going to scare them away."

She laughs again. "One day, Tasha. You are going to fall harder than the rest of us, and I can't wait."

"Whatever you say. I'm waiting with bated breath for my prince." I flutter my lashes in the best imitation of a princess I can manage, but the gesture probably doesn't match the smirk twisting the corners of my lips.

"Have you got something in your eye?" Jo asks, leaning in to peer at me. "Need me to flush it for you?"

Clearly, my best attempt is pathetic. Fine with me. Princess is not one of my life goals, anyway.

"I've gotta get going."

Cherry's dark brown eyes flick over to me. "You're not staying to practice?"

We usually hang out and get in some laps and advanced drills after the foundations class is over. My eyes scan the wood and exposed steel beams of the old warehouse, lingering on the smooth surface of the track, begging to be skated on.

"Can't. I've got an interview for a summer internship." The nervous flutter that vanished during our class comes rushing back at the mention of the interview, and I hug my waist, trying to ease my twisting stomach.

Jo's eyes light up. "That's amazing. Where?"

Excitement is bubbling up, but I'm trying to keep it contained. This is my dream job, and I'm praying I don't fuck it up. "Everge-En in New York. Sustainable engineering." The company's goals and methods are a perfect fit with mine, and I'm not upset about the location either. I've always wanted to live in NYC. The off the charts energy of the city. There's room for everyone. It's been my dream to get lost in the anonymity. And New York is the perfect place.

"Fantastic. Well, get out of here. Go get yourself cleaned up and destroy that interview."

"Are you saying I don't look good?" It's hard to keep the serious look on my face as I pull off my helmet, letting the sweaty strands of my black and pink hair slap my face.

"Of course not. I'm sure Everge-En loves their engineers to show up covered in rink sweat." Cherry smirks at me until I break.

"Fair point. Well, have a good one. Say bye to the newbies for me and I'll catch you at home, Emma." I wave at my girls behind my back, pushing off my skates to glide over to the change room. My track suit will be fine until I head home to shower and change into something more professional.

I can almost feel the pile of the carpet shrinking under my aggressive steps as I make a tight circle around our living room. I've been making the rounds for the last fifteen minutes, and my eyes keep darting to my phone, taunting me from the coffee table. After checking to make sure the sound was turned on for the tenth or possibly hundredth time, I forced myself to put it down. I haven't been this nervous about anything since we made it to the regional derby championships last year.

When the soft chiming ringer starts up, I skid across the carpet, lunging for it. Realizing I need to compose myself, I drag a breath deep into my lungs and slowly release it as the chimes tinkle away again.

"Hello." I paste on a smile while I put on my professional voice.

"Natasha, hello."

My stomach clenches at the sound of Mom's voice.

"Mom?"

"Yes. Who did you think it was, Natasha?"

Who did I think it was? The interview isn't scheduled for another fifteen minutes and they're not calling me. They've sent me a link for a Teams call. I know this, but my thoughts are so tangled up with nerves that I assumed it was my interviewer calling.

"I have an interview for an internship shortly, Mom. Can't talk right now."

"Surely you can spare a few minutes for your mother. The interview can't be more important than your sister's baby shower. She's bringing a new life into this world." The passive aggressive jab is all too familiar, glancing off me.

The heel of my hand rubbing my temple does nothing to ease the pain creeping up behind my skull. Why would I ever expect her to understand how important this is to me?

"Actually, it's for a summer internship with a company I'm very interested in working for, so yes, it is important, Mom."

"An engineering job, I suppose?" The disdain is so heavy in her voice it has no problem traveling through the phone line.

"That is the degree I'm working toward. So yes, Mom. It's an engineering company."

"Oh, Natasha. I was really hoping you'd come to your senses and move back home after you finished your degree. Your father would really like you to join the company until you find a husband. I don't suppose this job is in Grand Rapids, is it?"

"No, it's in New York." It might not be the only reason I'm so excited about this opportunity, but a little distance from my family definitely has its appeal.

She scoffs. "Anyway. The reason I called is..."

I glance at the clock on our wall, watching the second hand travel around the face as the amplified tick tock sound drowns out her words.

"I've gotta go, Mom. I can't be late for this interview. Call you later."

I won't, but I'm sure she'll forget all about it until the next time she calls me, trying to get me involved in helping to plan my sister's shower. It's not that I wouldn't help if either of them would actually be interested in any of my ideas, but I know there's zero chance of that happening. Our styles don't exactly mesh.

"Natasha, don't interrupt me."

"I have to go, Mom. Bye." I wince as I end the call, but I wouldn't put it past her to stall me until I'm late for my call, so I've got no choice but to hang up on her.

My eyes flick away from my phone at the sound of a key scraping in the lock. The door slides open ever so slowly, and my friend's blue eyes peek through. She spots me still sitting in front of my phone with a back so straight you really could shove a ruler down the back of my shirt. I try to ignore my roommate as I listen to the polished HR lady outline the responsibilities of the position. Emma mouths sorry at me and tiptoes in, shutting the door behind her with a soft click, and heading for her room.

"That sounds great, Rebecca." She introduced herself by her first name and gave me a warm smile that helped settle the jangling nerves that my conversation with my mother had induced.

"Did you have any further questions for me, Natasha?" she asks, glancing down to where she's been periodically jotting notes.

"I think you've covered everything thoroughly. I appreciate you taking the time to interview me."

"It's been my pleasure. Now, I want to let you know there will be a delay in the next step of the hiring process. If you're selected to move on, it may be a couple of months before you hear anything. Ms. Grayson is the Managing Engineer in charge of the interns and she's off on maternity leave for another six weeks. But she will reach out to everyone she's interested in moving forward with, and I feel comfortable letting you know that you're a top candidate. I understand if you've moved ahead with another opportunity in that timeframe."

My nerves ratchet up another notch. This is my dream position. My top choice. I'll pursue any other opportunities that come my way, but it's going to be rough not holding out for this one.

"I appreciate the notice."

"Perfect. You will receive an email within the next week or two to let you know if you've been selected. At that time, I'll provide you with further information regarding the timeline. Thank you again, and I'll be in touch."

"Looking forward to it. Thank you."

"Goodbye."

"Goodbye."

Before my finger has even touched the button to end the call, Emma is flying out of her room, pigtails bouncing behind her as she skips toward me.

"Well. How'd it go?"

Her eyes are shining, and she's bouncing on her toes. Her excitement warms that snowy tundra of disappointment that my phone conversation with my mother left behind. At least some people in my life understand the significance of this opportunity. Not everyone is lucky enough to have that.

"It went well. I think. The HR lady said there's a good chance I'll move on to the next round, but the process is going to take longer than usual. The manager in charge is on leave."

Her pink-glossed lower lip pushes out in a pout. "Of course you will. You're the bomb dot com. You're a hundred per cent the best person for the job."

She wraps her small arms around my waist, giving me a squeeze that has my hands hovering in the air beside her, not quite sure where to put them. I'm not much of a hugger. Not a particularly common move in the Deveraux household, but my bestie is a hugger, so I've gotten a little more accustomed to the move. I finally drop my hands to her shoulders, giving them a pat.

"Thanks."

"For what?"

"For being there for me. Rooting for me." I swallow hard, trying to force the words past the golf ball sized lump that's formed in my throat. "I really appreciate you."

"As you should." She pulls away. "We need to celebrate. Champagne or Whiskey?"

"Um, neither. It's only two in the afternoon."

"You're right. Better make them Mimosas."

Before I can protest, my friend is darting off to the kitchen, moving with the smooth grace of a cat.

Mimosa's it is, I guess.

CHAPTER THREE

STARS COLLIDING

JACKS

"I can't believe Jordan wanted to go to a roller rink for her birthday. I didn't even know these existed anymore." Dev cranes his thick neck around to nod at me from the middle row of seats.

Aspen makes a wide swing to maneuver the spaceship he borrowed from his dad into one of the spots at the end of the lot. I can't imagine having six siblings. At the same time, having that group behind you... might make it easier when you're going through a difficult time. I shove the pang in my chest deep down to its usual spot. Not the time or place. It never really is the right time.

An ugly brown rectangle of a building looms over us as we spill out the wide doors, shoving at each other. There's a retro-looking sign over the door that reads Roller Park in orange, brown, and yellow. Either they were going for a certain vibe, or this place hasn't changed in forty years. Ah well, I'm always up for a good time in any shape or form.

"Yeah, they shut this place down for a decade, but since roller derby has made a comeback, some guy who owns a few of the bars downtown bought it and reopened it," Aspen says.

Interesting life choice.

A wall of sound hits us as soon as we step through the sliding doors. Loud poppy music, the digital dings and beeps of arcade games and the swoosh and clatter of roller skates. My head starts bobbing to the beat of Olivia Rodrigo's newest hit. Some of the guys might make fun of me, but I can vibe to her music. I've never been ashamed of the things that bring me pleasure.

"Ooh, popcorn! I'm gonna go get some popcorn."

Beau grabs my arm when I wander in the direction of the delicious smell of fake butter.

"Dude, we've gotta check in and get skates first."

"Fine. Spoil sport."

"You're such a child. Want me to get you a balloon too?"

"They have balloons?"

He socks me in the arm.

"We better go." I catch sight of Jordan's red curls bouncing through the crowd. She drove in with some of her book friends, and let her boyfriend deal with all the hockey bros. I don't blame her. The crowded van was noisy as fuck. I'm not saying fifty per cent of it was coming from me, but I'm not saying it wasn't either. "Red shirt, incoming," I hiss at Beau.

He just rolls his eyes at me. Clearly, he doesn't understand the gravity of the situation. Jordan is an amazing
lady, but she doesn't have any problem keeping the entire
team under control.

"What are you two doing over here? Come, come. We
need to get everyone's shoe sizes so you can get your
skates." She waves her arms at us like she's trying to herd
an unruly clutch of baby chicks.

I give her my biggest smile and a sharp salute. "Yes,
ma'am."

"Don't call me ma'am, Jackson James Vaughan." She's
got her pointed chin tilted up as she stares me down. I
take a step back, throwing my hands up in surrender.

"Oh shit, you got full named, better get in line, Jacks."
Seb's teasing is music to my ears. I think he might have
done something stupid with his girl, cause he's been
broody again. At least he's still with us. Not completely
checked out like he was for a while last year. It was kind
of scary seeing one of my closest friends like that.

"Don't test me, Sebastian." She turns her laser glare on
him, and I can almost feel the heat easing off me.

"Exactly, Sebastian." My words come out in a singsong
that's probably going to get me punched, judging by the
glower on his face and the twitch of his fingers.

"Ugh. You guys are too much. Aspen, deal with your
friends. I'll be skating."

He grabs her arm, rolling her in for a kiss so hot you can
see her anger melting away, before turning his attention
on us. "Okay, boys, give your shoe sizes to the nice lady
behind the counter."

The pixie like girl with blonde pigtails behind the counter eyes us like a rabbit facing a pack of wolves. Sure we're big and maybe a little rowdy, but we're all housebroken. Someone slams into my back, throwing me off balance. My hands shoot out to grab the counter, sending a small stack of papers fluttering away.

Mostly.

"Sorry." I wince, hopping up and sliding over the counter to help her pick up her papers.

She's staring at me with wide eyes and a gaping mouth.

"Can I help?" She gives me a small nod, so I turn to the guys. "Yo, assholes! Cut the shit out and give the nice lady your shoe sizes."

"21!" Beau calls out. "Nice try, here's your elevens." I pass him the ugliest pair I can find in his size, and the look of distaste on his face is a win in my books. If he's not wearing spendy kicks, he's got on some designer fancy man shoes with his bespoke game day suit. A day in orange and brown roller skates will be good for him. Humbling.

He grabs a sanitizer wipe from his back pocket, wiping them off before he picks them up between two fingers, waiting while I hand out skates to the rest of the guys.

The girl has recovered by the time I'm done and she's back to efficiently dealing with the other customers. I slip a ten into the tip jar that has a picture of a roller skate imprinted on it. After Dev shoves Beau into the counter, upsetting a mug full of pens, I add a second one. Hazard pay.

"Thanks," she calls to me as I swing back up and over the counter.

"You're welcome..." I turn back to her, eyes drifting to the name tag pinned to her orange polo shirt. Why does everything have to be orange in this place? "Emma."

I flash a quick smile, heading off in the team's direction. They're easy to find, voices booming above the crowd even in this noisy place.

Everyone's settled into a party room near the back. With our experience lacing up skates, you'd think they'd all be ready to go, but nope. Still fooling around. Jordan's bright curls are visible out on the rink. She's got a few of her book friends with her, plus Jazz, who works at the coffee shop on campus. The team has been out to her bookstore on multiple occasions to help with events, so I've met all of them before. Thankfully, I haven't slept with any of them. The book besties are off limits.

Aspen finally gets everyone corralled and out on the floor. Feels weird to be skating on the smooth surface that is decidedly not ice, but it's fine. I pump my legs and test out the brakes. Number one rule. Know how to work the brakes.

Seb pulls up beside me. He's looking a little lost again, so I shove him, and he goes skidding to the side.

"What was that for?" He glares at me.

I bob my eyebrows a couple of times. "Race you."

He shakes his head, but I take off anyway, letting the wheels eat up the floor. He curses under his breath but takes off after me. I know he can't resist a challenge either. You don't get to the top level of college hockey without a competitive nature.

I pick up speed, weaving around the other skaters. Most of them are mediocre at best and wobbly drunk at worst. There's a handful of girls that could be hockey players themselves. They're at least as fast as us and pulling off some fancy moves. Skating backward, doing little spins, and weaving around each other in perfect formation.

That spurs me on faster, and I test out my limits when we get back to our starting point.

"Beat you." I crow at Seb, skating backward.

"Jacks! Watch out," Aspen calls out to me.

I spin around too late, crashing hard into a soft body. Gravity claims me, but I grab the girl I collided with, twisting in midair to take the hit. My shoulder screams, taking the brunt of the fall, and my head snaps back, slamming into the hard floor.

I blink, my vision wavering, and there are... "Stars...," I whisper.

"Crap. Did you give yourself a concussion, asshole?"

The words have a smile twitching my lips, but I force my eyes to focus on the concerned face hovering over me. She might think I'm an asshole, but she's still worried about me. Her hair is a contrast of black and hot pink, braided back to reveal the slick shave of an undercut on each side. Her dark lipstick matches her hair, but her eyes... they're the palest of blue, fading to almost white around the pupils. Like stars.

"No, you've got stars in your eyes." Lifting my arm to show her has me wincing at the lightning bolt of pain. Shit.

She pulls back, startled, and those stunning eyes meet mine for a brief moment before she's back to gently prodding at me. "Back. Neck? Anything hurting?"

Her small hands are surprisingly strong, pinning me to the floor as I struggle to sit up. "I'm fine. I don't have a spinal injury. It's just my shoulder."

Her gorgeous eyes narrow, then run down my body one more time, and I have to beg my dick to behave. He doesn't care that I'm flat on my back in the middle of a roller rink that's probably seen more bodily fluids than I care to think about. Or that there's lightning searing my shoulder. Nope, there's a hot as fuck lady with her soft body pressed against him in all the right places.

Thankfully, before I can embarrass myself, she swings her leg off and stands up, offering me a hand. I don't need her help, but I grab it anyway, wanting to feel her skin against mine. Once again, I'm disappointed. She's wearing little fingerless leather gloves with gold lightning bolts on the back.

I've never believed in fate, but the stars and lightning are all trying to shove it down my throat. I need to know who this woman is.

"I'm not usually one to help assholes, but I feel like I should at least help you off the rink and check you over. Make sure that thick head of yours doesn't have a concussion, since apparently your friends don't seem too interested in helping you."

I swing my head around, spotting the team in various places. Some of them are still skating. Some are back in the party room. Dev collapsed on a carpeted bench on the sidelines, massive shoulders shaking with laughter. Gee, thanks.

"I don't have a concussion." Unfortunately, I've had those before, so I'm familiar with the signs, but I follow her anyway, wanting to find out more about this punk goddess. "Are you a doctor?"

She snorts. "Not a chance."

Black fishnets lead up to a perfect ass in black denim cutoffs. It sways in front of me as she leads me...who knows where. Who cares, as long as I get to see her naked underneath me at the end of the night. Something's wrong with that thought... Right, supposed to be staying away from one-night stands. But this girl. Fuck, she's hot.

"So, how are you going to check me for a concussion?"

She finally reaches her destination, a small room near the counter where we grabbed our skates.

"Emma."

The pigtailed blonde turns her head. "What's up Tash?"

Tash. She has a name. Nice. It'll roll off my tongue nicely when I'm making her come on my dick.

She throws a thumb over her shoulder at me. "This jerk crashed into me, so I'm just gonna borrow the office for a sec, check him out."

Emma smirks at me. Maybe the mouse has more sass than I thought under there. "No problem. Go easy on him."

"I won't," she singsongs back.

"Perfect. I like it rough," I say.

I don't know what I was expecting her response to be, but it was not the tilt of her head followed by a slow, assessing look. She pushes her lips out. "Not sure you could handle me, surfer boy."

Oh fuck. The smile spreads all the way to my eyes. "Don't worry about me, Starlight."

She shoves me through the door into a small office and the door swings shut with a click, muffling the raucous laughter and general noise of the rink.

Her hands are insistent, but not rough, pushing me down into an office chair. There's a cluttered desk with an ancient laptop across from a shelving unit full of gear. Not the ugly rental skates we got. Sleek boots in black, pink, and rainbow. The helmets are just as colorful, surrounded by assorted sets of pads. Knee pads and elbow pads to match the skates. Each cubby has a handmade name tag underneath. Baby Slice, Kitty Cut, Tasha Scar. Nice. A Star Trek fan. What is this place?

I sweep the room one more time, searching for a clue, and my eyes snag on the posters tacked up on the far wall. Girls kitted out in all the gear are crouched down on their skates, ready to launch right out of their pictures. I hop over the posters until I find the one I'm looking for. Tasha Scar. There she is, stars softening her eyes even with the menacing glare she's giving the camera. Her gear is all purple and black, and she's wearing the fishnets and shorts look she's sporting now. But the part that really catches my attention are the socks with a

Star Trek comm badge pattern on them stretching to her knees. Lakeview Ladies of the Fight is splashed across the bottom graffiti style.

"You're a derby girl, Tasha Scar." I turn to look at her and she's reaching up to a cupboard over the desk, leaving her bare torso inches from my face. I can feel my resolve to lay off the ladies, crumpling like a candy bar wrapper.

When she turns back around, she's clutching a big red first aid bag to her chest protectively. "Yeah, what of it?"

"That's so fucking hot."

Her face twists in confusion for just a second, before she snorts out a laugh. "You are an enigma, Sunny."

My brow quirks up. "You can call me Jacks. Then I'll be less of an enigma. It's actually Jackson, but my friends all call me Jacks."

A strand of pink falls over her shoulder as she tilts her head, assessing me. "Well, we're not friends."

She pulls a swab out of the bag, dabbing at my forehead. I hiss through my teeth at the sting. I didn't know I'd cut myself.

She can call me whatever she wants as long as I get to spend more time with her.

"Well, I'm going to call you Sunny. You look like you just flew over from California anyway, so it fits."

"I didn't."

Her small fingers make quick work of a bandage wrapper and I inhale for a different reason when she presses it to my forehead. "Didn't what?"

"Fly over from California. Sorry to say I've never been. I'd love to, though, one day. I'm actually from Canada. Ontario. Not that far from Michigan." The words all kind of tumble out. I'm not usually this eager to share personal information with girls I just met.

"Well, that's less fun."

"Maybe so, but it doesn't make me any less fun."

She pulls back. "You keep saying stuff like that, but are you all talk or do you really want to take me on?"

I'm teasing, because there's something that makes me want to provoke some sort of reaction from her. However, I'd be one hundred percent willing to back up the words with action if she showed the slightest bit of interest. "Oh, I would take you on, right here, right now if you'd let me."

Her x-ray vision feels like it's piercing all the way to my soul as she blinks those icy blue eyes at me.

"I can't say I'm not tempted, but I'd hate to take advantage of you in your injured state."

"I'm not injured. Typical day for me."

"You crash into unsuspecting women and hit the floor on the regular?"

"Nope. I crash into fully suspecting men and try not to hit the ice."

Her head tilts back, revealing a long pale length of neck I'd love to sink my teeth into. Not like vampire styles, just you know a light nip. "You're a hockey boy. Of course. That explains everything."

"What exactly does that explain?"

"Cocky attitude, disregard for the people around you, that ridiculous mop of blond hair." She flicks black nails tipped in purple at my head.

She thinks my hair is ridiculous. I'm hurt. "Hey, I care about the people around me. I just got caught up in the moment. My friend Seb has been in a bit of a rough place, and I wanted to cheer him up. We were racing and I..."

"Didn't pay attention to the people around you."

Touche. She's got me there. I nod. "Fair. I'm sorry. I should have been paying attention." Her eyes widen as if she wasn't expecting me to own up to my actions.

"But... I can make it up to you." The innuendo laden words slide out easily, matching the slow smirk that twists my lips. Judging by the way she crosses her arms over her chest, maybe I should have kept that thought in my head. Way to confirm her fuck boy opinion of me. Not that she'd be wrong.

"Yeah, okay. You definitely don't have a concussion." She straightens up, but the warmth of her hands doesn't leave my shoulders. "See, here's my problem. I've met guys like you."

"Enlighten me. What am I like?" I throw up air quotes.

"Pretty boy athletes."

"You think I'm pretty." I latch onto those words like a dog with a new stuffed toy it's about to rip to shreds.

"See. You know how good looking you are. And guys like you don't have to try. Hot athlete just looks at a girl and she drops her panties. You don't have to put in any effort and personally, that doesn't sound like a good time to me. I've had enough mediocre sex lately to have zero interest in that situation."

What kind of moron is giving this dark goddess mediocre sex? "Well then, baby. How about we make a deal? I don't come until I've made you come three times."

"Take off your shirt. Also, don't call me, baby."

"What?"

Her hands wave me on. "Take off your shirt. I want to see what you're offering."

My shoulder screams when I reach back to grab the hem of my shirt, but I power through and peel it over my head, not even sure why I'm obeying her command.

She nods.

"You're making me feel like a piece of meat."

"That's all you are. If we do this, that's it. One shot. No feelings, no seconds."

"Maybe I do have a concussion, and I'm dreaming."

Her mesmerizing lips crack the tiniest of smirks. "Pretty sure I'm real. Want me to prove it to you?"

"Fuck yes."

With that, she turns her back on me, spandex shorts clinging to that juicy ass as she clicks the lock on the door.

This can't be happening.

Chapter Four

Full Of Surprises

Tasha

H ockey boy is still sitting there staring at me as if I'm going to transport out of here any second. This is my space. If anyone is leaving, it's him, but I make the mistake of letting my eyes drift down his body, and there's a lot, taking up too much space in the small office. Hockey might have given him a little too much confidence, but it also gave him a body that's begging to be explored, and that ink. That was unexpected on the golden boy. His left arm has an entire solar system twining around it. Stars, constellations, and...my stomach clenches at a familiar sight gliding across his chest. The Enterprise-D. Very unjockish of him. The careless hockey boy is a Trekkie. Full of surprises.

His face is laser sculpted as sharp as his body. But then he's got full lips in a deep shade of rose, and thick eyelashes that balance out the harsh lines. Those arms...yum. This could go one of two ways. He's either going to be the worst lay I've ever had or he's going to back up those words with action and rock my world. He doesn't utter a word while I study him, but the corners of his lips curl up in a lopsided grin that's more goofy than cocky. The eager puppy vibes make me think I'll be able to keep him heeled. Maybe train him up a bit.

Where did that come from? I'm not training him. If I do this. It's just a onetime thing.

"Well?" He arches a brow at me that's a slightly darker blond than the rest of his hair. "Have you made your decision?"

Of course, I've already made my decision. I don't know why I'm even still standing over here. "I locked the door, didn't I?"

It only takes a few small steps to get back to him, and I drop my hands to the smooth skin of his shoulders. As I'm leaning in to test out how those lips will feel against mine, I'm whisked into the air and spun around at a dizzying speed. He drops me into the office chair and grips the side of my shorts, tugging them down my hips.

I'm so surprised I go along with it, lifting my hips off the chair so he can slide them down my legs. His knuckles trail across my bare skin, sparking flames everywhere they touch. A needy moan hisses out when he drops to his knees between my legs that are still clad in my signature fishnets.

"What are you doing?" I was counting on maybe a quick fuck on the desk or against the wall, but his hot breath tickles as he takes his sweet time rolling the fishnets down, planting soft kisses on my legs as he goes.

Instead of diving right in, he's massaging my quads. God, that feels good. My thighs were already burning from my workout this morning when we came to the rink.

I jump and my eyes fly open when his tongue slides up the sensitive skin along the inside of my thighs. At this rate, I'll be soaking by the time he nibbles and sucks his way up to my pussy.

I slip my hands into the waves of his hair and it's as silky as it looks. Maybe the overlong cut isn't so bad after all. He shakes his head and pulls his mouth away, leaving me chilled and needy when I try to tug at him, hurrying him along.

"Maybe you're in charge the rest of the time, but not here. Not with me."

My pussy clenches. I'm usually the one that takes charge in the bedroom, but this. The commanding tone of his voice. The sharp bite he punctuates his comment with is really doing it for me.

"What do you say? Are you in?" There's a hint of challenge in his tone, as if he knows how hard it is for me to resist a dare.

He's fuzzy through my haze of lust, and words seem hard, so I nod.

"I'm going to need you to say it."

His mouth is inches from my pussy that's still covered by a thin layer of satin and sheer purple lace, and he flicks his bright blue eyes up to me, waiting for my response.

"I'm in." My head dips in a nod. I'm so in.

"Tell me what you want?"

Ugh. Just get on with it. "Your mouth." I let my legs fall open wider, sliding down in the seat, trying to bring myself closer to his face. His fingers squeeze my thighs in a grip that might leave behind prints, not letting me get closer.

"Where?"

"On my pussy. Lick me, pretty boy. Please." I can't believe I'm begging for it. From him, but it's worth it when he buries his face in the damp seat of my underwear.

"You're wet already, Starlight. Naughty girl."

He sucks on my mound through the panties until I'm desperate, bucking my hips at him. His fingers hook through the waistband, and he yanks them down my legs, burying his face in my warmth at the same time. Finally.

My hands are gripping the arms of the chair, warmth spreading through me like liquid fire. The expert strokes of his tongue stoke it higher and higher until I'm almost levitating off the rough mesh fabric of the office chair. It adds another layer of sensation to the mix.

A spasm runs through my entire body when he sucks my clit into his mouth, swirling his tongue around it in rhythmic circles. He doesn't protest anymore as I grip his hair, pulling him in closer.

I'm clenching on air, feeling empty as his finger toys with my entrance, teasing me. He pulls it away when I try to sink down.

"Please."

"Please what?"

"I need you inside me." His cock would be great, but I'll settle for anything to fill up the emptiness at this point.

"Do you?" He teases me again, barely breeching my opening before pulling away again.

"Stop fucking with me, Jackson."

That does the trick. That long digit slides in as he continues to suck on my lips and clit. It's almost like he can read me, backing off when the pressure gets to be a little too much. Upping the intensity when I squirm into him until he's lapping at me with the perfect amount of pressure that has me spiraling.

My thighs are starting to shake as he adds a second finger, plunging them in and out. I'm right at the edge when he closes his teeth on my sensitive clit. The hint of pain sends me over the cliff. I throw my head back with a scream, as my walls quiver around his fingers that are still sliding in and out of my slick channel. Stars flicker behind my eyes as my head falls back.

Thank fuck I'm sitting down, because I'm pretty sure my legs wouldn't hold me up right now.

"That's a good girl." His words send another spasm through my spent body.

When I drag my eyes open, he's still down there, looking up at me with a satisfied smirk on his pretty face. Those words. That praise. It should have my hackles rising. It should make me angry, but I'm too satisfied to care. Or maybe. Ugh. Just maybe. I liked it. Letting someone else take control of my pleasure for a change.

"One." He won't let me escape his eye contact as he slides those fingers between his plush lips, then pulls them out with a pop and holds a single digit in front of my face.

A knock on the door pulls me out of my daze. "Tasha. You okay in there?"

I stifle a laugh. She probably thinks I'm being murdered in here.

"I'm good, Em. Be right out."

Jackson says, "We're really good." His words are almost a purr, and I slap my hand over his mouth. It's still damp with my juice. I'm not one to be ashamed of my sexuality, but c'mon. This is the derby office. God, I'm never going to live this one down.

There's a giggle on the other side of the door.

"C'mon." I shove at his shoulders. He winces. Crap. He hurt his shoulder out there, didn't he? "Sorry, but we should really get out of here."

"You sure about that?"

"Yes. A hundred percent sure."

"Your place or mine?" I'm not a huge fan of that cocky grin on his face.

"Neither," I say, rolling my fishnets back up my legs. "I've got things to do."

"Well then, how am I going to give you your next two orgasms? I promised, and I'm nothing if not a man of my word."

I sigh, looking up. The ceiling fan spinning in circles reminds me of how my head was feeling just a moment ago. That was pretty amazing.

"I'll be at Clash Club tonight with the girls. Show up and I'll consider letting you finish the job." I give him a wink as

I wiggle back into my shorts and don't look back, pushing through the cheap wooden office door.

Chapter Five

You Lost, Pretty Boy?

Jacks

"Baby needs an ice pack after playing with the little girl?"

A cold sting sends a shiver down my spine when Lucy slings the ice pack at my chest. Sometimes I think he really is the devil we nicknamed him after. "Fuck man. Who hurt you?" I pick up the offending thing, pressing it to my shoulder to ease the pain. The floor of that place really did a number on me, not that I'd admit it to Coach or anyone on the physio team. How'd you hurt yourself? Fucking around at the roller-skating rink. Nope. Not admitting to that.

"I was being chivalrous. I saved her from suffering my painful fate."

"Only cause you slammed into her in the first place." Sebastian is slumped on the couch, arms crossed over his chest. The dark clouds are back on his face. Maybe I didn't help as much I thought.

"Semantics. You gonna come with me tonight?"

"Club Clash? Not really my scene. Besides, I have an assignment to work on."

Aspen took Jordan out for a private birthday dinner after we left the roller rink, so I'm left with this crew. "Dev, Beau??? C'mon guys." I'm not above begging. I really want to finish what I started with Tasha.

Beau swipes an imaginary speck off his pristine black sweater that probably cost more than my car. "I don't think I can handle that noise right now. Not after the roller-skating rink." Fair point. He's overstimulated. Let him have some time to decompress.

"Dev. C'mon. You owe me."

He looks up from the book he picked up off the coffee table. "For what?"

"Being a general dick."

"Fine. Whatever." He goes back to his book. Some sort of self help nonsense. Not my bag.

"Yes!" The ice pack hits the carpet with a soft thud as I get up to find something to wear. Punk is not exactly my typical look, but I'm sure I've got some black jeans and t-shirt in there to sort of blend in.

"Really, Jacks?" He's already bending down to pick up the ice pack I abandoned when I turn around.
"Sorry, Bo-Bo." I know it'll itch at his brain until he picks it up himself if I leave it there, so I dart back to clean up after myself.

Dev stands out in his blue track pants and white t shirt stretched across his bear-like chest, but no one is going to mess with that scowl or those biceps. He actually looks like one of the bouncers at the door. I'm still getting weird looks in spite of the dark jeans and black tee I threw on.

No, I do not fit in with the crowd of tattooed, pierced dancers hanging out in the place. There's probably a pharmacy's worth of hair dye represented in all the colors. One guy even has an entire rainbow of tall spikes running down the center of his head. Looks kinda like a cool dinosaur. Not that I would ever say that to his face. Pretty sure I'd get punched, judging by the scowl pinching his pierced brows together.

"Gonna get a drink," Dev says.

He abandons me to grab a soda, leaving me scanning the crowd in search of that particular mix of pink and black that I want to run my fingers through. Not easy in this place.

I weave around the people leaning against the brass railing bordering a sunken dance floor, scanning the crowd writhing to the beats.

My shoulder twinges as I bump into somebody for the second time today.

"Watch it."

"I'm sorry." I pull my distracted gaze away from the dance floor and meet a pair of soft brown eyes looking at me with confusion.

"You lost, pretty boy?"

"I was looking for someone." I almost ask the woman if she knows Tasha, but that would be ridiculous in a club this size.

"Here? You sure you're in the right place?"

Now I'm sure that my camouflage has failed me.

"Yeah. She said she'd be here tonight."

A slow smile curls up her red lips, softening the stern lines of her face. And is that recognition? She could be a hockey fan.

"Are you Tash's hockey boy? Nice."

I press my lips together, trying to suppress the smirk twitching at them. She told her friends about me. I wonder what she said to them. "You know Tasha? Where is she?"

The woman standing behind the brown-eyed beauty has a protective hand on her shoulder, but not the familiar hair or starry eyes I'm looking for.

She shrugs. "She'll find you when she feels like it, Sunny."

The smirk breaks free. I kind of like that she's got her own special nickname for me.

"C'mon. Please." Any information would help, but nope, she's shaking her head. She's going to leave me hanging.

"Nah, I don't think so. I'm Cherry by the way, and this is Jo." The girl with the blue and blond bob waves at me from behind Cherry's shoulder.

She accepts my offered hand for a quick shake, then pulls me in close. "Treat our girl right, or you'll have the entire team after you, pretty boy."

As if their friend didn't totally steamroll me in the office at the rink. I shake my head. "Don't worry about her."

They let out a synchronous snort at my expense. "Pretty boy is smart. Nice to meet you."

"You too," I say, even as they're turning back to each other. Well, I guess I'm being dismissed.

Now to find Tasha. I've lapped the club a few times with no luck when the music shifts into a new song and the crowd parts. The tiny blonde that emerges is familiar and my face breaks out in a grin when I spot her friend trailing behind her, attached by their linked hands. She's still wearing her fishnets, but she's swapped the shorts for a purple and black plaid skirt that barely covers the top her thighs. Her hair is tucked into two messy buns on either side of her head.

I step toward them as they break free from the crowd. "Ladies."

A set of pale eyes meet mine, and she smirks. "Sunny, I'm surprised to see you here."

"You invited me, didn't you?"

"Yeah, but I didn't actually think you'd show your face at Clash."

"So, it was a challenge?" I step into her, leaning in close to hear her over the insistent thump of the music. "Big mistake. I love a challenge."

"So you said before." She's been thinking of my three orgasm offer. I like that. I can't wait to make good on that promise. If she'll let me.

"Are you ready to get out of here now? Or you wanna stay and dance for a bit?"

Her eyes widen again. Maybe she was expecting me to drag her out of here, away from her friends, as soon as I laid eyes on her. As much as I'd like to do that, I know how important girls' night is. I wouldn't interrupt it at all if she hadn't invited me.

She looks at Emma, then back at me, considering.

Her friend shakes her head, holding her hands in front of her face. "Don't look at me. Jo and Cherry are quite happy over there." She waves her hand at the ladies I ran into earlier who are now twined around each other, joined at the lips. "And Ace should be showing up at any moment."

Tasha nods. "Let's dance for a bit. Show me your moves."

"I thought I already did that."

She rolls her eyes at me, ignoring the innuendo and turning around to make her way to the crowded dance floor, not checking to make sure I'm following her.

It's tight, but I can untangle the puck and steal it from a jammed up crowd of players in the middle of a game. Busting through the tightly packed bodies on the dance floor to get to my prize shouldn't be a problem. The air is charged with so much sexual tension you could probably power a small house with it if you could just figure out how to harness it.

Tash has got her arms waving, head dropped back as she sways to the beat, getting lost in the music. I scooch in behind her. It's not that I don't enjoy watching her lose herself in the tunes, but I don't want her to forget about me. Needy fucker that I am.

The farther I moved into the mass of dancing students, the hotter it was. But now, pressed up against her, I'm absolutely scorching. She tilts her head back, giving me the tiniest of smiles when she realizes it's me. Permission granted, I slide one arm around her waist, splaying my hand out over her bare stomach. A little shiver ripples her across skin as I make small circles with my thumb. My other hand grips her hips through her skirt.

She drops her hands back to rub my shoulders, and I'm lost. Her hips are gyrating in a teasing dance, brushing my length with each twist until I'm painfully hard. My hand slides up the front of her shirt until I'm brushing the bottom of her lace-clad tits. Man, I want to rip that piece of flimsy fabric off her so I can get my hands on her breasts.

Since that isn't exactly a viable option, I spin her around. I can't take any more of the torture she's meting out on my poor dick. My hands slip to her ass, pulling her into me, so we can sway together, but this move may have been unwise. Now I've got her heated core pressed up against my cock rather than her ass. Not better.

Needing something, anything, I lean in to meet her lips. I nip at her bottom lip, slipping my tongue in to tangle with hers. She meets me, nibbling at my lower lip, and digging her nails into my back. One hand makes its way to her front, dipping down to rub the soft mound overtop of her skirt.

She moans, grinding into me, and panting into my mouth. I glance over her shoulder. There's gotta be some-where to hide out in this dark club. Some secret corner

I can take her. If we were at Wright's I'd know just the place.

As if she can read my mind, she steps back. Our lips break apart and I lean in, trying to follow her, recapture the kiss.

"Follow me." The words are rough around the edges, like the frayed edges of the denim shorts she was wearing when I saw her earlier. All of her. The memory of her sweet taste has me groaning under my breath.

I let her lead me to a shadowy alcove at the back of the club. There's a set of stairs over our heads that must lead to an employee area, because they're blocked off with a locked gate. The space is surprisingly empty. It seems like prime real estate for doing deliciously nasty things. I may have let her take charge to find a spot to hide away in, but now that I've got her here, she's going to listen to me.

My body crowds into hers, pressing her up against the wall, and her hands find their way back to my hair. She was definitely lying when she said she didn't like the length. My scalp tingles as her fingers twirl around the strands, and her hips flex forward, ramping up my need to an insane level.

I made a promise, and I always keep my promises. Her skin is silky under my touch, and I move my fingers down to slip just under the front of her little skirt. She moans into my mouth, arching into the still chaste touch. That's the last chaste touch she's getting. The hem of her skirt provides little in the way of an obstacle, so I slide my hand under it on a mission to prove my skills to her.

My fingers flex on her waist when I finally hit the jackpot. Her damp panties are proof enough that she's into this, as if her moans aren't proof enough. I've gotten my fair share of compliments on how skilled I am with my hands, but I find myself wanting to prove it to her. No one else's past compliments seem to mean anything.

She rubs against my hand as I make soft circles around her clit.

Her lips clash with mine as she rocks against my hand.

"Fuck, Sunny. You're good with your hands."

There it is. I smile against her lips, pushing her panties aside to find the jackpot. She's slick with need, coating my fingers in her heat as I slide inside. One finger, then two thrust into her and she follows my rhythm with frantic thrusts of her hips.

Her skin is satiny under my palm as I follow a path under shirt all the way to those perfect tits. I moan into her mouth as my hand closes around her flesh. They're gorgeous, overflowing my hand when I pull her bra down to get better access. My thumb toys with her nipple, testing to see what she likes. Soft circles are good, harder rubs too, but when I squeeze tight and twist, she gasps, and I can feel her pussy clenching around my fingers on the verge of an orgasm.

"I'm going to need you to be quiet, Starlight."

A bead of sweat drips down my forehead as I add a third finger, wishing it was my cock. That can wait, though. Her first.

"You can come now." I whisper in her ear as I make a hard thrust, circling her clit and pinching her nipple again until she screams. She buries her face in my chest to muffle the sound like the good fucking girl she is.

Her pussy is clenching around my fingers, trying to keep me there when I reluctantly pull out. But her legs are trembling, so I slide both hands around to grip her ass, keeping her steady on her feet. I lean in to nip at her earlobe. "Two."

"Holy fuck, Jacks..." Her words trail off as she gasps, and I can feel her heart pounding in time with mine.

"You good?"

"Yeah."

"Ready to go? Or you wanna keep dancing." I smirk, knowing she can barely stand at the moment, much less dance.

She pulls her head off my chest, meeting my gaze. I can almost see her pulling herself back together, spine straightening one vertebra at a time.

"I think I'm ready to go."

"Can you make it to the car, or do you need me to carry you?"

"You're not fucking carrying me out, Sunny. I can walk on my own."

There she is. It feels good to bring her to her knees, but I love it when she stands tall and puts me in my place almost as much. I'm not sure if I like her calling me Jacks or Sunny better. They both sound amazing on her lips.

Some of her hair broke free of the adorable buns, so she tucks a sweaty strand behind her ear with a hand that's still a little trembly. Can't hide all her tells from me. "I should say bye to my friends."

"Of course."

I wait patiently for her to say her goodbyes, even though my cock is screaming at me to get her home and in my bed. We both perk up when she makes her way back over to us, hips swinging as she flows through the crowd all liquid grace, accompanied by her blonde friend.

"All good now? You ready to let me keep my promise?"

Her eyes are still soft and hazy from her orgasm, but her lips are bracketed by tight lines as if she's annoyed about how much she enjoyed that. "Fine, but you're coming to my place."

Something warm and unfamiliar spreads through me. Excitement maybe? I haven't been this excited to take a girl home since high school. My mood darkens at the thought of her. The girl I thought was the one who turned out to be the not-even-if-we-were-the-last-two-humans-after-the-zombie-apocalypse girl.

"Sure, Starlight. I'll follow you anywhere."

She rolls her eyes at my cheesy line. Emma pulls her in for one last quick hug before bouncing off toward a guy that does a worse job of fitting in than Lucy or me. He's got on dress slacks and a light blue polo shirt, but that doesn't seem to bother her. She jumps up, wrapping her arms around his preppy neck and planting a kiss on him. I guess opposites really do attract, because in spite of her blonde pigtailed hair, and tiny stature, she's dressed in a short pleated black skirt and Doc Martens.

Tasha shrugs at my confused look. "Don't ask me. C'mon. I've gotta get my coat before we get out of here."

She grabs my hand, dragging me after her with impressive speed and dexterity. All my years spent honing my reflexes are in use, making sure I don't plow into someone else on the way out. They might not be as nice as she was about it.

She's dragging me out the heavy black front door of the club before I've even had time to grab an Uber. A harsh gust of wind whips my damp hair off my forehead. The fresh air hits my skin in a chilly rush. Feels amazing after the dense heat inside.

"Let me grab us a ride."

"Nah, I've got it. White Civic. It'll be here in two." She's got her phone out, nibbling on her lower lip. The deep color hasn't faded even after the night of dancing and kissing. I'd love to see if it has the staying power to last after her lips have been wrapped around my cock.

It takes all my control to keep my groan inside at the thought. It would be nice if that happens, but I'm not expecting it. I promised her one more orgasm before I even get one, and I want to be wrapped up nice and tight in her pussy when I come. At least for the first time. First time? I don't do second times. Why is that thought even creeping around in my head?

"I would have gotten it."

"I'm sure you would have, but I did it first."

She drops her bomb, winks at me and slips into the car that's finally going to take me to the place I've been dying to visit all day.

CHAPTER SIX

TONGUE ACTION

TASHA

I don't bring just any guy back to my place. There are pros and cons of bringing a guy here vs going to his place or finding a dark corner of a club. Hockey boy has somehow earned my trust. Maybe it was the first two amazing orgasms that softened me enough to lead him up the wooden staircase to our place. Emma and I share the top floor of a nice house in the suburbs. Gives off heavy soccer mom vibes, and not a lot of students live in the area, so it's a great place to get away from the chaos.

The family who owns the house is super nice. They live downstairs and are the exact opposite of my family. Warm and loving. They've got the whole package. A set of adorable twins that I actually kind of like, despite my fear of children in general. And their golden retriever. It's easy to see why I've been comparing Jackson to Max. All big floppy tongue and silky ears. His entire goal in life seems to be to get his wet tongue all over you... I guess the two resemble each other even more than I thought. A laugh shakes my chest at the decidedly unsexy picture that forms in my head.

"What are you laughing about?" The man in question asks from behind me, and the chuckle turns into a full-on snort.

"Oh, I don't think you want to know."

"That sounds ominous. Tell me or I'm going to think you brought me back to sacrifice me to the Satan worshiping family that lives here."

I snort again and peer at him over my shoulder, trying to gauge if he'll be able to handle the comparison. "If you must know, I was thinking about how much you remind me of Max."

"Max, who's Max? Is he your boyfriend, cause let me tell you I'm not into getting punched for someone else's mistake."

He sounds way too alarmed by the prospect. "Is that something that's happened to you before?"

There's a panicked look on his face, and he's got those big blue eyes fixed on a spot over my shoulder. Boy should not play poker. Unless maybe it's with me. It doesn't surprise me in the least that he's left a trail of pissed off boyfriends in his wake.

The door swings open and I walk inside, twisting around when he doesn't follow me in. He's peering over my shoulder and his shoulders are tense, arms hanging ready at his side like a boxer waiting to get rushed. "You planning on staying out there all night? Or are you a vampire? Do I need to invite you in?"

One side of his mouth quirks up, but he's still a little tense when he says. "Would you?"

"Would I what?" Why is he talking in riddles?

"Would you invite me in if I said I was a vampire?"

Another giggle sneaks out. "Depends. Are you the ravishing me and taking delicate sips of my blood type of vampire, or the drain me of my lifeblood kind of vampire?"

Now he's laughing too. "What do you think?"

"I guess you'll have to come in and show me." His bright eyes are shining with laughter under the porch light, but he still makes no move to come in.

"What is going on with you?" My keys jingle as I drop them on the hook by the door.

"You didn't answer my question. Who is Max?"

"Oh, yeah no. He's the golden retriever that lives downstairs."

His shoulders sag and he steps forward before pausing again. "Wait, so you're comparing me to a dog?"

"Yeah. He's all golden and waggy. Seemed appropriate. Not to mention all the tongue action."

"Oh, my god. That was not what I was expecting." His shoulders start shaking and then we're both laughing until we're gasping for air. At least he made it in the door, though. A step in the right direction.

When I finally get myself together, I shut the door behind him, sliding the lock shut with a click. This is not how my one-night stands usually go.

"Tongue action, eh?" He straightens himself up to his full height, towering over me. I'm not a short girl, so it's strange to have to look so far up to meet his eyes.

"Yeah. You know. Cause you seemed pretty interested in licking me earlier, even though we'd just met. Kinda like Max." My words take me back to the office at the rink, and my nipples harden just thinking about it.

His eyes fall to the rock-hard buds pressing against the sheer black top I've got on over my lacy bra. "Right. I do like licking you. If I remember correctly, you seemed to enjoy it, too."

He takes a step in closer, dropping his hands to my shoulders and leaning down to capture my lips before I can answer. I moan out my agreement against his mouth. His hands trail down my arms in a shivery trail until he reaches my wrists. He circles them in a hold that's somehow both gentle and aggressive at the same time. He pulls my arms above my head, stepping in until I'm backed up against the full-length mirror beside the front door, never breaking contact with my lips.

The smooth surface is cool on the exposed skin of my back as he shoves me against it. Every single muscle in his torso is pressed into me, and it's so fucking hot. I can't wait to get his clothes off to see what's underneath. I got a look at those unreal abs, but the rest of him is still a perfectly wrapped mystery.

My tongue slips in to tangle with his as I fumble for his zipper, but unexpectedly, he stills my hand, pulling away from my mouth. "No. If we're going to do this, then I'm in charge for the night. Remember?"

I flick my gaze up to look at him through lust-hazed eyes. Is he serious? "What?"

"I told you before that I'm in charge in the bedroom, so you're going to have to give up control to me if you want that last orgasm. Can you do that, Starlight?"

"Um." I hesitate for a moment. I'm usually the one leading the way during sex. I know how to get myself off and I know what works for me. At least I thought I did. The commanding tone in his voice has my body vibrating with need. My breath is coming faster, and my heart racing harder than it ever has before. I guess I can give it a shot. For one night. Can't hurt, right? "Okay."

He reaches out, tilting my chin up. "Good." His hands punctuate the word, finding the hem of my shirt and dragging it up over my arms before I have time to catch my breath. My bra goes flying after the shirt a moment later, and he's groaning as he stares at my chest.

"Fuck, Tasha." There's a ravenous look in his eyes as they devour my tits. Definitely a boob guy. "These are incredible."

I drop my head back, closing my eyes when his hands close over them. Long fingers expertly pluck and pinch my nipples and his thigh slips between my legs, settling against my heated center. I grind down on him, seeking friction as lust burns from my sensitive nipples to low in my belly.

"Uh, uh. Did I say you could do that?"

The frustrated whine that comes out of my mouth is surprising, but I still my hips, enjoying his game even though it might kill me.

Cold air hits my chest when he lets go. Then he spins me around to face the mirror, and I shut my eyes to avoid looking at the heaving mess that he's already turning me into.

Goosebumps pop up under his hands as he slides them back up my arms. His fingers tangle with mine for a moment and then he presses my palms against the wall on either side of the mirror.

"Don't move those hands." And I don't even though there's nothing I want more than to touch him back.

He traces circles down my spine. "Nice ink." I shiver as he trails the lines of the wings of the phoenix that stretch across my back. "Beautiful, just like you."

My shoulders tense for a moment, relaxing when he doesn't pursue it any further, because the inspiration for that tattoo is not something I talk about casually. Especially not with some guy I'm never going to see again after tonight.

I'm on fire by the time he makes it down to the curve of my hips, slipping under the waistband of my skirt. My hands fly off the wall with the force he uses to yank the skirt off.

"What did I tell you?"

"But you..." I try to protest.

"Hands back where they belong." Why am I so into this? A sharp smack accompanies the faint sting as his palm makes contact with my ass, and my pussy clenches.

"That was just a warning. Keep those hands there or I'm going to have to take things up a notch. Got it?"

I nod. That sounded like a threat, but I'm almost tempt-ed to disobey to see what that means.

"Starlight, I need an actual answer."

"Yes. I've got it."

"Good. That's a good girl."

I wince a little when I hear the tear of my fishnets ripping, but I'm not surprised. I go through way more of those than I'd like, but sometimes you have to make sac-rifices for style. His rock-hard thigh nudges mine apart.

Now I'm standing there, legs spread wide open, hands planted on the wall, eyes closed to avoid looking at myself in the mirror. I have zero problems with my body, but it's still a little weird to be staring at myself in the mirror completely exposed like this. So vulnerable, laid bare for him. But when he grips my hips in a hold that borders on painful, my eyes fly open, and I see everything. The pink flush sweeping from my chest up my neck to my cheeks. Eyes glazed, and lips parted. His large body hovering behind me.

But when one of his hands shifts to my abdomen, the prominent veins standing out as he circles my clit, I'm lost. Lost to the sensations of him taking charge of my body. Lost to the burning heat racing through me. Lost to him.

Chapter Seven

Warp Speed

Jacks

S he's wet. So fucking wet for me. I release my grip on her hips for just a moment. Just long enough to rip open the condom with my teeth and slide it over my aching length.

I'm poised at her entrance, legs trembling. "You good." My voice is raspy, and my eyes are as glazed as hers.

"Yes. Fuck me, Sunny. Please."

A small smirk spreads my lips. I love hearing her beg. And this isn't the last time I'm going to make her do it tonight.

"Remember. You don't get to make the demands." I warn her sliding just the tip in to her heated channel before pulling it back out.

She bucks her hips back against me, trying to draw me back in, so I give that lush ass a smack. It jiggles under my touch.

I need to feel her come around my cock, so I release her hips to reach around, sliding one hand around her torso in an agonizingly slow slide until I reach her clit once again.

Her legs twitch, still sensitive from my earlier attention, so I adjust the pressure until her breath is coming in pants.

She's almost there. On the brink. I can feel it, so I pull away, ignoring her protests.

I notch myself at her surface again, plunging to the hilt in one vicious thrust that rocks us both forward. Her sweat slick hands slide down the mirror again. I still my hips for a moment, reveling in my first feel of her wrapped around my dick.

Her full tits fill up my hands. Nipples hard under my fingers. I knead, and pinch, and I've never felt anything so good. So perfect.

My hips start to move in a slow rhythm as I slide in and out of her. Her eyelashes rest on her pale cheeks, but I need to see those eyes, those stars.

"Open your eyes, Starlight. Look at me."

"Only if you..."

"If I what?"

"Harder. Faster."

That's one command I'm willing to obey. I draw myself all the way out before filling her all the way up in one vicious thrust. Her eyes fly open meeting mine in the mirror. Pale blue to bright blue. It's the perfect combination.

My continued thrusts have her orgasm building again, and so is mine. The tingle at the base of my spine roaring to life and begging me to let go. Not until I feel her surrounding me with her release.

I slide one hand back down her smooth stomach all the way to the place where we're joined. Fuck that's hot. I haven't had enough mirror sex in my life. I never thought I'd want to be one of those weirdos with a mirror on the ceiling above my bed, but this is so fucking hot. Watching her tremble and fall to pieces under my hands as I find that spot again. The spot that's going to have her screaming my name.

She's so ready, so close that all it takes is a few quick flicks and she's in pieces, shattering around me. Slick heat accompanies the pulsing of her pussy, clenching around me and bringing me with her as she screams my name, clawing at the mirror.

I let go, spilling inside the condom as I keep thrusting inside her needy warmth. I groan, barely able to hold myself up, as my brain shorts out.

I'm standing there, stunned, as my mind comes back online. Her hands are leaving a damp trail as they start to slip down the wall, and I realize the tremors are coming from her legs. We both groan as I slide out of her.

Once the condom's been tied off, I scoop her up in my arms.

"Hey, what are you doing?" Her voice is thready with exhaustion.

"Going to lie down. Where's your room?"

"I can walk." I'm gloating a little at the weak protest. Her head is lolling on my shoulder as if to disprove her words.

"I know you can, but I want to look after you. Now if you don't tell me which room is yours, I'm just going to pick one and if your roommate comes home to find us in her bed, not my fault."

"You're impossible." She's trying to hide the small smile that's twitching at her lips, but I catch it when I look down at her to brush a lock of hair away from her mouth. "It's the door on the left."

She throws her hand out to point in the general direction of her room. An abstract canvas with a silvery starburst on a black background is hanging from the door. It has a very galactic feel to it, almost as if we're traveling at warp speed on a starship. Kind of the way I feel after everything that happened today.

"Did you paint that?"

"Huh? Oh no. Cherry's the artistic one. She painted a mural at our derby practice track. It's incredible. I can't paint."

"It's gorgeous, just like you."

I drop her on the patchwork quilt that covers her bed.

"You know you can turn down the charm now. You literally have me in my bed." She scrabbles her legs, struggling to squirm under the blankets.

I reach down to help her out, pulling aside the sheet and blankets to find another fleecy one underneath the quilt. She must run cold.

"Can't. There's so much charm trapped inside I have to let it out or I'd explode."

Her little snort is growing on me. It was cute at first, but now I'm finding myself eager to tease it out of her.

"Must be hard to be you." The last word comes out around an enormous yawn as I'm tucking the blanket up under her chin.

"Oh, it is. You have no idea." I plop down on the side of her bed, wanting to join her but unsure if she's going to be ok with me staying the night. It's not something I'm usually into, but I'm so tired, and she looks so soft and cuddly that I really don't want to pull my clothes back on and leave her behind. Besides, we can probably sneak another round in tomorrow morning if I stay. "Can I?" I pull back the corner of the blanket, and my shoulders relax when she pats the space beside her.

"Get in, Sunny."

The sheets are cool against my skin, so I slide in closer to her, spooning her. She wiggles that gorgeous ass back to settle against my dick. He twitches in response. You think he'd be tired after all that, but nope. I'm not as tired as I thought either, settling an arm around her waist to pull her in tight against me.

The intoxicating scent of her hair invades my senses when I bury my nose in it. I'm not sure why I even asked to stay. I never stay the night, but there's no place I'd rather be right now than here. With her. It dawns on me that I'm going to have to leave in the morning, and never see her again. The thought twists my guts into knots.

"Fuck, Starlight." I look up at the ceiling. "Don't tell me that's the only time I get to do that. I couldn't handle it." The only response I get is a soft snore.

Fuck. I'm a goner. I would promise her anything. The world, my hockey career. My first-born child. Anything for another taste of this perfection.

CHAPTER EIGHT

DON'T FEED THE STRAY

TASHA

My bed is so warm and soft when the gentle chimes of my phone alarm ring out. "Mmmmm." I mumble, snuggling back into the... wait, what? There's a heavy weight resting across my arm and something else hard pressed up against my back.

What is happening? I shove at the arm and the hand slides a little lower until it's resting on my tit. My naked tit. Oh, my god. There's a guy in my bed.

"Morning, Starlight." The words come out in a raspy grumble that has no place in my bedroom while the bright sun is peeking through the slit in my curtains.

Sunshine. Hockey boy. Right. Why exactly is he still here? I don't let guys sleep over in my bed. No matter how good the sex is. And man, that was some incredible sex. Probably the best I've ever had. Who am I trying to fool? It was hands down, miles above the best sex I've ever had, but that doesn't mean he should still be here. A tingle lights up my body when he shifts, his thumb idly brushing my nipple. Nope.

I shove the offending arm off, sitting up so fast my head spins for a moment. I had like two drinks last night, so I don't even have alcohol as an excuse for breaking my cardinal rule.

"Awww. Where are you going? I was going to offer you number five."

Right. He went above and beyond last night with four orgasms instead of the promised three, waking me up in the early hours of the morning for another bout. Overachiever. I like that, but this I don't like so much.

"Nope. Get up. I've gotta go."

Obviously, he's not understanding the seriousness of the situation, so I jerk open my black curtains and yank the sheet off his body.

Immediate regret.

The bright light highlights every single ridge and curve on his glorious body. No wonder I forgot the rules.

"Hey." He blinks at me. His full lower lip pushes out in a pout, tempting me to take a bite of it, and I notice the red marks on it. May have already accomplished that task.

"Get up, Sunny. I've got things to do."

"Better things than multiple orgasms?" There's a hopeful look in those eager eyes.

"Yup."

"Fine. Your house. Your rules."

I have to look away from the sight of every muscle rippling and folding as he pushes himself up into a sitting position. I'm afraid he'll suck me in like a black hole if I stare at him too long, so instead I fumble around on the floor with my eyes half closed, gathering up his clothes. He catches the bundle I toss at him with lightning reflexes.

"That's right." Maybe I let him take charge last night, and maybe it was fucking amazing, but it's not night anymore and I need to take the control back. Get this runaway train of a situation back on the tracks.

I grab some clean yoga pants and a Ladies of the Fight polo out of the closet.

"Fuck."

The words throw me off as I'm yanking a pair of lacy purple underwear up my legs.

I spin around. "What?"

My eyes follow the light trail of golden hair running down his torso that leads straight to that massive dick of his. My pussy is clenching just remembering how well it stretched me out. He's just sitting there completely naked and eyeing me with a glazed look in his eyes while said appendage twitches.

"Are you sure you don't want one more round?" He made me beg for it last night and now he's the one doing the begging, but I'm not giving in to that desperate-puppy-begging-for-treats look in his eyes.

How is this happening? He was the perfect candidate for my one night only rule. The ultimate player. A cocky hockey player who knows just how good looking he is. He should have left me with nothing but a pleasant soreness between my legs and a scorching memory to revisit with the help of my vibrator. Instead, he's still here in the morning asking for seconds. This. This is the reason I don't let guys stay over.

"Nope. One night, remember? We both agreed to that. Now get up and get out."

I punctuate my point by sliding my shirt on over the sports bra I wrestled myself into.

He sighs. "Fine."

Kitchen. Get to the safety of the kitchen. I thought Emma would have stayed at Ace's house last night, but apparently, I was mistaken. The faint smell of coffee drags me along.

"Hey, babe. Looks like you had a good night. Hockey boy treated you right?"

"Shhhh. He's still here." I hiss out the words so he doesn't hear us talking about him.

My friend's big blue eyes widen. "He's still here?" Her hand reaches out, and she places a cool palm on my forehead. "Are you okay, Tash? Should I call an ambulance? You don't let guys stay the night."

"Ha ha. You're hilarious. I must have fallen asleep. It wasn't like I invited him to stay over."

"Maybe not, but you also didn't kick him out as soon as he pulled out. This is a momentous occasion. We should celebrate with..." She spins around, rifling through the treat cupboard of the kitchen. When she turns back around, she waggles a box in my face. "Raspberry Pop-Tarts."

I just roll my eyes at her.

"What are we celebrating?" The deep voice rumbles behind me and I turn around to see Sunny standing there wearing nothing but the black denim that looks like a costume on him. He's got one arm stretched up to brace himself on the door frame, leaving his obliques on display.

"Did you lose your shirt?"

He looks down. "Guess so. You tossed one of yours at me, and I didn't think it would fit so well. I mean, I'm sure I could rock me some black mesh, but I didn't want to tear it like I did those fishnets of yours."

"Morning, Baby Slice." He has the audacity to wink at my best friend before strolling out of the kitchen. Bare feet and black jeans hugging that tight hockey butt is a good look on him.

"You're such a traitor. Are you flirting with him?" I round on Emma.

"I'm not flirting. You know I would never do that to Ace. Just think it's funny that you let him of all people stay over."

"I didn't exactly let him. I just didn't... stop him. I must have been exhausted. It's all this internship stuff, and finals coming up. I'm just stressed out. My brain's not quite functional."

"Uh huh." There is nothing in her tone that says she believes a word coming out of my mouth.

"Why are you here, anyway? I thought you'd have stayed over at Ace's last night."

"Well, we had to do the Foundations today, and I forgot to bring any spare clothes for the rink."

I can barely see her through the narrowed slits of my eyes. "Don't you have like an entire second wardrobe stashed at his place?"

She shrugs and one side of her lip curls up in a smirk. "I didn't have what I needed there."

"Sure you didn't. So, you came home to grill me?"

"I'll never tell."

I step into her. "Yes, you will. If you want a ride to the rink today."

"Fine. Cherry and Jo told me I should come home to check on you. Couldn't have you getting axe murdered by the hockey boy."

"And you think you could have stopped an axe murderer?" I wave a hand up and down her tiny frame. Sure, she's a demon on wheels, but she'd definitely still be the first one to get murdered in a horror flick. Blond hair, big innocent blue eyes. The only thing missing is her virginity.

"Hey, they don't call me Baby Slice for nothing." She zig zags her hands in what I think is a terrible impression of the star of a karate movie. Not sure. I don't watch too many of those.

"And..."

"And what?"

"What else did Cherry and Jo tell you to do?"

Her eyes flick around the kitchen, everywhere but at my face. "If you must know. They wanted me to find out how your night went. I had no idea he'd still be here."

"There it is. Digging for dirt. You three are so nosy." I turn my back on her to pour myself a cup of coffee. I'm gonna need some caffeine to deal with this conversation.

"We're your friends, Tash. We care about you, and we know your sexual experiences of late have been lackluster. You gotta understand we're just looking out for our girl."

"What kind of idiots have you been sleeping with?"

Hot coffee spills over my mug, splashing my hand when I whirl around with a gasp. "What are you still doing here?" At least he's got a shirt on now. I'm not sure I could have held out any longer if I had to keep staring at those unreal abs.

"I was just putting my shirt on and then I heard that you've been sleeping with morons that don't know how to please a goddess such as yourself and I got a little riled up."

I barely keep the laugh in. "Ok, well that conversation was not for your ears, and now that you seem to have found your lost shirt, how about you get out of here? I'm sure you've got things to do. Hockey practice or something. I don't know. Video games, watching porn. What do you guys do in your spare time?"

"You think we're sitting at home watching porn together?" His eyes light up. "Is that what you girls do? Can I come?"

"I think you already did." Emma slaps a hand over her mouth at the lasers I shoot in her direction, but Jacks makes no effort to hide his amusement. His laugh is rich and hearty. Free and easy.

"You're right. How about some breakfast? Are those Pop-Tarts?" His grin could probably power an electric car. "I love Pop-Tarts."

The toaster chooses that moment to pop up, revealing two sugary items that have no right to call themselves breakfast. Emma snatches the little frosted squares up, drops them on a plate, and hands them off to him before I can protest. How dare she give my Pop-Tarts to my one-night stand? Feeding the stray will only encourage him to come back.

"You're not staying for breakfast." I march over to the duck shaped paper towel holder on the counter. My vicious yank rips them down the middle rather than along the nice perforation lines.

He protests when I go to grab his plate, but eventually I snag it and slide his tarts onto the paper towels before shoving him toward the door.

"Okay. Out you go."

"Can I at least wait in here for my ride?" He's fumbling on his phone to call for a ride, I assume.

"Fine."

His hand closes around my upper arm when I spin to walk away, sending a shiver of heat through me. Every time he touches me, I remember what it felt like to have those talented hands all over my body.

My eyes fly open when he pulls me into him, dipping his head down until his lips clash with mine.

Teeth nibble at my lower lip, and a tongue caresses mine in a heated slide. I let myself lean into it, pushing up to my tiptoes as he curves down into me. The kiss deepens as we explore each other.

"Want to do this again sometime?" He mumbles the words into my lips as he snatches another kiss, and an alarm bell dings in the back of my brain.

"No. No. We can't. One night. That was the deal. Go on. Get out of here." I back away from him.

The look he gives me is the equivalent of one a dog would give its owner when they leave on vacation, and there's a tingle of something in my chest. Do I feel bad for this hockey boy? What is wrong with me? It's not like there aren't several dozen — hundred?—other girls waiting in the wings. He will not be going without anytime soon. Get yourself together, Tash.

Chapter Nine

Thin Ice

Jacks

I 'm still yawning as I follow the smell of bacon into the kitchen. Our big bruiser of a defenseman is standing in front of a sizzling pan of the good stuff. Which is better? Bacon or the Pop-Tarts I scarfed down on my Uber ride home after that amazing night last week that's lingering in my head. Bacon Pop-Tart sandwiches? Probably not nutritionist approved, but sometimes you gotta live life on the edge.

"Lucy! My man. You really know the way to a man's heart."

The grumbling sound coming out of him is likely his attempt at a conversation, but he doesn't bother to turn around.

"I'd marry him, but I'm not sure if I'd ever be able to convince Tasha to sleep with me again if I did that. Maybe she's into the forbidden love thing, though. What do you think?" Something about that girl got stuck in my head, and I can't shake it. It's only been a week, though I'm sure I can find someone new to satisfy the itch. Except my mind keeps drifting back to her in a way I haven't felt since she-who-won't-be-named. That's exactly why I need to forget all about her. Look what happened the last time I let someone get too close.

The silence has me glancing around the room at my teammates who are all here, including Aspen? And none of them are laughing at my joke.

"Have you not checked your messages yet today? You've got bigger problems than getting some girl to sleep with you."

Now I'm getting a little concerned. I pat the pockets of my loose black track shorts and come up empty. "I don't know where it is. What's up? Why are you here, Aspen? If I were you, I'd be back home in bed with that fiery redhead of yours. Married sex getting boring?"

Aspen's eyes flash at me. "Don't talk about her like that." He tilts his head up to the ceiling and takes a deep breath. He knows I'm only messing with him. I'm in love with his girlfriend Jordan in the same way the rest of the team is, but there's no way I would ever fuck around on him for real. "Emergency team meeting. Ten o'clock. I was just about to come up there to drag your sorry ass out of bed."

"What." I groan, rubbing my hand over my face. "We were supposed to have the morning off."

"Yeah, we were," Seb shoots me a glare from his spot leaning against the island counter. "Thanks for that."

"What? What did I do?"

Beau tosses his brand-new iPhone at me, and I snatch it before it can suffer a most horrible death at the hands of our grey tiled kitchen floor.

I click on the screen, typing in his lock screen password. The screen is open to the school newspaper. Hockey Jocks Behaving Badly...Again is the headline silently judging me in black typeface.

I scan the article, my name jumping out at me in screamy text, accompanied by a grainy picture of me at Club Clash last week. Thank goodness you can't see Tash's face, but my head is turned to the side enough to identify me by my profile. And it's very clear that my hands are up to indecent things. "Are you fucking kidding me?"

A couple of players last year got arrested after getting drunk and acting like dipshits downtown. They broke a window at a local restaurant and got caught on camera. It got clicks, so some paparazzi wannabe started digging up dirt on the rest of the team. Every little thing we did was scrutinized. The spotlight never landed on me, though, and the articles died down this year after Lennox and McAllister graduated. They were the OG shit disturbers that got arrested.

Looks like someone's trying to stir the pot again, and I'm the one with a target on my back. It mentions me sleeping with a girl, not remembering her name, and then moving on to some public indecency with some other girl. Fantastic. This is not what I need right now.

"This is fucking bullshit. I have never promised a girl anything more than one night. This article is making me out to be some kind of alcoholic asshole who goes around lying to women to get them in bed. Fuck this." I hold back before I chuck Beau's phone at the wall. Not the phone's fault.

"No, but you also don't remember their names and faces. And you know better than to do that in public. Thankfully, this is just a college article, but what if you got caught in public with your dick out next year? As a professional athlete, that would be splashed all over the internet. This one's on you, Jackson. You've got to learn to be more responsible."

I really hate the disappointment in Aspen's voice. I hate it when people are upset with me and do everything in my power to avoid that sinking feeling in my gut that I've let someone down. Or the entire team in this case.

"This is just one stupid article, though. Nobody's going to care as of next week. It'll be fine. It'll all blow over and everyone will forget the whole thing ever happened."

The look Coach is giving me when I walk in the meeting room at the rink has my balls shriveling up. I'm not loving the glares and grumbles coming from the rest of the team seated around the intimidating dark wood conference table.

I slink to the end of the table as far away from my angry looking coach as I can get.

"Vaughan, get your ass over here," he barks at me, and I force my legs to carry myself over to the seat across from him that he's gesturing at.

"We've got a PR problem, and we're going to deal with it right now before it gets any more out of hand. What were you thinking, Vaughan? Fucking around in public, sleeping with the daughter of Tim Richmond and forgetting her name?"

My stomach pitches and a cold sweat pops up on my skin. "What?" The name sounds familiar but I can't place it.

"You heard me. Tim Richmond, Lakeview alum, former NHLer and most importantly one of the biggest donors to the hockey program. You should know better than that. I'm disappointed in you. How many times have I told you boys to keep your dicks clean? You know I mean that in more ways than one."

"But it was just a one-night stand. She's not accusing me of doing anything against her will or anything, right?" My heartbeat is pounding so hard in my ears I can barely hear the buzz of voices from the rest of the team. I would never do anything like that, but what if she had accused me of something like that? That would have totally fucked my career. I seriously need to lay off women this year.

"No, Jackson. But that doesn't mean her words won't hurt the team. She's making the entire team out to be a bunch of assholes who don't give a shit about the school, women, or the alumni who sponsor us." I'm not stupid. I know they're the ones who provide us with this state-of-the-art facility. "This is not a joke."

Sin, the PR assistant for the team, glances at me through her dark glasses. "Not to mention you've already been drafted by Seattle. After their PR nightmare with O'Grady last year, they're not going to take you on if they think you're going to risk the image they've just started to clean up."

Now there's bile collecting at the back of my throat. My contract. This girl could lose me my place on the team I've been dreaming about joining since I heard my name called in the draft.

"No. They wouldn't do that, would they?" My eyes flick around the room, seeking anyone who's going to deny this claim. But all I see are sympathetic looks mixed in with the occasional judgy raised eyebrow.

"They might. They've been laser focused on fixing the PR nightmare that got them dropped by some big name sponsors. If they think you're going to fuck around and mess with their new family friendly image, they will drop you. There are plenty of talented players out there."

"Fuck." I drop head into my heads. "What can I do?"

"First, you're going to write a public apology to this woman. What's her name?" Sin peers over the top of her glasses at me with one brow arched. I can feel her eyes searing straight through my skin, and I know she knows. "Well?"

I bury my face in my hands, pressing my fingers into eyeballs as if I can will the knowledge into my brain. "Uh, Karen?"

"You still don't even know her name. It's Kiera. Kiera Richmond. Daughter of Tim Richmond. Don't forget it again." She announces each damning syllable as if she can sear the information into my brain merely with her words. Judging by the intense look in her eyes, I'm inclined to think it's a distinct possibility.

Wow. I really am coming across as the asshole here. "I won't," I mumble, still afraid to look up from my hands. What's the point? I know what I'm going to find there. Disappointment, ridicule, and anger that I fucked up everyone else's morning off.

"Good. So, you're going to write that apology and have it printed in the paper, and you're going to pick up some volunteer work. I have a list of charitable organizations the college is involved in. You're going to pick one and show up every week, so everyone can see what a good guy you really are under all your man whoring tendencies."

I'm not sure Sin even believes her own words, but I guess that's not her job in PR, is it? She doesn't have to believe in us, she just has to make us look good. She slaps a piece of paper down in front of me with the heading volunteer opportunities on it.

I keep my groan on the inside. Between school, training, practices, games, I'm already tapped out.

She pinches her thin lips up in a vicious little smile. "You can use all that time you've been spending on one-night stands and put it to good use helping people for a change."

Hey, I help people. I help people all the time. I help the team win games. I help my friends—looking at you, Sebastian—get their heads out of their asses. And most importantly, I help women have the best fucking orgasms of their life. I think about the four I provided Tasha with, and my eyes roll back in my head at the memory of her. Those lean muscled arms, the challenge in her eyes that was fucking delightful to conquer, and those tits. Fuck me, why can't I stop thinking of her and those luscious tits? I've never had this issue before. Not since...Well...Doesn't matter. That's so far in the past, it's like it happened to someone else. Tash, on the other hand, is fresh in my mind and for some reason, I can't shake her loose.

"Vaughan. Focus!" Coach snaps at me, yanking me out of my head. "You with us?"

"Yes, Coach." I nod and do my best imitation of my usual grin. Probably looks more like I'm heading for the gallows, but that's all I've got in me at the moment.

Sin pushes up from the table, leaning down with her palms pressed into the wood. "You've got until tomorrow to write your apology. I've circled three volunteer opportunities on that list you can pick from." She taps the piece of paper she gave me.

I give her a weak nod and glance at Coach.

"Consider yourself on probation. You're on thin ice and if we catch wind of any shenanigans, you're facing a suspension or worse. Don't test me."

Suspension. You've got to be kidding me. The murmurs of my teammates are too loud to drown out. They're pissed too. If I get suspended, it could seriously fuck up our very real shot at the champs this year.

"I won't." It's not in my nature to be serious, but I have zero desire to get my ass kicked today, so I'm going to refrain from choosing violence.

"Same goes for the rest of you. To the rest of campus this year, we're the Angels, not the Lightning. Keep your noses clean and stay the hell out of trouble. Dismissed."

His chair scrapes across the floor as he stands up, turning his back to us.

I stall, dropping my head on the table and waiting until the shuffling and cursing have quieted. Sure enough, my squad still has their butts in the seats, waiting not so patiently for me to acknowledge their existence.

Seb gives me a tight smile and a nod. His eyes are begging me not to fuck this up. I know he doesn't think I'm aware of how important this is to him, but I am. Most of his season last year got totally fucked by his injury. He needs this win, and he needs all of us to be supporting him 1000 percent. So that's just what I'm going to do.

I hold up three fingers in a boy scout salute. "I swear I'm good. From this point on, consider me an angel. No more one-night stands. No more fucking around. I promise." No more Tash? No. I can't. Look at the shitstorm I almost dragged her into with that picture. What if the article had named her, or you could see her face in the pic?

Dev snorts. "Right."

"We've got your back." Aspen, the backbone of the team, gives me a punch in the arm.

"Girls are trouble, man." Cole's quiet comment has me whipping my head up to look at him. The newest member of our team was a transfer this year. He had some trouble with his last team that he's never fully explained to any of us. But even though he's moved into our house, we hardly see him. Clearly, he's seen some shit, though, and I'm going to make it my mission this year to get to know him better.

Man, I'm going to miss the fuck out of these guys next year. Hope my new team is half as awesome. If I manage to keep my shit together to make it there.

CHAPTER TEN

SKILLED WITH HIS HANDS

TASHA

"Thanks for coming with." I'm glad Cherry and Jo were able to help today. They can't come every week to whichever Habitat for Humanity project I'm currently working on, but they do what they can because they're that awesome. I love these projects, but everything is more fun with my friends around.

"My pleasure. You know I like building things. And wearing the lumberjack shirt is good for my sex life." Jo winks at Cherry.

"Like you need help with that. Me, on the other hand. Ugh."

"Hookup didn't go so well last night?" Jo asks.

"Uh no. No, thank you. He couldn't even kiss me without slobbering all over my face. No way was I going any further than that. Not my bag."

"I still don't understand why you won't go back for seconds from the hockey boy that gave you, and this is a direct quote, 'The fucking best sex of my life.'" Jo throws up air quotes.

I smack Jo on the arm as we step through the front door of the skeleton of a house we're currently building. It's been two weeks since I slept with Sunny, but my mind keeps straying back to the things he did to my body.

"Morning, Glen." He's so stoic I may never know if the older man overheard my loudmouth of a friend. Here's hoping he was so engrossed in his work he missed that little tidbit.

The poor guy looks up from the plans he was studying carefully, and his eyes crinkle the slightest bit at the corners. He dips his head in his version of an enthusiastic greeting, touching the brim of his well-worn hard hat. Glen and I get along perfectly when my friends aren't blabbing about my sex life.

"Morning. Got a recruit today. He's all yours."

I try not to complain about extra help on the job site. Volunteers are not always easy to come by, but you never know what you're going to get. Could be an experienced handy person or it could be a sorority sister who's never touched a hammer in her life trying to fulfill a volunteer requirement. Or worse, trying to get a little grease on her panties by sleeping with one of the construction workers. Don't get me wrong, I never have a problem teaching someone the ropes, but only if they actually want to be here, and I've had too many experiences where that was not the case.

"What time are they going to be here?" I flick my wrist up to check the time. Five to nine.

"Nine." He swivels his head to glance over my shoulder. "Starlight?"

My mouth drops open at that name coming from that voice.

Cherry, the traitor, bursts out laughing.

"Well, looky who it is," says Jo with a smirk.

"What are you doing here?" I rub my temples before turning around.

The object of all my recent dirty dreams holds up his hands, backing away a couple of steps. "I'm here to volunteer. Pretty sure I'm in the right place." He waves at the space, empty beams still open at the sides are letting the sun shine down and glint off that mess of gold hair on his head.

"Are you stalking me?"

I notice his eyes flicking nervously between my face and my hands, glancing down to see... The hammer. I burst out laughing.

He drops his hands, looking puzzled. "For the record, I'm not stalking you. I picked Habitat For Humanity from the volunteering list, but I had no idea you volunteered here too."

List? "Why were you picking from a list?"

He messes his hair, still staring at the black hammer with white star stickers all over the handle that I'm slapping against my palm.

"Maybe you could put the hammer down and we can chat?"

"I'm not going to hit you with it. Unless I find out you are stalking me, so just be forewarned." But I place my hammer down carefully on the workbench to my left.

"Got it. No funny business. I promise. I'm supposed to meet Glen here."

Glen grunts behind me, not turning away from the wall he's working on.

I toss a thumb behind me. "That's Glen, but if you're our new volunteer, then you have the pleasure of working with me today."

"Really?" He arches a brow and the fear that had tightened his features has softened into something else. I can almost feel his eyes caressing my curves as they rake down my body.

I snap my fingers at him. "Hey. Eyes up here. We're here to work. Come on."

He trails after me to the back area that's set to be the kitchen. "We're working in here today."

"Mmm hmm." When I whip my head around, he's got his eyes glued to my ass in the black leggings I wore. Comfort first on the job site. "Stop checking out my ass and come here. I'm assuming you're not here of your free will, so I'd hate to have to report you to whomever is making you pay your penance building houses for families in need."

"How did you..." he trails off.

"Lucky guess, which you just confirmed. What exactly did you do to earn this hard labor?"

His long legs are encased in tight denim that looks like it's earned the wear and tear rather than come fashionably distressed. He's leaning against a beam with a big, goofy grin on his face. Apparently, he's unperturbed by my questioning.

His eyes are squinched up. "You really don't know?"

"Should I?"

"Some girl I slept with ratted me out and they ran an article about the team in the paper. I got the brunt of the blame, so they need me to prove I'm an upstanding member of the community." His face scrunches up, and the look in his eyes is wary. "There might have been a picture of you in the article. You really didn't see it?"

"What? What picture of me?" Why would there be a picture of me in the school paper? I didn't even know we had a school paper.

He's staring at his feet, rubbing his hands down the front of his jeans. "From the club."

"The club? Like Clash? Why would anyone care about that?" Then the memory of my face buried in his chest to muffle my screams comes to mind. Oh shit. It's not the first time I've fooled around with someone at a club, but maybe the alcove under the stairs wasn't as private as I thought. My face heats when I imagine pictures of my lady parts getting spread around the entire student body. "How bad is it?"

"You can't see your face or anything, and they don't mention your name, but you can tell it's me." My heartbeat eases up when he flashes his phone at me. The photo is pretty poor quality thanks to the low lighting at the bar. You can't tell it's me, but his face is visible, and you can see one of his hands under my shirt and the other up my skirt. It's pretty obvious what we're up to.

"That's not that bad. What did you do to this girl to make her write an article about you?"

"Well....," he winces, "I brought her home."

"And...?"

"Forgot her name and that I'd already slept with her. It was before I met you."

"Oh, that's harsh. Still doesn't seem like breaking news." Why exactly did he feel like he needed to explain that last part to me? We're nothing to each other. My stomach gives the tiniest flip. I don't think I ate enough breakfast this morning.

"She's the daughter of one of the athletic department's biggest donors." The crack of his knuckles has me wincing.

"Got it. You're a master of good decisions, I see."

"Hey, I didn't know. I never promise girls anything. This one just came back to bite me in the ass. But you're not mad about the picture?"

"What's there to be mad about? It's not like you can see anything." I shrug, letting my arm fall to my side.

"I don't know. All I know is that the shitty behavior of the team last year has blown this whole thing out of proportion. I've got to be on my best behavior for the rest of the year."

"So now you're my problem."

The sound of a saw cranking into gear tears apart the weighty silence that had fallen between us.

"That's not fair. I'm here to help, and I'll help. Whatever you need me to do. I'm yours, Starlight."

"Okay, Sunny. First thing you can do is stop calling me that, and second, you can grab a Phillips-head number three out of the toolbox by the front door."

He bobs his head, ducking into the front room to root through the toolbox. He's a little more subdued and obedient than the last time I saw him. Do I miss the over-the-top flirting and goofy smiles? Doesn't matter. I turn around to assess the work I've got to get down today. Glen slipped me a list of tasks that are easy enough for a noob.

"Got it. Where do you need me?" I'm pleasantly surprised to see him standing there, smiling with the correct screwdriver in his hands. He must see it on my face. "Thought I'd screw that one up, didn't you? I've got skills you don't even know about, babe." There's that winning personality.

He is skilled with his hands. I can vouch for that. A shiver runs down my spine. The sex was amazing. "Much worse. Never call me that again."

"Whatever you say, Starlight." He winks at me. "Where do you need my hands?"

Everywhere. Stop it, Tasha. "Follow me."

"Hey, you breaking for lunch?" Jo peeks her head around the corner, eyeing the two of us up.

The bright sun beaming down on is proof that it's noon already. Time has been whizzing by surprisingly fast. Sunny managed to keep his mouth shut for most of it, and I kind of missed the deep rasp of his voice. But he worked hard, and he clearly knows what he's doing with a tool.

He wipes the sweat off his forehead with the back of his forearm and the corded muscles of his biceps bulge out from the bottom of the black t-shirt he's wearing. "Lunch time already? That went by fast."

It did. He's right. Not a single complaint. He did everything I asked, and we got a ton accomplished this morning.

"We'll be right there, Jo."

She disappears again and I reach up, swiping a hand across his forehead that's still a little tacky from sweat. He startles for a moment when I make contact, then drops his eyes closed, leaning into my hand.

"You have a little dirt here." I scrub at the spot with my thumb.

His hand comes up to close around my wrist, and heat creeps up my arm at his touch. What is with me? I'm never like this.

The dirt smear gets a little bigger with my touch, and I snort. "Think I made it worse."

He just shrugs and smiles, eyes still shut, with a thick layer of long lashes resting on his cheeks.

"Tash! You coming?" I drop my hand at the yell and Jackson blinks those startlingly bright blue eyes at me.

"Coming!" I yell back and head off through toward the front of the half-finished house. "I hope you brought food, because I did not bring enough to share."

"Oh, don't worry about me, Starlight. I never go far without snacks. I left my lunch bag in the car, though. Wanna come with?"

I shrug. He brushes by me as I let him pass by and the air between us is charged.

The car he stops at is about fifty percent goldish paint and fifty percent rust. I'm not sure it can even legally be called a car in its current state.

The front door creaks, and he wedges his huge shoulders through the tight space between the seats. He grabs a reusable grocery bag out of the back seat, grunting when he squirms back out and holds up the faded red bag with a flourish.

"You like doing things the hard way?"

The triumphant smile turns a little wicked, and there's a glint in his eyes that I recognize from the one night we shared. My lady parts are tingling at the memory.

"You know it." And then he winks. As if that's something real people do.

I scoff at him, turning to my sleek black Mercedes parked next to his. "Is that thing even roadworthy?"

"Don't say things like that. You'll hurt Mabel's feelings."

I can't help peeking over my shoulder. His hand might be patting that monstrosity, but his eyes are locked on my ass. "Mabel? You named your car?"

"Of course. She's been with me through thick and thin. Good times and..." his sunny smile falters for the first time and there are shadows darkening his eyes. "Not so good. She's a good car."

I find myself wanting to ask about those not so good times, but we barely know each other, and I plan on keeping it that way. Although now that he's gotten himself stuck on volunteer duty on my project, I might be spending more time with him than I ever have with a one-night stand.

He shakes off the melancholy so fast I'm not even sure it was there in the first place. "Where are we eating?"

I gesture to the house. "We've got some folding chairs in the kitchen area. Not exactly glamorous, but we do fine."

I duck into my own car to grab my lip balm, and when I shut the door with a soft click, Jackson lets out a low whistle that blends with the wind swooshing across the job site.

"That's your car? Nice. What year is it?"

Right. Sometimes I forget how out of place the shiny vehicle looks for a college kid. It's not that uncommon around here. It is a private college after all, but most people do expect way more Mabels than Mercedes.

"It was a present." My shoulders tense up as if I'm expecting an attack.

He throws his hands up in the air. "Hey, I'm not knocking it. I was just hoping for a drive." One of his hands reaches out to pat his own beater as if he's reassuring the car he's not going to cheat on her. It's kind of adorable and my shoulders relax right back in a way they rarely do around strangers.

The last thing I want is to be judged by someone for my family's wealth. It's not mine. I didn't earn it and I have no claim on it, but I do have a healthy trust fund from my grandmother that I gained access to on my 19th birthday. She's the only relative that ever really cared for me, so I'm glad I can use her money to pay for school rather than relying on my parents. It pissed my mother off so much when I said I was going to use Gran's money to pay for my education, leaving her and my father with zero influence on my chosen major.

"You wanna take a ride in my car?"

His lips twist in a little smirk as if he's trying to hide the laugh that wants to come out. "I could offer you a ride on something else in return if you'd like."

My nipples tingle at his words. I don't think I can be around him and all his tempting sexuality. I'm too weak. There's no way I'm going to be able to resist going back for seconds if he keeps this up. Especially having stripped down to a white t-shirt that bares those edible biceps of his. Man, the things he could do to me. He could destroy me. In more ways than one.

"Get your mind out of the gutter. I was not offering rides of any kind. Let's get back in before my friends think you've thrown me into the trunk of that heap."

"I would never. Unless that's your thing?"

Ugh. "You're impossible. Come on." This boy seems to be incapable of opening his mouth without something flirtatious coming out of it. Why do I find it so endearing?

Cherry and Jo give me a series of not-so-subtle winks and smiles when we hit the kitchen area and Glen won't make eye contact. Lord knows what my friends were saying while we were out of the room.

I ignore them, busying myself with pulling things out of my purple lunch bag while Jacks plops down in a chair, spreading his legs about a mile in front of himself. My eyes inadvertently trail up their length to the bulge in his pants that he's not trying to hide. He catches me looking and grins without adjusting his stance one iota.

"How's your morning going, ladies?" I ask my friends, studiously ignoring the man beside me, even as he pulls a mind-blowing amount of food out of his grocery bag.

"Oh, we're having a fantastic time. Cherry was just saying we should hit Sweets after we finish up for the day. Grab some food."

I can practically see Jackson's tail wagging as he smiles at me. "I'd love to come." Then his smile dissolves. "But I promised Seb I'd hang with him tonight." He purses his lips, looking up at the ceiling. "Maybe I could cancel."

"I'm pretty sure you weren't invited."

He looks a little crestfallen, and I regret my words as soon as they've fallen from my lips. He has been a huge help today without a single complaint. Maybe I was a little harsh there. He did say he had plans, though.

"Welp I'm all finished, how about you Jo?" Cherry turns to her girlfriend who is still munching on a bag of cheesy popcorn.

Jo crumples the bag closed. "Right, me too. Glen asked to finish that section of the bathroom, right?"

"Sure did." Cherry turns back to me, brushing crumbs off the front of her hot pink t-shirt. "We're going to get back to work. Enjoy the rest of your lunch." Her smile is all bright white teeth.

"Uh huh." I roll my eyes at her, letting her know I'm on to her little game.

"See you later, hockey boy."

"Definitely," he says before turning back to focus his attention on me.

"So, how'd you get involved with Habitat? Any chance it was mandatory volunteer work like me?" Just like that, he's blown right over my earlier rude dismissal. Smiling at me again before he stuffs half his huge sandwich into his mouth.

"Definitely not." I hesitate for a moment, poking at the leftover cashew noodles I brought for lunch. "I...I'm in engineering. Structural engineering. It's a good volunteer opportunity to get some hands-on experience with building." A tiny fraction of the truth, and not really what I'll be doing in my career.

He narrows his eyes at me, Adam's apple bobbing as he swallows his way too large bite. Did he even chew? "There's got to be more to it than that. I used to ref the mites and squirts when I was in high school." The little crinkles at the corner of his eyes make them look even warmer. "That was so much fun. I wish I had time for it now. Maybe once I graduate, I'll be able to help with some camps and local teams during the year instead of just over the break. But I did that because I loved it. Hockey is my life and my love and it's such a great feeling watching kids work hard and develop that love of the game."

His honest passion is written all over his face, and I find myself wanting to share a little piece of myself in return. "I guess I feel the same way about building and designing. I've always loved taking things apart and putting them back together. Building something amazing out of different parts. LEGO was my number one toy when I was a kid, so yeah. When I got the opportunity to help out here, it made so much sense." Not that my parents have supported me any step along the way.

"So, what do you want to build? Houses, other buildings? What's your dream job after you graduate?"

"Hmmm. I'm into sustainable engineering. One of my class projects was to incorporate sustainable features into a community center. Things like that. City buildings. Recreation centers, libraries. Places I can picture people gathering, sharing the space, working together. I dunno. That's ultimate goals. But right now, I'm looking for a summer internship after we graduate. I had an interview for my dream job, but there's a bit of a delay in the hiring process, so it's kind of wait and see." I shrug, looking down at my cold noodles, surprised he pulled that much information out of me. Sharing is not one of my strengths.

"That's so cool. I love that. And I bet you'll get the job."

"You don't know anything about me. I could be at the bottom of my class, barely passing."

His mouth tugs down at the corners and his fingers tickle my scalp when he reaches over to tuck a wayward strand of hair behind my ear. "I bet that's not true. I'd be willing to bet almost anything that you're right up near the top of your class. Even my chocolate bar."

The crinkle of a wrapper has my ears perking up, and I look up at the shiny brown and gold wrapper in his hands. He breaks off a tiny square of chocolate and pops it into his mouth.

"What's that?"

"Only the best chocolate bar on the planet, and I'd know because I'm a connoisseur."

"Really. The best?"

"Yes. It's a Caramilk bar. Milk chocolate with a gooey caramel center. No one even knows how they get the caramel in there. One of life's greatest mysteries." He winks at me.

I snort. "I've never had one. Where'd you get it?"

"From home. My mom sends me care packages of Canadian chocolate bars you can't get here. And ones you can, because they just taste better."

"Really?" I reach into my bag, pulling out a Kit Kat. I didn't bring anything from my special collection today, but I snap off a bar and hold it out. "Trade?"

He tilts his head to the side, considering, then breaks off a few bars and hands the strip over. When I tug on the small piece, he clings to it as if he's reluctant to let go, and his eyes widen when he does.

Gooey caramel spills out, oozing down my lip as I nibble at the piece. The sweet, rich flavor explodes on my tongue.

He laughs, reaching out to swipe at the caramel with his thumb, holding it in front of my mouth. My lower lip tingles at his touch and for some crazy reason, my tongue darts out to lick it off.

His eyes darken, and he shifts in his seat. "You're doing it wrong."

"What?"

"You have to eat the full square. Although. There are definite perks to your method." He pops the thumb I just licked into his own mouth to finish cleaning it off and the gesture has an intimacy to it that's unsettling.

"We should get back to work." I stand up so fast my head spins for a moment, and I have to blink a couple of times to get my head right.

"What did you think?"

"Huh."

"Of the Caramilk."

Right. Chocolate. "It was incredible. Maybe not best ever, though. I'm a Heath girl myself."

"Oh, I'll win you over." His promise has me hurrying off to find something to hammer.

Chapter Eleven

Fair Play

Jacks

"Spot me, Woodsy."

Aspen flips me off when I interrupt his set of squats, but I need to talk to him, so he's gonna have to wrap it up and get his ass over here. He's the most reliable one on the team, and I've been on my best behavior, so I think I deserve a little of his time.

"Let me finish my set, asshole. The world does not revolve around you."

"Huh. That's weird. Way to burst my bubble, bro."

He rolls his eyes at me, and finishes his set with a grunt, but I know my friend. He's strolling over as soon as he finishes wiping the sweat off his brow with a white towel. His shadow falls over my face as he settles behind me, hovering his hands below the bar. He can't resist helping someone in need. That's why he's the captain.

The ridges of the bar rasp against my palms, and I start my first set of reps. The burn of my muscles as I push them to their limits is satisfying. Takes my mind off the uncomfortable thoughts swirling around in my brain.

"What's up?" he asks when I take a rest break between sets.

"What do you mean?"

"You would usually have Seb spot for you. I'm assuming you have something on your mind that he can't help you with."

"How'd you get so smart? Was it all those books? Should I read more, or do I just need to get a hot book-worm for a girlfriend to gain information by osmosis?"

"Do you really want to be running your mouth like that when I'm holding your life in my hands? Now get to your point or I'm going to leave you here." His threat is empty. He's the nicest guy on the team and he would never let harm come to a single one of us.

"Fine. So, you know that girl?"

The bar clangs as I drop it on its rack, sitting up and spinning around on the bench to face him. I can't quite get into this while I'm lying there.

"Kiera?"

"Who?"

"Kiera, the girl that's holding your balls over the fire right now numb nuts."

"Oh yeah. No, not her."

"You're an idiot."

"Probably true, but no. I'm talking about Tasha. The derby girl. Best fucking sex of my life. Remember?"

"No, thank goodness. I don't remember the best sex of your life." His green eyes are squinched up in confusion. "What about her?"

"Did you not hear what I said? Best fucking sex of my life. My dick is never going to be the same again." As long as it's just my dick this will be fine. I can handle it.

"What's the problem? Get to the point. I've gotta finish my workout. Jordan has a thing at Top Shelf this evening."

"Whupaw!" My whip noise is subpar, but the guys laugh and that's when I notice they've all drifted closer to be a part of my private conversation with Aspen. Of course they have. Nosy fuckers. "Ow, dude, that fucking hurt." I pout at him after he slams his fist into my shoulder.

"You deserved it," he says.

"What do you think, guys?" I turn to the rest of them since apparently, they're planning on listening to our conversation anyway, I may as well get them involved. Sure, it's a terrible idea to take advice from a bunch of single players and one single fucker who is currently brooding over a girl from his past. I glance at Seb. He looks okay right now, but he's got some shit going on.

"I think he's solidly whipped." Beau chirps in, squirting some hand sanitizer on and rubbing it in. "But looks like you're heading for the same fate yourself, so good luck with that."

"I am not. Did you not hear what I said? Best sex ever. I'm not planning on giving her a ring anytime soon, but I would like to get into her panties again." Those little lacy panties I'm dying to rip off her.

"Well then, what's the problem?" Dev looks confused as he pauses mid calf stretch.

"You mean other than the fact that he's supposed to be keeping his nose squeaky clean right now? No women, right? Isn't that what you swore up and down?" Seb's glowering at me.

"Actually, you said no women. I said I was going to be more selective. And I don't think you guys are understanding my point. Think of the best sex you've ever had and times it by infinity. That's how good it was. The problem is she isn't into repeats. We agreed on one night only."

"So, your usual deal? Hate to tell you this friend, but maybe the sex wasn't as good for her as it was for you? Have you ever thought about that?" I wanna punch the sympathetic look off Woodsy's face.

Could Aspen be right? Was I shitty in bed? I think back to that night. "Nah bro, I made her come like four times." Lucy lifts a brow, and I shake my head at him. "No way. She is not the type of girl who would fake an orgasm. She takes what she wants, and she's not afraid to tell it like it is. No way would she fake it. Especially not four times."

"Well, then I guess she pulled a you on you. She one and doned you. How's that feel?" Aspen asks.

His words hit home hard, roiling my stomach. He's right. No matter what my intentions were, I hurt Kiera. I was a thoughtless asshole, and I probably deserve this. "Like shit."

"Exactly. Maybe you should just forget about it and move on. Lay off the hookups entirely or find another girl or two to get you through the year."

I could probably go through the motions and find someone else, but for some reason, no one has caught my eye since my night with Tash. It's unsettling how much she's gotten under my skin already, but I don't think I'm ready to let it go. "I don't think you're understanding. It was like mind blowing. Earth shattering. I need another shot. Plus, think of it this way. If I'm only sleeping with one girl, then I don't look like such a piece of shit player. I still get sex, but I'm not causing trouble for the team, man whoring all over campus." Maybe I'm trying to find an excuse to make this work, but it's valid. There may be a slight twinge deep down that I haven't felt in a long while, but I don't need to give in to that. I can make this thing work on a purely physical level.

"I guess you need to try harder then. Woo her."

"Woo? What are we in a Jane Austen movie?" I'm not that surprised to hear that word come out of Aspen's mouth. He does read a lot of schmancy romance books with his girlfriend.

"Whatever dude." He shakes his head. "Just trying to help."

My cheeks puff out with a resigned exhale. "Okay. I'll bite. How would I go about wooing her? For just sex type purposes. Not like dating or anything, since neither of us is interested in that."

"Buy her some flowers, or a book, or share some of your secret Canadian chocolate stash with her."

Share my chocolate? I don't share my chocolate with anyone. Other than that one time. With her. Wait, I shared my chocolate with her? "Don't think flowers are her thing. Not sure about books. We haven't exactly gotten to know each other. That's really the crux. I need to convince her to take a second ride on my cock. Fuck her so hard, she'll never want to get off."

Dev groans. "Thanks for that picture. I'm gonna need to bleach my grey matter later. I'm out of this convo." He turns his back to us, popping his earbuds back in.

"How about you delve deep into your own twisted brain? How would you convince yourself to go back for seconds if you were a girl?" Seb asks.

"I don't fucking know. I thought the sex spoke for itself. That's all I need. One more shot. A chance to remind her of how good it was and then propose some sort of arrangement. No strings."

"Good luck with that. Now let's get back to your set. Enough gossiping like ladies at a wine club masquerading as a book club." Aspen lays down the law.

I settle back down on the narrow bench, inhaling a deep breath and closing my hands back on the bar. I just need one chance to convince her. We'll see each other at the build again on Sunday, but that doesn't seem like the best place for my mission. How do girls catch my attention? Wearing my jersey at games. Cheering me on and lying in wait to catch me on a winning high. That usually works. Stroking my ego often leads to stroking my dick.

Would that even work on her? And if so, how would I go about it? She's not a hockey player. The picture from the office at the rink of her looking smoking hot in her derby gear flashes in my head. But Tasha Scar is a roller derby girl, isn't she?

Chapter Twelve

Smash And Dash

Tasha

I slump back on the couch after snapping my laptop shut with a little more force than necessary. Three video interviews today have just about drained me of all my mental energy. Thank goodness we have a bout tonight. I'm going to need to get some of my pent up aggression out somehow, and that is a safe place for it. Good luck to anyone who wants to challenge me tonight.

Two out of three of the interviews today were duds. The companies just don't align with what I'm looking to do with my degree. A lot of the big names don't value sustainability and innovativeness the way I do, but they're the ones who can afford to take on multiple interns, so the competition is less intense. One of them even offered me a job on the spot. Their HR rep said he'd email me the paperwork and I have a week to decide.

The safe thing to do would be to take one of these. It's just an internship. Not like I have to commit my life to them. But getting into Everge-En would give me a golden ticket. A clear path to my dream job, not to mention working on a project I can feel proud of. Rebecca, the HR manager, emailed me saying I made it to the next round of interviews, but she hasn't given me a clear idea of when that will happen.

Nobody tells you how complicated being an adult is going to be until you're deep in the trenches trying to figure out the rest of your life when you can barely figure out what to cook yourself for dinner.

I've been restless all day, and now finally we're here, lacing up and getting ready for a bout. I need this so badly. Get rid of all this nervous energy. I shoot up out of my seat as soon as my boots are laced, pushing off to the other end of the little former classroom that doubles as our change room. I'm glad we're on home turf tonight. It's always nice to be on the familiar track.

"What is with you today?" Emma asks. She's leaning back all casual in her seat, hair pulled up into cute blond ponytails that are absolutely not representative of her viciousness in a bout. She's small but fierce with a wicked set of elbows.

"It's this internship. I still haven't heard from them, and I want it so bad."

"I know. They're probably obligated to interview all the suitable candidates, even though they decided on you before your interview was over."

I roll my eyes at my bestie but appreciate the support. "Thanks, babe, but I'm not sure it works quite like that."

"You've had a couple more interviews, though, right? You'll get something. Zero doubt about that."

"Yes, but this is the one I want. They have offices in Seattle and New York, as well as one in Cali. It's small enough to be able to make change without being obscure, and it's perfect. You know the community building project I worked on for my end of term assignment last year? That's exactly the sort of project they work on. I can take all my ideas and find a good home for them at Everge-En I want this job so bad. But I've already got an offer from MG Tech. The smart thing to do would be to accept that internship, gain some experience, and then move on to something more in my niche, right?"

"That would be the safe thing to do," Jo says, slapping the Velcro shut on her elbow guard. "The smart thing would be to follow your heart and wait for a job that's a better fit. I know you Tash. You wouldn't be happy at some big, soulless corporation. You're also way too much of a bad ass bitch to play it safe. Go big or get the fuck off the track, right?"

I smile as warmth spreads through me like liquid honey, sweet and golden. She's right.

"Listen to my girlfriend. She knows best. You're incredible, and you've worked your ass off to get where you are.

You can totally do this." Cherry holds out a hand for a high five.

Our wrist guards bang together as I slap her palm. "Thanks ladies. You're the bomb."

Cherry is snapping her chin strap shut when she turns back to me, and I don't trust the gleam in her eyes. "Now, if you want something to get your mind off the job, why don't you bang out that excess energy with your hockey boy?"

I roll my eyes at her. "He's not MY hockey boy. And you know that's not my thing."

"I know, but I still don't quite understand why. You said it was amazing. Sounded like he was into a repeat performance. Go for it. It's not that complicated."

"I don't do relationships."

"Doesn't have to be a relationship." My eyes flick to Jo. She's pulling her fingerless gloves on, and checking that her pads are secure. "Keep him as your boy toy, your cock on lock."

Did I hear those words come out of her mouth? "Are we in a dirty Dr. Seuss book? Cock on lock? You're deeply disturbed."

"And that, my friend, is why you love me. Two fucked up peas in a pod." The lopsided smile on her face is deranged. "Seriously, have you never had a friends with benefits type situation?"

"He's not my friend." I snap. "And even if he was, those things never work out. Someone always catches feelings. Not me, of course, but that's why I keep it simple. Smash and dash. Oh god, you're rubbing off on me."

We all burst out laughing, but her words are still traipsing through my brain when it's time to hit the track.

The crowd is small but enthusiastic and I smile when the cheers ring out as we skate out on the smooth surface.

"The moment you've been waiting for. Your home team, The Lakeview Ladies of the Fight." Lana's deep voice rings out over the scratchy PA system and the room goes wild with cheers and clapping.

Love this shit. I skate backward, waving at the audience scattered across a mix of old wooden bleachers and camp chairs brought from home.

"Watch it," Izzy hisses at me when I skate into her, almost losing my footing. She's been gunning for the star on my helmet all year, but I'm still the best Jammer on the team, and I won't let myself get distracted by her pettiness.

"I'm sorry." I can't even look at her. My eyes are glued to the handful of guys in the front row of the bleachers. They've all got muscles bulging out of the purple tank tops that match our jerseys. They've even got Ladies of the Fight painted across the front in childlike scrawl.

A huge smile is on Jackson's face as he holds up a sign that says. "Make it so, Tasha Scar." Then he spins around to show me my derby name and number written on his back.

Seriously? Emma shoves me and whispers in my ear. "This might be the best night of my life."

I shake my head at her and get into position, trying to ignore the hockey players that came out to cheer us on. Unfortunately, they're so loud and they take up so much space they're hard to ignore. Especially the blond one with the smile as bright as the sun and the body made for dirty, dirty things.

CHAPTER THIRTEEN

LADIES OF THE FIGHT

JACKS

This is amazing. The roller derby track is in a former school, so it's got an underground vibe to it. The bleachers are still intact, and the stank of decades of sweaty bodies and stinky feet clings to the walls. Nothing we're not used to. Beau did some research for us and bringing our own camping chairs seemed like a much more comfortable option. Not to mention we got here early enough that we're in the front row right in the action.

When the girls came out, I cheered louder than anyone else in the place, and I'm still smirking as she's lined up behind her team. She's got the jammer star on her helmet. I did my research I know what it means.

She's gotta lap the members of the opposing team to score points, and some of the women on the other team look fierce. They've got black and white uniforms adorned with skulls, and a few of them tower over our girls. Tasha's tall but her muscles are of the long, lean kind. She's strong but not bulky. There's an intense look on her face as she crouches down poised on the toes of her skates.

The whistle blows and they're off, immediately converging into small packs and holding out their arms to block the jammers from getting by. It's fierce.

The jammer from the opposing team tries to break through the triangle formed by three ladies from the home team, but they hold strong. They're not the ones who are keeping my attention, though. I'm locked on Tasha. Her arms are bare, revealing the stormy pattern of stars and a single lightning bolt shooting down her right biceps. It's like it was meant to be. If I believed in any sort of fate.

A tall, mean looking lady hits her hard, rocking her back, and I suck in a breath, not letting it out until she steadies herself and ducks down to scoot around the woman. Man, she's fast.

There are shouts of encouragement and praise from all the derby girls, and the noise from the crowd is much louder than you'd think. What they lack in size, they're making up for in spirit. Of course, having several rowdy hockey players in the front row helps, but even without us, the enthusiasm is infectious.

Her arms pump as she moves those sexy, fishnet clad legs back and forth, searching for an opening around her wall of opponents. When she finds it, she shoots forward, pushing off her heels to deke around the blockers. Her friend Jo shoves aside a rival, letting her pass and her arms fly up as she coasts around the track.

My knowledge of what's going on is still pretty basic, but I can tell she's killing it when they reset for another bout.

"This is fantastic!" Beau shouts in my ear. "Level me up to superfan status."

I grin back at him, slapping him with double high fives as we stand up, clapping.

"TASHA SCAR!!!" I shout out, uncaring of the eyes swiveling around to find the source of the noise. The lady herself turns to look at me and her face is bright pink. I'm sure she'd blame it on the exertion, but I think she might be just a tad embarrassed. Score one for me.

The helmet shadows her face, but I still catch her eye roll as she shakes her head and turns her attention back to the match.

We're on our feet cheering as the Ladies of the Fight huddle in the center of the track, hugging and clapping each other on the backs. It's a very familiar sight, if a little less rowdy than the ones we get into on the ice.

They shake hands with their opponents, do a quick victory lap, and then disappear behind the stage that still stands at one end of the gym. I imagine the beaten-up wood surface has witnessed many a crappy high school performance in its day.

The audience gets to its feet and some people are shuffling out while others are standing around mingling and chatting.

Dev yawns, stretching his massive arms over his head. "Can we go now?" he mumbles.

"No way. We've gotta stay to congratulate our team."

Seb's eyebrow is reaching up almost to his hairline. "Really? That's why you want to stay? To congratulate the team we've never heard of before today? Don't bullshit us."

Aspen laughs. "Yeah, where's your lady?"

"Where's yours?" I shoot back at him. "I thought Jordan might show that gorgeous face of hers here. Even though books are more her thing, I thought she might be into all the lady power here?"

"She's got an exam to study for, otherwise she might have come. Don't try to distract me, though. We all know why we're here. Just admit it."

"Right," Beau says. "You wanna rebang the hot roller girl. It's cool we can wait."

There's the sound of a throat clearing behind us and I turn around to find my Starlight.

She's got murder in her eyes. "Rebang? Is that even a word? I don't like to stereotype, but it might be a good idea for you hockey boys to study a little harder if you still need to work on your grasp of the English language."

"Yes! You're perfect. Never change." Aspen steps into Tasha with his hand held out. "Hi, I'm Aspen. Team captain and, therefore, unwilling handler of these fools." He's not kidding anyone. We know how much he loves keeping us in line.

She's stripped off the pads and helmet, but she's still wearing her derby clothes. The frown pinching her eyes together is as dark as her deep purple lipstick. The color that's looked fucking fantastic ringing my dick in my dreams. It's about time I made those dreams a reality.

Her hand slides into his in a firm shake before she swings around on me. "What are you doing here?"

Her tone is sharp, but I don't let it dim my smile. "I came for the derby, Starlight. Heard it was a great time. Turns out it was even better than promised."

"Uh, huh. But it's over now. Why don't you boys get yourselves off to whatever pursuits your evenings usually consist of?"

She's trying so hard to dismiss me, but the harder she tries, the more I want in. "Oh, we cleared our schedules for you. No plans for the rest of the night."

"Really?" Her petite blonde friend sidles up to her. "We're riding that adrenaline wave, so we were planning on heading out for a little dinner after this. You boys are welcome to come if you'd like." She has to tilt her chin way up to look at us, but I'm no longer fooled by her innocent appearance. I saw the way she held back the other team. Baby Slice has a vicious side.

"Emma." Tasha rounds on her friend and I'm surprised she doesn't grab the other girl by the pigtails. I wouldn't put a stop to it. That would be fucking hot as fuck.

"We'd love to. Where are we going, Baby Slice?"

I'm rewarded with a bright smile and blue eyes sparkling with mischief. "We're going to Ethel's. Know it?"

Of course I know it. The little mom and pop diner downtown is the campus hot spot for greasy breakfast the morning after an overindulgent night out. You'll be lining up for an hour in the morning, but the evenings aren't as busy, so we should be able to grab a late-night table. The thought of some homemade food is fantastic. It helps fill the void of my mom's home cooking.

"Who doesn't? We'll be there."

Tasha is staring at the ceiling, probably questioning her choice of friends.

"Anyone need a ride?"

"Nah, we're good. Thanks for the offer, though. See you boys there." She winks over her shoulder as Tash drags her away, whispering furiously.

CHAPTER FOURTEEN

QUALITY DICK

TASHA

"I can't believe you invited them. This is supposed to be girl time. Post match recap, easing off the adrenaline fun times. Not rowdy hockey dude time."

"Really, Tash?" Emma's trying to keep up with the furious pace of my much longer legs as I lead her to my car. Icicles are forming in my hair from the frigid December air, but I was too stressed out to blow dry it after my shower. "Like you don't pick up some rando fifty per cent of the time to burn off the excess after a bout. I'm just doing you a favor and bringing along a sure thing. And by sure thing, I mean a guaranteed orgasm. Something of which you are desperately in need of. How long has it been?"

"I don't know. A day? Not that it's any of your business."

"I didn't mean self inflicted. You need some dick. Good dick. Not shitty dick."

Ugh. The thing is, she's right. I want to burn some of this energy off with someone, but my last few attempts have been lame at best. And Jackson. He's my cosmic opposite. A bright ball of sunshine to my shadowy night sky, but he sure gave me an incredible time.

"I don't need dick." There's heavy emphasis on the word need.

"Of course it's not necessary to your existence. I'm not questioning your feminine independence. You know that. You're just being obstinate, and I'm not having it. Quality dick is hard to come by and you deserve some, my friend. We destroyed the Killers out on the track tonight. I'm not telling you to marry the guy, but one repeat or a little cock on lock wouldn't hurt you. You have all the power. He's dying to get in your pants for another round. Make your own terms. Put up some boundaries. Whatever you need to do, but enjoy that fine piece of hockey ass. If I didn't have Ace, I would a hundred per cent take one of those boys out for a test drive."

"I'll think about it."

Her squeal pierces my eardrum, and she bounces on her toes. "Yes!"

"What are you so happy about? You're not sleeping with him?"

"Yes, but you'll tell me all about it, and I can live vicariously through you."

"I'm not telling you all about it," I say, sliding into the smooth leather seat of my car and stroking the wheel.

"Yes, you are. Don't mess with me."

She's probably right. I don't keep too many secrets from my roommate and bestie. I don't know why this thing between us works. We're complete opposites, for the most part. If anything, Emma's way more like Jacks than I am. They'd either make the perfect couple, or they'd drive each other and the rest of the world crazy. Alas, she's already taken, and I guess I'm stuck with him. Maybe. Still haven't decided for sure if I'm going to let him take another shot. We'll see how well behaved he and his hockey friends are tonight.

The diner sits tucked away at the end of a residential street. It's in a big old white house with a peaked roof in the front and cheery yellow curtains hanging in the windows. Ethel lives upstairs, but her son runs the place now that her husband Merv passed away. She still stops by to visit and help, though, claiming the energy of all the college students keeps her young. But if you give her a bit of time, she'll start telling you about her escapades when she was younger. She's led a wild life, and her stories far outrival anything we get up to.

The bell tinkles our arrival and sure enough, Ethel turns to look at us as we traipse in, stomping the dusting of snow off our boots. The strawberry color of her curly hair is somewhere between pink and red and she's wearing a glittery red apron trimmed in white lace. It gives her a distinct resemblance to Mrs. Claus.

Her son Ron marches over to greet us. He dips his head in a stiff sort of bow as if the place is a five-star restaurant instead of a cozy family diner. "Follow me."

I glance at Emma and shrug, following him into the back room. The large bodies of our new friends dominate the small space and they're laughing and talking already. No sign of any booze, just a couple pitchers of ice water and white coffee mugs.

The boys are all spread out around the right side of the worn pine table, so I head for the seat at the far end.

"Starlight, I saved you a seat." Jacks pats the seat next to him and I'm still hesitating when Emma shoves me forward.

Fine. I keep the scowl on my face but squeeze into the seat next to him. The window behind is chilly and my shoulders shimmy with a little shiver. I should have dried my hair.

"Chilly?" He frowns. "Shouldn't have sat beside the window. Here." Something fleecy and warm drapes around my shoulders and a sweet coconut smell engulfs me. *Mmmm.* Smells delicious. Unbidden, the memory of his muscular body flexing above me as he buried his cock deep inside my heat pops into my head, and a shiver of another sort rips through me. Down girl. It's just the post bout adrenaline.

"I'm fine." I shrug his jacket off my shoulders, regretting it immediately when the icy air hits my mesh-covered arms. Maybe I need to wear more layers, so I won't have to rely on guys for extra clothing.

He leans in, his words tickling my neck. "I'll leave it there. Feel free to borrow it if you decide to choose comfort."

I'm going to choose violence if he keeps reading me like that. The thought of letting him in makes me uncomfortably squirmy. He doesn't know me, and he doesn't need to.

"Fanfuckingtastic bout ladies!" Cherry comes roaring up with Jo, eyes bright and lips swollen. They must have had trouble getting out of the car, because they left right after us. After two years of fighting their feelings for each other, it warms even my stony heart to see them together.

"Wasn't it?" My smile comes out to play. This I can celebrate.

"You've got a dimple." A hand reaches out, hovering over my cheek, not quite touching my face. The heat from even the hint of contact has me feverishly warm.

That comment clears the offending dimple away. I'm aware of how much it softens my face and makes me look younger, so I do my best to keep it in check. "And?"

"It's adorable. I want to plant a kiss on it and then continue to map out the rest of that gorgeous body with my lips." His voice drops to a whisper, but he doesn't kiss me or make any other moves. I almost wish he would. I don't know that I'd resist.

"I'm not adorable."

"No, but your dimple is. You? You're stunning, a fucking work of art."

Is he even serious with that? Who says shit like that? He must notice my skeptical look.

"What?"

"Are you for real?"

He looks down, then back up, pats himself down. "Pretty sure I am."

A snort of a laugh sneaks out, and he smirks.

"Hey, I'm not a liar. I'm not saying anything that's not true."

"It's not the sentiment, so much as the words." I'm not self effacing or insecure. I know I'm good looking, but still those words are a lot. Just like him. Everything about him is a lot. It's like his personality is so big it's crowding the fence I keep around myself. Leaning on it a little more with each joke, each smile, and each gesture. The gate is creaking and swaying under his weight until I'm afraid it's going to crack all together.

"I call it like I see it, but if you want me to stop, I will. If I'm making you uncomfortable, it's over." He throws his hands up in the air. "I don't want to be some creep coming on to you against your will."

My head shakes back and forth almost of its own accord. "No. You're not." If there's one thing he's not, it's the creepy guy staring at me from a dark corner. Nope. The only thing that about him that makes me uncomfortable is my own reaction to him.

Chapter Fifteen

Hot Teacher, Horny Student

Jacks

That snort laugh was fucking adorable, and it was also the moment I knew I had her. Before the reluctant agreement that I wasn't creeping her out. Before the cautious circles she started tracing on my knee under the table, and way before I slipped my hand onto her leg, sliding it up her inner thigh.

She tucks her bottom lip between her teeth to keep the sounds inside that I really fucking want her to let loose. Maybe not in the restaurant, though.

She finally pushes me away when the food arrives, but not before I've reached the prize. I swipe my fingers along the soft mound at the juncture of her thighs and find her panties soaked. She covers her moan with a cough, pushing my hand away before I can explore further, but now I know it's a lock. I'm going to get the chance to taste that sweet pussy tonight. Even if it's only one more time, she's not going to resist.

I hope it's not a two off. I'm afraid I'm about to get addicted to this woman with her prickly exterior and fiery passion. It feels like we were designed to fit together. In the sex department, at least.

Who am I kidding? It's not just the sex I'm seeking from her. That feeling I got when I teased the dimple out of her was intense. It was more. Something I haven't felt for a girl in years. Something I don't want to feel because it's scary. Because if you love someone and they leave you, it fucking hurts. There's a hollow ache in my chest that never goes away. It's a reminder of what love can do to you. I'm terrified but can't seem to make myself stay away.

"Jacks. The ladies are going to think we don't feed you. Slow down." Aspen's words still the hand that's shoveling meatloaf down my throat. It is really fucking good meatloaf, granted, but that's not why I'm eating so fast.

"Don't worry. They shove a plate through the slot in my door once every day or so." I laugh off my crappy table manners.

"Somehow I don't think you'd have grown that big and strong on scraps." Emma smiles at me, and I catch Tash glaring at her out of the corner of my eye. It doesn't escape me that her plate is almost clear too. She went for the burger and fries. Good choice. Now I get the pleasure of her delicate little tongue darting out to clean the grease off her lips.

I almost reach over the table to smack Lucy when he orders a slice of apple pie with ice cream. Admittedly, it is delicious pie, but he's just doing it to cockblock me since I'm his ride home.

"He'll have that to go." I tell Gemma, the redheaded granddaughter of Ethel. She's working at the diner while she gets her degree at Lakeview. She's smoking hot, but thankfully I have enough brain cells left even after all the hockey hits to not fuck where I eat. That would be a terrible idea.

"Hey! I wanna eat it here."

I ignore the big man and smile at our server. "Just the bill, please."

She looks between the two of us, then her eyes trail to the girl by my side and a slow smile inches up her cheeks. "Sure thing."

"What's the rush, Jacks? Got somewhere to be?" Aspen asks.

"Yeah, your mom stopped by. She slipped a key in my back pocket earlier." He pushes up on the table and I'm a little worried he's going to bust some shit up in here. I'd hate to get banned from this place. The food is way too good to risk.

I throw my hands up. "I'm just kidding. Ease up, dude."

He sits back down with a glare, and I laugh. Narrow escape. Not so easy to rile up the calm and collected mature one of our group, but I know everyone's buttons to push. For some reason, I can't help but use that knowledge way too often for my own health.

"Let's get out of here," Jo pushes up from her seat. "All this testosterone is killing my post derby vibe. C'mon, sweetie pie."

"Don't call me that in public," Cherry hisses. They'd be kind of adorable if I wasn't fucking terrified of them. Especially after seeing their vicious skills earlier today. If they do that for fun, I imagine they'd take great pleasure in dismembering me if I did anything to hurt their friend. Same for Emma.

Beau throws the bill on his card and takes cash from everyone for their share. Then, when the girls have walked off toward the door in a secret huddle, he tosses all the cash on the table as a tip for Gemma.

I catch up with the girls before Tasha slips out the front door and disappears into the night. I snag her arm, pulling her into my chest, and sliding my hand up to rest on her shoulder in a light grip. "Come home with me," I whisper in her ear. Strands of her black and pink hair have escaped her high ponytail and are tickling my nose, so I reach up to brush them away and tuck them behind her ear.

She squinches her face up. "I have to drive Emma home."

Her friend must have supersonic hearing or something cause she turns around. "I'm going to get Jo to drive me over to Ace's. You don't mind, do you, Tash?" her eyes are wide with faux concern and innocence.

Tasha sighs. "You know I don't. I'll see you tomorrow."

"Yes, you will. I can't wait to chat."

"So?" I ask again.

"Okay. I'll come home with you, but I'm driving myself and there are going to be some rules."

"Rules? Like spicy librarian rules. Ooh or hot teacher, yes. Can we play hot teacher, horny student?"

"What? No. Not what I was talking about." She rolls her eyes at me, pressing her lips together to avoid giving me that smile I'm dying to see again. "We'll talk when we get to your place. What's your address?"

"Here, give me your phone." She purses her lips, frowning, and finally digs it up from... between her cleavage. Oh my god. She had her phone tucked away between the best set of tits I've ever seen. Wish I was there right now. Soon. I'll get there.

Mabel creaks when Dev throws his big body down onto the stained velour, and cracks open the cardboard takeout box with a flourish.

"Are you gonna eat that in here?"

Dev glances up with a surprised look.

"JK." I laugh. "Enjoy." Maybe if I had a sweet ride like Tasha does, I'd care about my friends eating in it, but Mabel was meant for enjoyment. A few crumbs won't hurt her.

I bang on the glove box to get it to pop open and snag a Mars bar out. Gotta have a snack for the ride home. On second thought. I pause, rooting through my stash and pull out a Coffee Crisp.

Dev reaches for it, and I smack his hand away. "Not for you."

"Fuck you."

"Fuck you too. Eat your pie."

The drive home feels like it takes forever, but I'm pretty sure it was my fastest time ever. I scan the road in front of our place, but there's no sign of Tash's fancy ride.

"What's with this girl?"

"She's hot as fuck. I'm sure that can't have escaped even your notice." Even as the words come out, I know they're a lie, or at least a half truth. She is hot, but she's so much more than that. She's so smart and driven. I've got my own ambitions, so I can appreciate how passionate she is about her degree and her future career. And she's prickly on the outside but cares so much for her friends and her teammates, too. She's just my Starlight.

"Yeah, well, she's not the only hot girl on campus. One of many."

"Not like her."

My friend tends to be the strong, silent type, but the look he's giving me right now is a little too intense and perceptive for me. It's like he's reading things about me I've barely admitted to myself.

CHAPTER SIXTEEN

HOT AND HARD FACTS

TASHA

H e typed his address into my contacts, along with his number, listed under the name Horny Student. That cannot pop up on my screen. I'll change it in the morning. It would totally be like one of those videos where people show texts from their dogs. I'll leave him for an hour and get a hundred texts from Horny Student. No thanks. I'd never live that one down.

I get all the way to his house and pause before pulling up beside the curb. I'm contemplating turning around and getting the hell out of there when I see movement on the big front porch. There he is, swaying back and forth on a big wooden porch swing, one leg hanging over the edge, one bent up beside him as he slouches in the seat, waiting for me.

I guess there's no point in turning back now. I've been spotted. It's fine. I've got this under control. I take a deep breath and start walking up the path. My car chirps behind me as I hit the lock button, and Jackson shoots to his feet when I hit the steps.

"Thank fuck," he says. "I thought for a minute you were going to back out on me."

"I did too."

"But that would have been a crazy thing to do. We're fucking incredible together. You can't deny that."

He's leaning in for a kiss, pausing when his forehead hits my outstretched palm. As much as I want to lose myself in him, I need to lay down the ground rules first.

He flicks his eyes up to mine, brow pinched in a frown, one eyebrow curved like a question mark.

"Ground rules."

"Ah, yes. Rules. Like eight simple rules for fucking my hot derby girl."

"Keep that up and rule number one will be Not Happening."

"Sorry. I'll be good. Promise. What do you propose? Should I get my lawyer to draw us up a contract, a la Fifty Shades?" He cups his hand around his mouth, whispering as if the squirrels are going to overhear him.

"You're ridiculous. How about we keep it simple? I'm afraid your brain will explode if I try to stuff more information in that clearly overloaded grey matter."

"Do you think I'm some kind of dumb jock just because I'm pretty?"

"No. You just already seem to have a plethora of thoughts spilling from your mouth constantly, so I figure you don't need me to add to the burden."

He laughs, raking a hand through his golden hair. It looks so soft with the porch light shining down on it. I want to reach out and sift my fingers through it, but rules first. "Ok, simple. No catching feelings. We're not dating, we're not girlfriend and boyfriend. This is all about the sex. Can you handle that puck boy?"

His lips pinch down a bit at the corners before the thousand-watt smile is back. "No strings attached sex with the most stunning woman I've ever met? I think I'm up for the job." He glances down at the tent already forming under his sweatpants and man, I forgot how massive that thing was. How good it felt destroying me.

"Are you sure? Compliments like that reek of someone trying to impress."

"I'm not allowed to tell you how stunning you are? That's no fair. I'm only stating a fact. A cold, hard, objective fact. Or maybe it's hot and hard." I should roll my eyes at that ridiculous line, but he's just so damn charming he pulls it off.

I sigh. "Fine. Compliments allowed. Second rule is whenever one of us wants to end it. Whenever this is not fun anymore, we're done. No quibbling or begging. Just done."

"That's fine, but I've got a rule of my own. No lying to get out of this. If we really aren't enjoying it anymore, fine, it's over, but no lying to me or yourself to get out of it. If the sex tonight is as fantastic as it was last time,

I'm imagining we can ride this out for the rest of the year. Unless, of course, you meet someone else. That's different." He shifts on his feet, hands flexing at his side.

"I'm not going to meet anyone else. Don't worry about that." Now that I think about this, it is the perfect arrangement. I get to enjoy great sex with the guy who I already know is going to give me a good time. I don't need to look for random hookups or suffer sloppy kisses in pursuit of a brief release. And he really seems to be on the same page as me, with zero interest in an actual relationship.

I glance over his shoulder toward the front door. "One more thing. Can we keep this between just us?"

His eyes widen. "Like, a secret?"

I shake my head. "No. What I meant was I'd rather we don't sleep with anyone else. We've both had our fair share of sexual partners, but while we're together, can we agree to only sleep with each other?"

Oh, his lips curve up in a slow smile, and I can feel his eyes as they trail down my body. "You want to be exclusive with me?"

That word hints at so much more than I want this to be. "I guess you could call it that. Exclusive sexual partners. And if we want to sleep with anyone else, we tell each other and cut ties. What do you say?"

"A hundred percent. I'll save all my boners for you. And maybe my hand if you're not around. Is that okay?"

"Sure." He's such a man child. What person over the age of twelve even uses that word?

"So, we've got a deal?" His smile is getting bigger by the second, stretching all the way up to crinkle the corners of his sky-blue eyes.

"Deal." I hold out my hand for a shake, and he reaches out, but when his rough hand closes over mine, he jerks me in until I'm pressed up against him. He dips down to meet my lips in a fiery kiss.

I reach up to grab his cheeks as if I'll lose myself without something to hold on to, but he circles my wrists and jerks them behind my back. I miss his lips already when he breaks off the kiss, leaning in to whisper in my ear. "Oh, yeah. Almost forgot my other rule. In the bedroom. I'm in charge. Remember? Is that still okay with you?"

My eyes flutter open to meet his gaze. This should be a deal breaker. I've got a tight grasp on every area of my life. After years of living under the weight of my parent's rules and expectations, I broke free. But there was something so liberating about turning this one thing over to him. My pleasure. So I nod.

"I didn't hear you," he says.

Ass. "Yes. You're in control."

A self-satisfied smile twists his lips. "Good girl."

A shiver runs through me, and I feel myself falling, and then... what the fuck? My legs disappear from under me as he yanks me up and drops me over my shoulder.

"What the fuck, Jacks." He pins down my legs when I kick at him. The world bounces under me as he bounds into his house, through the living room, and past an astonished roommate I haven't met yet.

The dark-haired guy rises to his feet. "Hey, what the hell is going on, are you, ok?"

I'm swung through the air when Jackson turns to face him. "She's fine, Cole. Mind your damn business."

"I wasn't talking to you."

"Way to kill the vibe, dude."

Every single hard, muscled ridge of his body drags along my sensitive skin, lifting my shirt as it goes. I yank the shirt down when my feet hit the ground.

"Go ahead. Tell Cole I didn't kidnap you to have my nefarious way with your sweet, innocent body."

I turn to his roommate, not quite meeting his eyes. "I'm fine, but you know what? I appreciate you stepping in. Not every guy would have the balls to walk into a situation like that. Don't let this ass make you feel bad about your concern."

Jacks looks chagrined. "Fair point. Sorry, Cole, but she's my willing victim. Everything that happens tonight is a hundred percent consensual, so when you hear her screaming for me to stop, don't break into my bedroom."

"Ow, that hurt." He grabs his shoulder where I punched him.

"Too much information. I think you've effectively murdered the mood. Maybe I should head home for the night."

He grabs my hand when I turn toward the door.

"No fucking way are you leaving, Starlight."

"You know what? I'm going to go hit the library. I've got a final to study for, anyway. You two do, whatever." He waves a hand at us. "I'm gone. I don't want to hear about it."

Cole stands up with a disgusted look, heading for the door, and Jacks turns back to me. Shivers follow the finger he trails down my cheek and under my jaw.

"Now where were we?"

CHAPTER SEVENTEEN

THAT'S A WIN

JACKS

H er glares turn to giggles while I'm racing up the stairs with her bouncing on my shoulders. The mattress dips as I drop her on my bed. She doesn't strike me as the giggling type, so the feat spreads a warm glow through my chest. Any time I can make someone smile or laugh is a win in my books.

I crawl up between her splayed legs, lowering myself until my weight is hovering inches above her. My cock twitches as it brushes against her molten core, begging to be let in.

She pushes on my chest. "Seriously. How did that not kill the vibe for you? I think I need a minute to recover from your roommate's attempted rescue."

I groan, palming my dick, but sit back on my heels. "Wanna watch something on TV for a bit?"

She slides up from underneath me, propping her back on the cheap pine headboard. "Sure."

The remote slips off the bedside table when I fumble for it with hands still clumsy from unfulfilled lust. She grabs my ass and gives it a squeeze when I lean down to scoop it up.

"Hey. You can't be grabbing me if you don't want me shoving my cock so far inside you that you can't walk for a week."

Her mouth drops open, and I follow the movement of her tongue gliding along her bottom lip. She slowly tilts her head up to look at the ceiling. "Forget it. I don't know what I was thinking. I need you inside me. Like now."

Fuck yes.

I still the hand she has tearing at my zipper, pinning her down with a stare. "I don't think so, Starlight. Don't you remember the rules? Now. hands over your head. Grab the headboard."

She hesitates for the barest of moments. I can see the struggle in her eyes. She doesn't want to give up the control. I get that. I really do, but I will make it so worth her while. Her eyes skate down my body and she squirms before slowly reaching her arms up above her head. My chest swells, so I reward her by reaching behind me to drag my shirt off in one smooth movement.

"Good girl." Her lip twitches at the praise, but she keeps her hands over her head while I take in the sight before me. Too many fucking clothes. My fingers toy with the hem of the black cropped t shirt she's wearing. The words Dream Wife are slashed across her chest in red.

Her head tilts back, exposing the long, lean line of her pale throat as my fingers trail up her sides. I peel her fingers off the headboard to whisk the tee off. Unfortunately, she has a long-sleeved velvet and mesh number underneath. It reveals blocks of tantalizing skin, but I can't wait to touch her. See if the smooth skin is as soft as I remember, so I tear it off, and it joins the tee on the floor, leaving her in a black lacy bra that's pushing those delicious tits up.

Her hands fly down to my shoulders when I bury my face between the soft mounds. My eyes flick up to her face, and she pulls them back when I arch a brow at her.

The straps of her bra are soft and satiny under my fingertips as I slide them along it, snapping it open at the back. I slip the straps down her shoulders, tossing the bra to the side. Her breasts fall free from their prison, and I catch them in my palms, dragging my thumbs over her already taut nipples before leaning in to capture one between my lips. Her back arches, and a soft moan travels straight to my groin as I toy with her rosy nipples, giving each one equal attention.

She's a gasping, squirming mess when I finally leave that beautiful chest behind. Her abdomen is mostly bare of ink, but there's an occasional scattering of freckles, so I make sure to kiss each one until I get to the black pleated skirt riding low on her hipbones. Two black stars peek out of the waistband, one on each hip, and she arches up to meet my touch when I peel the skirt down, tracing each piece with my tongue.

The fishnets are the last thing to go. I'm going to need to stock up on these so she has some extras at my house, because I am way too impatient to be gentle with them. Sure enough, there's a tearing sound as I rip them off.

She doesn't even protest, just squeezes her legs together until I shove them open to reveal the prize. Almost there. I duck in to press my lips to the barely there triangle of black fabric covering her pussy. I suck her already soaked mound into my mouth before tearing the thong down her legs.

And there she is, finally exposed to me. I trace the Coliseum wrapped around her left thigh, followed by the solar system etched into the skin on her right one.

The gorgeous art, however, has got nothing on the pink lips of her perfect pussy already glistening and ready for me, but I'm not rushing this. I've been waiting so patiently for a second taste of her sweetness and I'm going to enjoy every moment.

I part her lips with my thumbs and duck down to bury myself in her heat. She's already clenching at air, so I slide a finger into her ready channel, while my tongue laps at her clit. Her core clenches at my single digit, so I add a second, getting her ready for my aching cock. Her thighs flex around my head and I can feel them start to tremble around me as I coordinate my licks and thrusts in a steady rhythm.

"Holy shit. Fuck, Jackson. I need you inside me." Her hands fall back to my hair and her tugs leave painful stings behind that ratchet up my own desire, so I let it be.

"Not yet." I mumble the words into her core, and she mewls when my lips close over her swollen bud. I suck on her clit, feeling her trembling increase around me. My free hand makes its way back up to knead her tit, and one sharp twist of her nipple tears a beautiful scream out of her as she comes. Her walls clench at my fingers and I pull them out, needing to feel her wrapped around my cock.

Her hair has come loose from the elastic, and a halo of messy strands surrounds her flushed face. I need to see those stars in her eyes when I plunge my cock inside her.

"Eyes on me, Starlight."

She drags them open, meeting mine with an unfocused look, chest heaving. Her mouth drops open, eyes tracking my fingers as I slide them between my lips to suck her honey off.

The sound of my zipper rips through the room, and I drag my pants and boxers off in one go. I slide open the drawer to my bedside table, fumbling until I find a foil packet. It crinkles under my fingers as I bring it to my mouth, tearing it open between my teeth without losing eye contact with her.

My dick is impossibly hard and aching as her gaze falls to it while I sheath the sensitive skin in latex.

Clothes off, condom on and poised at her entrance moments later, I lean in, tilting her chin up until her glazed eyes meet mine. "Good?"

She presses up against me, trying to spear herself with my cock. "Yes. Get inside me already."

Perfect. I've got her just where I want her. I slam my hips into her so hard it rocks the headboard into the wall with a bang. Liquid heat surrounds me, and the remnants of her orgasm have her fluttering around my hard length. I'm not going to last long at this rate.

The bite of pain from her fingernails digging into my back ramps up the pleasure. The building tingle of bliss that's creeping up my back. When I can't get any deeper, I grip the backs of her muscular thighs. She's loose and pliable under my grip, surrendering her body to me as I push her legs up, burying myself as deep as I can go. I'm so far inside her body I'm trying to imprint myself in her mind, too.

Her gorgeous eyes are wide again as I reach that spot deep inside that's going to have her coming harder than ever before. The white stars around her pupils are shining brighter than ever as her body rocks back with every plunge.

"I need you to come for me again." My voice has gone dark and growly, fading out at the edges as I plead with her. "Come on, Starlight. Come for me."

Her breath is coming in rapid pants, and her fingers are digging into my ass as her head falls back with a thready gasp.

The pressure builds to a crescendo and I bend down to capture her lips as the explosion rocks me. Our slick bodies slide together in a perfect rhythm. The pleasure shatters me.

"Starlight." I groan, as her walls clench at my cock, milking every last drop from me.

I rock my hips in a few last slow pumps before I crash down, wrapping my arms around her to hold her tight as I fall to my side. I'm not quite ready to slip out of her warmth yet.

Her eyes flutter open when I tuck a strand of sweat-soaked hair behind her ear and her soft lips give under mine.

She's smiling at me dreamily, a faint shadow of her dimple showing, and something twists deep in my chest. I could wake up to that smile every day and never get sick of it. A chill races down my spine at the thought. That's not right, this is just sex. Nothing more. I'm never giving my heart to someone again.

I pull out of her and roll to the side, sitting up on the edge of the bed to remove the condom. A small snore sounds behind me as I stalk to the bathroom to clean up.

A smile twitches my lips and I make the mistake of looking back at her. She's passed out right where I left her. Shit. I'm in trouble.

CHAPTER EIGHTEEN

No Shame In His Game

Tasha

The need to pee is warring with the warmth of my bed, but the urgency wins out, and I yawn. A heavy weight on my chest thwarts my efforts to sit up, and I glance down to find an inked-up arm resting on me. A light dusting of blond hair is visible in the grey light of the dawn sneaking through a crack in the curtains. There's a hand resting casually on my breast as if he couldn't bear to be apart from it, even for the night. Guys are so predictable.

I laugh at myself. Trapped like a wild animal. If I can just get up without waking him, I can sneak out of here before he wakes up. That seems like the safest option.

He lets out a grunt as I inch out from under the weight, squirming and sliding until only the fingers remain. I scrabble for a hold on something as my ass meets the edge of the bed and I go tumbling off the side. The floor is jarring on my already sore spine after I took a hard hit during the bout yesterday. I wince, peering between my scrunched-up eyelids. And there he is. Electric blue eyes dancing with laughter.

"Whatcha doing down there?"

"Well, I had to pee, but you were holding me captive under your brutish forearm." I wave a hand at the offending arm, but the beautiful art distracts me. Colorful blues and purples weaving around the moon and stars. It's absolutely stunning.

"You're blaming me? Did I push you?" He swipes at the mess of blond hair that's creeping over his forehead.

"No, but..."

"That's what I thought. Go on then. You can use the bathroom down the hall, but don't blame me for anything you find in there. I have to share it with Lucy and Cole."

"I'm sure I'll survive. As long as there are no dead wives hanging from the walls."

"Dev's feet stink like a decomposing body, but as far as I know, he's never actually been married, so you're probably safe on that front. Cole, on the other hand, is a mystery. He could have left a trail of murdered spouses behind before he got to Lakeview."

I'm used to wandering wherever I like in my place, so I'm about to stroll out into the hall when something soft hits me in the back.

"Might want to put that on. You look hot as fuck in your own skin, Starlight. But I'm not sure you want the rest of the house to see you naked. Come to think of it. I don't want them seeing you like that. For my eyes only."

My hackles rise at the possessive bent of his words, but I probably don't want to put on a show for his roommates. I'm not going to prance around naked out of sheer obstinance. That would be ridiculous.

A sharp whistle sounds out as my fingers close over the piece of clothing he tossed at me, and I snap back upright. I drop the soft purple shirt over my head and turn to find him staring at me with a grin. He's unashamedly naked, sprawled out on top of the sheets. His hands are clasped behind his head, legs are spread wide, showing off some impressive morning wood.

"What's this all about?" I crane my neck back to look down, tugging at the back of the loose t-shirt.

"I didn't want you wandering the halls naked. Didn't we go over this?" He's still lounging on his bed, supremely confident.

"You didn't need to brand me with your name. I am assuming this is your name." Awesome. Just admitted to the guy I've slept with multiple times that I don't even know his last name.

"I'm not branding you." He laughs. "It was the first shirt that I touched. But I have to admit you look extra hot with my name painted across your back." His overeager dick twitches to punctuate his point.

"Put that thing away." I wave at the offending appendage. "It's distracting."

He makes no move to cover up. "Distracting, eh? I can think of a few ways to distract you."

"Ugh. I don't have the mental capacity to handle your nonsense right now. I'm a busy girl operating on not enough sleep." Images of bare skin, skilled hands, and that cock slipping inside me over and over are seared into my mind, reminding me why I didn't get enough sleep last night.

"If I didn't know any better, Starlight, I'd think you were trying to get rid of me. Teensy problem. This is my house."

"Exactly. That's why I'm leaving." I travel the room picking up stray items of clothing as I go. "Where is my underwear?"

"That?"

I follow his finger to find my thong draped over the bedpost. Huh? How did it get there? I map the angle of the throw out in my head as I'm reaching for it. He snags it off the post before I can get there, holding it behind his back.

"Gimme." I lean over him to grab it, and an arm locks around my waist, jerking me off balance until I tumble onto his naked length. My nipples tighten, begging for one last round before I leave. Nope. No time for that.

"Give it over. I have to get to class."

"I'll give you a ride to your place. Are you sure you don't want another round before you go? Maybe some breakfast?"

Even though my entire body is screaming at me to say yes, my brain is all hell to the no. "Let's get this straight. We don't do breakfast. That's not what this is about. And I don't have time to linger this morning. And you bet you're giving me a ride home."

He laughs and relinquishes my underwear to me, but not before leaning in to capture my lips in a kiss.

Tingles start on my lips, spreading like wildfire through the rest of my body. His tongue slips in to caress mine, and I'm needy and grasping within seconds. Fingers tangling in his hair to pull him in closer. Before I know it, I've clambered into his lap. My hips buck, grinding my insta-damp pussy against his hard cock. Fingers dig into my hips to yank me in closer and I'm reaching down to tug on the hem of my t-shirt. There's way too much fabric. Not my t-shirt. That's the reminder I needed.

Class. I need to get out of here. I break the contact between us, already breathing hard as I swipe a lock of hair off my face with a trembling hand.

"Shit. What am I doing?"

He groans, tilting his head back but lets me go. "Enjoying yourself?"

"Yes, but I have to go." It's not like me to get so lost in a moment. Lose track of myself and my priorities. The fact that this isn't the first time he's done this to me is making my skin a little itchy as I glance at the door. Even if I land my number one internship, I'm still going to need to maintain my grades to hold on to it. That's part of the deal, and I have no intention of getting lost in some guy because of his skills in bed. I've seen what losing yourself to a man can do to someone. My mother. My sister. Not going to be me.

"Are you sure?"

"Yes. I'm sure. Don't worry about driving me. I've got my car, remember?" How did I forget that fact before?

"Right. Yeah. At least let me walk you to it. Let me maintain my gentleman card for one more day."

I've got my panties and skirt on already, clutching my ruined fishnets in one hand and pushing his door open with the other. "It's fine. I'm good. I'll see you around."

"Fuck."

The word is accompanied by a thump that I don't stick around to investigate, already halfway down the carpeted hall.

A startled set of brown eyes meets mine when I leap down the last two steps, but then a small smirk twitches the corners of the guy's lips. He's a huge dude. Biceps as big as my thighs and barrel of a chest. Lucky, Devil? Something like that.

The sound of footsteps thundering down the stairs like a stampeding elephant kicks me into high gear, and I make a run for the front door.

I've made it all the way to my car when he catches up, arms shooting out to box me against my own car.

"Hey, wait. When am I going to see you again?"

I shrug, not willing to turn around to meet his eyes. Maybe that's the problem? Maybe he's hypnotizing me with his stare or something. Like a vampire mesmerizing its prey. Vampires are not my thing, but Emma has an obsession that she's always willing to share.

"I don't know. Casual, remember? What happens, happens." And what might be happening right now is I'm coming to my senses and keeping as far away from his charms as possible.

"Fine, Starlight. If that's how you want to play it. I'll text you." His hand curves around my neck and he drops a kiss on my forehead that has the hair on the back of my neck standing up.

"Cool. Can I go now?"

"Yup. See you soon." Heat emanates from him as he leans into me for one more moment before drawing away with a sigh.

"Drive safe."

I nod and slide behind the wheel before I can second guess myself. My car jerks forward with a squeal, protesting my heavy foot as I speed off.

The purple shirt draped over my chair catches my eye as I'm dropping my backpack on the desk at the end of the day. Emma is not going to let me live that one down. Coming home with a guy's name on my back. The bright yellow letters spelling out Vaughan are taunting me, so I snatch it up and toss it into the laundry basket, but not before pressing it to my nose for a deep inhale. The lingering fresh smell of a sunny summer day clings to the fabric.

I toss it away when my phone sings out with that special ringtone programmed to warn me when she calls. Can I get away with ignoring it? I squinch up my face and then sigh. It'll only get worse if I leave it. Ripping off the Band-Aid, I accept the call and start pacing the living room.

"Hi."

"Is that any way to greet your mother?" My pace increases at the immediate scolding that I should have been expecting.

"Hi, Mom. What's up?"

"Can't a mother just call her daughter to see how she's doing?"

A mother can sure, but not my mother. "Of course. I'm doing great. I've had a couple more interviews for internships."

She blows right by my comment as if she didn't just ask me how I was doing. "Your sister found out it's a boy, so now I'm going to have to reset the menu for her shower. You're still going to be there." It's a command, not a question.

"Yes, Mom. Why exactly does the gender of the baby cause a menu change?" I can't wait to show up for my sister's baby shower to celebrate her procreating with that asshole. It's public knowledge that he cheated on her while they were still engaged. But he's rich and well connected, so a pesky little thing like infidelity is easy to forget. And to have to face them all over the Christmas break, no less. Way to pile one horrific family disaster on top of another. At least I still have a few weeks to psych myself up.

Her shrill laugh scrapes at my eardrums as if I'm the ridiculous one, and she steamrolls right ahead. "I've booked it at the club anyway, so I'll talk to Pierre to make sure everything is just right. I'll have a few dresses ordered for you, so I can pick the most appropriate one when you get here on the Friday night."

"But I was planning on coming on the Saturday morning. I have practice on Friday."

"That won't do. I'll need you here to make sure any alterations get done. And what if there was traffic, and you didn't arrive on time? For your own sister's shower. No. You'll be here Friday night, and we'll have a family dinner. Maybe I'll invite the O'Rourkes."

"I can get a dress on my own. You don't need to order one for me."

Her laugh echoes through the speaker. "No, no, no. I'll make sure I get you something suitable."

"Fine." My will to fight is nonexistent at this point. It's not like I was planning on arriving in black lipstick and fishnets. I am quite capable of wearing clothes suitable for different occasions, but it's not worth arguing with the driver of the steamroller bearing down on me.

"Excellent. See you then."

She hangs up without another word and I collapse on the couch, mentally exhausted from a simple phone call. I'm not looking forward to a weekend of my sister pretending she's the happiest woman on the planet while Derek is railing his secretary behind her back. Or my parents pretending that they have any sort of bond that isn't marital obligation. Not to mention the O'Rourkes. No mystery why they'll be invited over. The parental units have been trying to push their son Chad and me together since we learned to walk. They don't seem to be aware that arranged marriages went out of style with the demise of petticoats.

It'll be fine. It's only one week. One mentally exhausting week of keeping up appearances and then. I'll make up an excuse to head back to campus early. A little alone time before my real family is back won't hurt.

Chapter Nineteen

Insider Information

Jacks

I never thought I'd be willingly hanging twinkle lights around a stuffed dragon's neck, but here we are. Big, macho hockey bros draping fabric on the walls and arranging displays of fake flowers between stacks of books.

"Not like that, Jacks!" I jump at the sound of Jordan's voice inches from my ear.

The lights look a little wonky with a heap of them piled on one side, and only a few draped down the other. They got tangled. I got impatient. My bad.

Aspen's girlfriend is objectively as hot as usual, wearing a black velvet dress with gold strings crisscrossing up to her tits. But by some miracle, I'm not even up for making a sly comment about her to piss off the captain. The girl living rent free in my head right now is taking up too much space.

"Jackson!" He anticipated the move I wasn't planning on making, and my hands are up in the air before the word is out of his mouth.

"What? I didn't say anything."

"I know what you were thinking."

Jordan's got some event going on at her bookstore tonight and as usual we got voluntold to help out. I could never say no to her anyway. She'd probably turn me into a frog or something. I'm pretty sure she's absorbed some magical powers from all of those books she reads.

She floats off after fixing my mess and I straighten the pile of nearly perfect books on the table she assigned me to. The lights were the extent of the responsibility I was trusted with, and apparently, I couldn't even handle that. Beau is arranging flowers in the window. And he's doing a frighteningly good job of it. I think, judging by Jordan's beaming face.

Laughter rings out and I turn to catch sight of Aspen spinning a squealing girlfriend around in his arms, and my stomach twists when I remember the last time I had that. I haven't thought of Lena in years. At least I didn't think I had. But now that I've met Tasha, I'm not so sure.

The constant string of casual flings was only filling a tiny portion of the void in my chest. But I never realized it until I found her. With her scowl that hides her adorable dimple, quick as lightning comebacks, and the way she doesn't take any shit from me. I think I'm falling for her, but I'm not sure she's ever going to be able to return these feelings, and I'm not sure my heart will recover if it gets shredded again.

It would have been nice to have invited her here. I'm not even sure if she's into books, but I bet she'd get along with Jordan. They might be different, but they're both kick ass women.

"Hey, Jordan. Can I borrow you for a minute?"

Aspen's brows pull together as Jordan slides down his body and he squeezes her in with a possessive tug. "No."

"Come on, man."

Jordan pulls away from him, stepping toward me with a sparkle in her bright green eyes. "Book recommendation. Now I know you're more of a sci fi guy than a fantasy one, but I talked to Grey that works here on weekends and he had a ton of suggestions for you. He's a Trekker like you."

"First of all, the correct term is Trekkie and second of all, I didn't come here for your spot-on book recs. It's more of a..." I glance between her and Aspen, shifting on my feet. I may have been talking to him about my need for Tasha in my bed, but I haven't been honest with him about the brewing need for more, and I'm not quite ready for his take on that yet.

Jordan picks up on the vibe and a smile spreads her crimson lips. "Aspen, can you unpack that extra box of L B Blaze's books from the back room? I want to make sure we're all set up for the signing tomorrow."

He hesitates for only the barest of moments before trotting off to do her bidding.

"Did you really need those books?"

Her entire face lights up with her laugh. "Of course not. What can I help you with, Jacks?" She claps her hands together, leaning in closer than the captain would like. "Is it a girl thing?"

Even though she dropped her voice to almost a whisper, I can't stop my eyes from wandering around to make sure none of the other guys are nearby. "Yes."

She's practically thrumming with excitement, but she rolls her lips together, dipping her head in a nod.

"We've been sleeping together..." I'm struggling to find the words.

"Uh huh. Wait. This is the roller derby girl, right?"

Of course she knows about Tasha already. Aspen can keep a secret, but not from her. They only started dating last year, but they've been best friends since they were practically in diapers. I drag in a deep breath. "Yes. We've got a thing going on. No strings attached, but for the rest of the year. Cause you know. I said I wasn't going to sleep around as much, and she's not looking for a relationship, so it's been working. Not to mention it's fucking incredible."

"The sex?"

It should be weird talking to Aspen's girlfriend about this, but somehow, it's not. "Yes. Best sex I've ever had."

She tilts her head, eyes narrowed. "Really? Interesting. Kind of like when Aspen and I finally got our shit together last year?"

"What? No, no, no. Don't go there. It's not like that. We're not like you two." My hands are thrown up in the air as I shake my head at her. "We have this agreement. Strictly casual."

"Ok, fine. What's the problem? Don't get me wrong. I'm happy to help you out, but if it's just a casual hook up thing, what kind of advice are you looking for? Need some ideas to spice things up? Are you boring her already? What's your kink?"

She spins around, grabbing my hand and dragging me to a section of shelves that have a disturbing mix of book covers featuring bare-chested men with almost as many abs as I do and cutesy cartoon people.

Her fingers trail along the spines until she lands on one of the chesty ones. "A little light bondage, or does your girl have a praise kink?" She picks up a pink one with a drawing of an adorable couple glaring at each other. "Exhibitionism? This one's got a smoking hot scene in a change room at a lingerie store."

"Wait. Hold up." I snatch the innocent-looking book out of her hands, waving it in her face. "This book. This innocent-looking book has a sex scene in a change room. Does not compute." I squint at the cover, flipping through the thing.

"Oh yeah. That one. That one is good stuff. Turn to page 128. Trust me."

I'm not one to disobey our queen, so I let the pages slide through my fingers until I get there and start reading. "Oh my god, Jordan. Does your boyfriend know you read this sort of thing?" I reach over and cover her ears as if that's going to do anything.

She laughs and pulls them away. "Of course. He reads them too. Very informative." Her eyebrow curves up along with the right side of her lips.

"Really... Any details you want to share?" Any dirt I can get on our team captain could potentially supply us with endless entertainment in the locker room.

"Well... Wait no." She pulls back, shaking a finger at me. "You're not going to distract me. You wanted to ask me about your girl. What's the scoop? What can I help with?" Her hands stay busy at the round display table in front of her. She's arranging books in neat piles and artfully adding little stars and flowers, but her eyes remain locked on mine.

"Ok. Ummm. Like I said, we're sleeping together, and it's great, but I want to hang out a bit, get to know her better. I would have loved to bring her with me tonight, but I didn't think she'd say yes. So, what can I do to you know get to know her as a friend too? She's a cool chick. And... I think I like her."

Her hands have frozen in the middle of rearranging the books and the smile has spread to both sides. There's a suspiciously knowing look in her eyes. "Uh uh. You should get her a present."

"Like flowers? Not sure she's a flower kind of girl."

The eye roll she levels at me says the words she's too sweet to say. Stop being such a dumbass. "No. Something meaningful, but small. Let her know you're thinking of her, and you know what she likes."

"Huh. Interesting. But aren't presents a little girl-friendy?"

"Friends give each other presents all the time."

"Fair point. Any ideas?" I shoot her a hopeful look. I haven't bought a girl a present since... well, since high school and if she thinks I'm a dumbass now, she'd be floored by how much of an idiot I was then.

She laughs. "No, Jacks. You're gonna have to figure that one out on your own. I can't do everything for you." The bright light in the bookstore glints off her sparkly gold shoes as she spins and walks away with a swish of her velvet skirts. I'm left behind holding a book open to a page that has the word cock glaring me in the face. My eyes trail down to the part where the guy is gripping the girls' hips tight and slamming her up against the door of the change room. Maybe I should take Tasha shopping???

I'm lost in my fantasy of what that would be like when my phone lights up with a notification. It's her.

My heart stops when I see her face peering through the window of Top Shelf, nervously swinging her keyring around her index finger.

Jordan swoops over before I can, unlocking it to welcome Tasha in with a huge smile. I rush to intervene. Who knows what might come out of her mouth after the conversation we just had.

"Hey, Starlight." I step in front of the redhead with open arms, pulling her in for a quick hug. Nothing ostentatious.

"Hey." Her eyes are dancing all over the store over my shoulder, taking in the sights.

"I'm glad you messaged me. I'd been thinking about calling you, but we've been so busy helping Jordan out here. Didn't think you'd want to be dragged into all of this chaos." Beau jumps on Dev's back as if to prove my point.

"We're finishing up here, anyway. Why don't you two go on next door? You can get some dessert or something. It's not like you were much help anyway, Jackson." One red eyebrow is curved up as she looks down her nose at me, pointing to the hall leading over to the attached restaurant.

"You're so welcome, Jordan. I'm glad you appreciated all my hard work."

She laughs at the pretend annoyance on my face. "You know I love you, but decorating is clearly not your forte. I'll be sure to invite you to help next time I need heavy boxes lifted, though. Gotta use of those muscles of yours." Her smile is sweet and spicy, just like the rest of her.

Aspen swoops in behind her, arms encircling her waist as he leans in to whisper something in her ear. Her laugh is low, meant only for him, and I take that as my cue.

"Come on. Let's leave these lovebirds behind."

Her hand is smooth under mine as I drag her through the store, keeping to the front, since the guys are all crowded into the back, goofing off as usual.

"Have fun, Jacks!"

"Stay safe."

My plan to sneak out is an epic fail. "Sorry." I turn back to Tasha, but her shoulders are shaking with laughter.

The swinging door leads us into a darker space. The bookstore is lit to make the books look pretty, while the restaurant is dimmer to set the mood for an intimate conversation.

I lead her up to the wooden podium where the hostess stand is located, but I make a detour by the glass fronted case showing off all the beautiful sugary treats.

"Check those out and pick your favorite before we grab a table." I turn to her anxiously. "That is, if you even want dessert."

"Oh, I always want dessert." Her eyes are locked on the treats and water wells in my mouth, but I don't think it's just the Death by Chocolate that has my mouth watering.

"Chocolate Brownie Bomb." We both say at the same time.

Our words are in sync, like our bodies were the other night.

She purses her lips, eyeing the treat.

"Wanna share? It's huge." I ask her. I eat more than my share of chocolate and should probably not indulge in the entire confection all on my own.

"Yes. Perfect."

The hostess with the curly black hair has the perfect smile for her job title. All big white teeth reaching almost to her eyes. "Welcome. Are you staying for dinner tonight?"

"Just coffee and dessert." I turn to Tasha after I say that. Maybe I shouldn't be speaking for her. "Unless you want a meal, Starlight."

"Nope. I ate dinner."

We get seated in the lounge area in low curved chairs squeezed close enough together that our knees are brushing and place our orders.

The soft light from the crystal beaded chandelier glints a rainbow of colors off the black strands of her hair. She shifts in her seat, running her finger around the rim of her water glass.

"So, what made you send me a message tonight?" I eye her curiously. "I'm happy to see you. Just a bit surprised."

Her finger pauses in its circle, and her face scrunches up. She looks so cute like that, concentrating. "I wanted to talk to you yesterday afternoon, but..." She shrugs. "It seemed silly so soon after I'd left you in the morning."

She was thinking of me. My body is light, warmth suffusing my limbs. "You can call me anytime. Did you have something in particular you wanted to talk about?"

The nail polish on her thumb is going to chip right off the way she's nibbling at it. "It was nothing. My mom called, and..."

A shadow falls over our table. I was so absorbed in drinking in every detail of her face I didn't notice him arrive.

"Mocha, extra whipped cream for the lady, and a peppermint hot chocolate for the gentleman." There're chocolate shavings grated on top of both of our drinks.

"And a Chocolate Brownie Bomb, two forks."

He places the white plate between us, and it looks almost as incredible as my date. Probably shouldn't call it that out loud.

"Thank you." She nods at him.

Our hands collide as we grab for the same fork. I close my fingers around it, leaning in. The fork slides through the warm brownie with ease, and a liquid chocolate comes oozing out of the center.

"I won the fork battle, so you get the first bite." Her eyes widen when I hold the morsel out in front of her mouth. She's got on a deep red lipstick tonight. "Open up."

Her lips part, and I'm dying to close the distance between us but slip the fork between her teeth instead. The moan she lets out is doing dangerous things to me below the table. If we keep this up, I won't be able to leave this place without embarrassing myself.

I take a bite for myself and it's amazing. Warm, dense chocolate is cooled by the spoonful of creamy chocolate ice cream I paired it with. Incredible.

"So, your mom." I encourage her.

Her nose wrinkles in distaste. "I don't want to talk about it."

Interesting. "Okay. Tell me something about yourself then. How did you end up at Lakeview? I'm sure there are plenty of excellent programs at other colleges."

Her tongue darts out to lick a crumb off her bottom lip. "There are. My parents wanted me to go to U Penn, take business at my dad's alma mater, but I fell in love with Lakeview the first time I stepped on the campus. Bonus that they have a fantastic engineering program."

The ice cream slides down my throat. "It is a beautiful college, for sure." I leave it at that, hoping she'll fill the silence. Not something I'm known for. Keeping my mouth shut.

"They said they wouldn't pay for it, but I knew I had my grandmother's trust coming to me, so I used that to pay my own way. She would have liked to see me here, defying my parents." Her eyes lose a little of their sparkle.

Sorrow tugs at my heart at the hint of her loss. "You lost her? I'm sorry."

"Yes. She was the only person in my life. The only one who knew the real me and loved me for it. She was her own person. Not afraid to be herself. And that's when I decided to start being me. Who I really am, not who my parents expect me to be. That's when I got the phoenix on my back. The start of my new life. My own life. I know that's what she wanted for me." Her head tilts up, eyes a little too bright as she blinks. I want to tell her it's ok. It's ok to cry, to let it out, but instead I listen.

"I think who you are is pretty fucking fantastic," I say. "You're fierce and strong, and you don't care what people think about you. You love your friends, and you look fucking hot in those fishnets and short shorts."

A laugh bubbles out of her. "Thanks."

"Tell me about your grandma."

She snorts. "She was a character. When they were young, she used to get up to all kinds of crazy things with her best friend Ellie. One time, she told me about how they went into town and there was a dance going on. Well, some guys came by on motorcycles and invited them to their place in the country. Of course, they were like legit bikers, and they ended up at their headquarters. She said the things she saw that night were imprinted in her brain forever. Her parents were so pissed. They were pretty wealthy and had certain standards for their daughter."

"Sounds like fun. What about your grandfather?"

"He was not the same. He didn't see the good things in her. Everything happened really fast. She never really knew who he was, but apparently, she had a great love before that, and when he left her at the altar, she didn't care anymore. She married someone her parents approved of, because she didn't think she'd ever love someone like that again, but it wasn't good. She didn't really get back to herself until he passed away. I was seven at the time, but that's the grandma I remember. The real one. Her true self. Not the one that was dimmed by a controlling man."

"How about your parents? What are they like?"

Her shoulders tense up. "They're not like her, that's for sure."

This conversation is clearly where she draws the line. Now I'm starting to see where she's coming from, though. Why she's afraid of love and wants to keep this distance between us that I'm already starting to hate.

"Families are tough."

My parents are amazing. It's hard for me to see where she's coming from, since they've been nothing but supportive of my dreams. But it's sometimes hard to think about them without thinking about the missing piece.

Chapter Twenty

Invasive Tribbles

Tasha

Arms wrap around me from behind as I'm staring at the coffeepot, willing the sweet liquid to drip faster. I smile, leaning back into the warmth of the embrace.

"Morning, Starlight." His voice is husky with sleep, and I tilt my head to the side when his lips graze my neck, teeth nibbling their way up to catch my earlobe.

I melt against him, closing my eyes and breathing in his fresh scent, mingling with the rich smokiness of the coffee. It only lasts a moment before I'm stiffening in his hold.

"Did you do this?"

His nose brushes my hair as he drags his head up. "Do what?" He drops a kiss on the top of my head.

"Get the coffee set up to brew this morning?" I wave my hand at the bubbling pot. My favorite stainless steel Picard tumbler is sitting beside it, ready for me.

"Mm hmm." His hands slide up under the soft tee I slipped on when I got up.

I brush his hands away, looking for an escape, but I'm caged in against the counter by his enormous body. There's a vice squeezing the air out of my lungs. I need air.

He steps away and I can finally breathe again. "Was that not okay? I'm sorry, I should have asked."

The coffee cycle finally ends, so I busy my hands pouring myself a cup. I snap the lid on and clutch it to my chest, feeling a little better now that he's not all up in my space.

"No, it's fine. I was just surprised." I busy my hands pouring myself some cereal and grabbing oat milk out of the fridge to add to it. Him making me coffee shouldn't bother me, but it just feels a bit too familiar. A bit too boyfriendy.

The easy way he moves about my kitchen grabbing himself some toast leaves my skin a little itchy. I shouldn't like having him here in the morning, but before I thought too hard about it, I did. His sunny smile first thing in the morning is kind of nice.

I try to relax as we sit down at the table to eat. It's not like I invited him to stay over, but he's been having car trouble, so one of his friends dropped him at my place last night. Since we're both going to the Habitat build this morning, it made sense for him to stay. We can drive in together.

After breakfast, we head down to my car and my breathing evens out in the crisp air outside. I'm being ridiculous. People stay over at other people's houses all the time without committing their lives to them. It was a practical decision, and the sex last night left me limp and boneless. No way I would have wanted to leave my cozy bed to drive him home after that.

The parking area out front is suspiciously devoid of Glen's familiar black pickup truck as we rumble up the unfinished drive leading to the build site.

I have to hide my yawn behind my elbow when I can't keep it under control. The night left me pleasantly sore, and tired, but oh so satisfied. I don't know what it is about this guy, but it's like he can read my mind, or maybe it's just my body. Heat races down my spine at the thought of what those hands can do to me.

Maybe he got a ride in from someone? Nope, the door doesn't give when I yank on it.

"Easy there, Starlight. You don't want to destroy the house before we've even finished it."

I sigh. "Where is he? Glen is never late."

Jack's fingers close over mine before I can slam my palm into the door, and the heat flares up again. My miscreant friends were out last night, so none of them signed up to volunteer. Now here we are. Just the two of us.

"Hey. I thought you were helping run this project? Don't you have a key?"

"No, we're not allowed on the site without an industry professional and that is Glen."

"And he didn't call or anything?"

I resist the urge to lean back into his chest when he slides it around my shoulder. "Nope." There're no missed calls or anything when I glance at my phone again.

His left arm tightens around my shoulder, thumb drawing small but distracting circles as I lean into him.

"Build is cancelled for the day."

There it is. I can't believe I missed it. An email sent to everyone who signed up to help today. Build cancelled for the rest of the week. For whatever ridiculous reason, it went to my spam account.

He leans in to my ear. "I guess that means we've got the day to ourselves. Whatever will we do with our time?"

I pull away before I can give in to the velvety promise in his voice. "Welp, I guess I'll drop you off at your place."

My fingers are tapping on the wheel as my brain races a mile a minute, trying to come up with an excuse to leave him at his place. School work, right? I'll just tell him I've got too much school work and I can't stay with him. I need to create some sort of separation from his magnetic pull. Distance. Distance is good. I'm getting way too attached to that goofy smile. This is not like me at all. School work. You got this Tasha.

Flakes of soft white snow were falling gently when we left my house, but now they're coming down so hard, we're driving into a wall of white. "Crappy day."

"Perfect day for snuggling up and swapping body heat."

My heart's racing in my chest faster than it should be. It's the whole driving in the snow situation, right? Not sure I believe myself. Maybe I'll be able to breathe properly once I get him out of my car.

The seconds stretch out as he sits in my car, hand paused mid motion on the door handle.

"Have a great day."

"You should come in." He leans in the opposite direction of where I need him to be. The warmth from his body encroaching on my space, leaving my skin tingly.

"I've got..." His mouth descends on mine, chasing away my planned excuse.

I can't think when he's crowding my space, fogging up the windows like a couple of teenagers who don't have anywhere else to enjoy each other's company.

The sharp bite of his teeth closes over my lower lip, nipping and tugging at it, leaving me breathless when he pulls away.

"Are you sure you don't want to come in?"

I'm not sure at all. He's not playing fair. Using my body against me. I'm just supposed to drive home now, all hot and needy. Fuck.

"I've got something for you."

My eyes dart down to the hard on pressing against his purple track pants. "Uh huh. Never heard that one before."

"Not that. Well, that too, but something else."

Now my curiosity is piqued. Perhaps he went shopping for something to spice things up? I shift in my seat, calculating in my head whether I can make it home in this state without skidding into a tree.

"Fine." All my well-rehearsed excuses vanish in a cloud of intrigue.

"Really?" He turns to me with surprise, and I can almost picture him bouncing in his seat. Honestly, if he'd had that eager look on his face a minute ago, I might have been able to resist him, but it's too late to back down now.

The house is surprisingly peaceful. Usually, the massive bodies of his teammates are sprawled over the furniture or fucking around in the living room. One of the reasons I prefer taking him back to my place, even though that can also be a bit dicey if Emma happens to be home to tease us. One reason to look forward to graduation. Hopefully, I'll be able to get my own place. Although if I end up in New York, rent prices might make that impossible. I'll probably be living with roommates for the foreseeable future. I can handle that to live in my dream city, though.

I glance around the place, taking in the black bookcase stretching to the ceiling on the right wall. Books only occupy three of the six shelves. I stroll over to check it out, running my fingers along the spines. One shelf is all self help type stuff and the other two are lined with hockey memoirs and fitness books.

"What's with the empty shelves? Hockey goons not into reading?"

"We're not goons. You'd think you'd know better than to judge a person based on their sport. I'm sure you run into stereotypes all the time, derby girl."

He has me there. "Good point. Sorry." I can admit when I'm wrong. "But still. Why's the shelf so empty?"

He ducks his head down, squeezing the back of his neck. "It was full last year. Aspen was the reader, but he took all his books with him when he moved in with Jordan."

"She seems cool. From what I've seen of her."

"She is amazing. Top Shelf is her bookstore, you know. Technically, it's still her moms, but she's been pretty much running it for years. When she's finished school, she's planning on officially taking over."

"That's great. I'm all for women-owned businesses. The world would be a better place with more women in charge. You know that statistically, when women are in positions of power, they more often than not spread the wealth and help others out. The positive effects are mind blowing."

He tilts his head, assessing me. "I did not know that, but it doesn't surprise me at all. My mom is proof of that."

That little flame that now seems to flicker in my chest whenever he's around flares up, spreading warmth through my chest. He really seems genuinely supportive of the idea. Feminist issues like that make a lot of men all squirrelly. The thing they don't seem to get is that giving power to one person does not mean that you're going to lose power. It's all a give and take. "What does your mom do?"

Warmth crinkles the corners of his eyes. "What doesn't she do? She's always been involved in school since we... I was little." The light in his bright blue eyes dims a little.

"She got involved and helped run the PTA. She always wanted to be there. To know what was going on, and she was always the first to help when there was a family at the school that needed a little extra support. That couldn't quite make ends meet. She helped with my hockey team and volunteered in the community. And then after..." His mouth twists down. "Anyway. She's incredible. I can totally see your point."

I open my mouth, about to ask him what he was going to say before the shadows took over, but that's not my place. He's not my boyfriend. It's dangerous to go digging too deep.

"Come on." He turns and heads for the stairs, not even checking to see if I'm following.

His long legs give him a solid head start as he takes the stairs two at a time. By the time I get up to his room, he's already settled onto the bed with the TV remote in his hand.

I plop down next to him, dropping a hand onto his thigh, and giving the hard, muscled length a squeeze. His fingers find mine, twining around them and preventing me from sliding up farther to see exactly how happy he is that I came in with him.

"Can we just watch something for a bit?"

I swivel to check out his face. Same cheekbones chiseled out of stone, same strong jaw, and flop of blond hair that's a little too long curling up at the back of his neck, but his expression is wrong. I don't know him well enough to read it. Anger, sadness, fear? I'm not sure what it is, but his brows are pinching together, and his Adam's apple bobs as if he's trying to hold something in. Like he's trying not to cry. I wish I could tell him it's ok. If he needs to cry or talk or whatever, he should be able to. But I can't. I can't even handle my own emotions. How could I possibly help him deal with his?

"Maybe I should leave." I try to extricate my fingers from his to slide away, but his hand tightens on mine.

"Please don't." He doesn't look at me, but there's a plea in his voice that I can't refuse. "Stay with me. We can watch something. Star Trek. How about that?"

"Hey. Didn't you have something to give me?" I arch up a brow, trying to distract him, tease him back into the mood that was consuming us both when we first got here.

It works for a moment. His lips twitch at the corners, but then the wistful look is back. "Can we save it for later?"

A whoosh of air exits my lungs. It's hard to say no to Star Trek. "Okay."

He scrolls until he finds The Next Generation. "Season Four?"

"Sure." I agree. Clearly, he needs this, so I'm not going to argue, and it is one of the best seasons.

I slide closer to him, and he tucks me under his shoulder, sliding his left arm around my waist. The flames dim to a comfortable glow, and I drop my head onto his chest.

The screen is black with the would you like to continue watching message glaring at us from the TV as I'm blinking awake. A huge yawn stretches my jaw when I glance over at the digital clock on Jack's bedside table. It's only two o'clock, but he looks so peaceful in his sleep that I can't bear to wake him up. Golden lashes rest on his smooth skin, and his arm is draped over me in a hold that I'd rather settle into than escape from.

Panic presses down on my chest, making it hard to breathe. I've got to get out of here. I shift and wiggle to get out from under his arm, trying not to wake him.

He sighs, rolling over and draping a leg over mine. What am I doing? Who cares if I wake him up? It's not like he's going to stop me. What am I afraid of?

I pick up the heavy weight of his arm and toss it off my chest. He startles awake, and his bright blue eyes land on me. Full lips spread in a slow, sleepy smile, full of a warmth that's all for me. It's too much.

"Morning, Starlight."

"It's not morning, and I've gotta go. Could you get your leg off me?"

It hurts a little when his big smile droops at my sharp tone, but he moves his leg.

He groans, swiping a hand down his face. "What time is it?"

"It's two. I've gotta get to the gym and then I've got an assignment to finish for Dynamic Systems." I don't even know why I'm hedging and making excuses. Usually, I would tell him straight out that I need to leave, but something about him makes me want to protect him from any hurt. He's so happy and carefree, but there's that vulnerable side of him that shows up now and again. It's like he's hiding the clouds behind all the sunshine, if that even makes sense. I feel like it would be so easy to crack that exterior, and I don't want to be the one to do that, because then I'd have to let him into my heart.

He arches his back in a long stretch that draws my attention to his abs when they peek out underneath his grey t-shirt. "I have to go work out, too. We should go together."

"What?"

Those perfect abs that have me fixated ripple with a laugh and his finger slides under my chin to tilt my face back up. "I said we should go to the gym together. We both need to work out."

"I'm going to the campus gym. Don't you have some super special gym of your own at the arena?"

"Yeah, but you can come. No one will care."

Pro: well-equipped private gym versus campus wide one that'll leave me fighting for every piece of equipment. Con: Sharing a small space with only members of the hockey team or worse, Jackson alone. Feels very intimate and not in the sexy way. Although that could be interesting.

"No. I've gotta get home. I'll see you around."

Decision made my feet sink into the plush carpet as I slide off the bed and head out.

"Wait." He calls after me.

He snags my arm before I make it through his door. "What?"

"I have to give you your present."

My eyebrow stretches toward my hairline. "Present? We don't do presents."

"Why not?" He tilts his head at me.

"Because we're not dating. I thought we were both clear on this."

"But we're friends. Friends can give each other presents." I resist the urge to smooth out the line that's popped up between his eyes.

"Are we?"

"Yes. We enjoy each other's company, and we hang out together for fun. Definitely friends. Besides, it's just a small, fun thing."

If I accept a gift from him, does that make this more than what I want it to be? I guess I give gifts to my friends. He's not wrong.

"Fine. What is it?"

"Don't sound so enthusiastic. It's not like I'm giving you the gift of herpes or something."

The joke eases the tension and I let out a laugh, a full smile stretching my cheeks. "Well, that's good. Ok. Hand it over."

"Yes! There it is." He reaches over to cup my chin, thumb tracing the dimple that I let pop up. "Love that smile."

I blow a breath out through my lips, turning my eyes up to the ceiling, not sure how to respond. "Well then. Hit me up."

He bounces on his toes. "Close your eyes."

I tuck my lips between my teeth, frowning.

"Come on, trust me."

A sigh hisses between my teeth. He's kind of impossible to refuse. "Fine."

The world goes dark, intensifying the rough feeling of his hands closing over mine. He flips them over and uncurls my fingers. There's a brief chill when he pulls his hands away and then... something soft and fuzzy is dropped on my palms. My eyes fly open, landing on a brown mound of fluff.

"Hey, I didn't say you could look yet."

"What is this?" I flip the stuffed creature around in my hands until it hits. "Tribble? Is this a Tribble?" I don't even try to stop the snort from bursting out.

"Yes. Do you like it?" His bright blue eyes are shining with eagerness that I don't really want to squash. And to be fair, it is a pretty thoughtful gift, and maybe that's what sets me even more on edge. If he gave me flowers or chocolate or some other impersonal gift with little thought behind it would be easier to blow it off. He thought about this and specifically got me something that he knew I'd like.

"Of course. Where did you even get it?"

"Etsy." That makes me laugh again. The thought of him going online and searching Etsy for Tribbles is kind of hilarious, but also a little terrifying that he did that for me.

"Didn't take you for an Etsy kind of guy."

"I'm a man of many sides. You haven't even seen the half of it."

I stroke the long fur of the stuffed creature, then try to hand it back to him. In my experience, gifts come with obligations, and that isn't what this relationship is supposed to be about. "Maybe you should keep him here."

I have the urge to brush the chunk of blond hair away when he tilts his head to the side, and it falls over his eye. He's studying me carefully, and my hackles bristle up my spine.

"What?" I snap at him.

"I'm just trying to figure you out. You're really not into accepting things from others." His insight is a little too close to the mark, so I turn away before he can analyze me even closer.

I give him my back. "I don't need anything from you, Jacks."

His hand curves around my shoulder and he leans in close, breath tickling the back of my neck. My head tilts to the side, giving him better access.

"Oh, I think you do."

"Not what I was talking about," I mumble.

"Nope, but it's what I'm talking about."

"I've gotta go." I tell him, trying to will myself into leaving his warmth and invitation behind.

"Fine." He sighs. "Coach'll have me by the balls if I don't hit the gym anyway, so I'll let you go this time, but you're taking Troy with you."

"Troy?" Did I miss some vital part of the conversation?

"Troy the Tribble."

"You named him?"

"Of course I did. It would have been rude not to."

"Okay, Sunny. I'll take your Tribble, but no more gifts, please."

"I can't promise that." His lips finally hit my neck, landing in a soft caress that he trails up to nip at my earlobe.

"If you keep that up, neither of us is getting out of here anytime soon."

His kisses reach the underside of my jaw, making their way along my chin until he reaches the corner of my mouth.

"And would that be so bad?"

I have to push him away or I'll get lost in the moment. In his heat. His hard edges and soft lips. "Yes. We've both got shit to do."

He sighs, pulling my lower lip in his. "I guess. You're my new addiction, though. I want my lips on yours twenty-four seven. I can't sleep when you're not with me. I... need you, Starlight."

His words finally break through the trance his body has put me in. "I'm leaving now." Pulling away is far harder than it should be with the pit of fear weighing heavy in my stomach.

"Goodbye, Jacks."

He reluctantly releases me from his hold. "Come to my game on Friday."

I can think more clearly when he's not touching me. "I don't know. I'm pretty busy right now."

"Please. I came to yours."

True. "I'll think about it."

"Good. I'll save you seats. Bring Emma or one of your other friends."

"I'll see."

"See you then."

"I didn't say yes."

"You didn't say no either."

CHAPTER TWENTY-ONE

TAPE IT UP

JACKS

"Dude. You need to ease up on those. You're going to hurl a rainbow all over the ice, and I don't want that shit on my skates." Dev glares at me.

"I'm not going to barf on the ice." I tell him, but the hand that's pouring the Smarties into my mouth stills. Maybe I need to stop. I crunch down on the colorful rainbow of chocolate. But it's hard to stop. They're the good Smarties from my home country, not the weird chalky things that go by the same name here in the US. I bet Tash would like them. I dump another bunch in my mouth, hoping she comes.

"What's with you anyway?" Aspen asks, looking up while his fingers continue to tug his laces tight.

"I invited Tasha to come to the game tonight." I shrug, chucking the rest of my third box of Smarties into my mouth. May as well finish what I started.

"Gotcha. Well, keep your head in the game. This is our last one before the break."

"Of course." My hands close over the new grip tape I picked up, and I start wrapping the handle.

"Pink? That's new." Seb says, looking at me curiously.

I glance down. "Yeah, it reminded me of..." I trail off. Shit. They're not going to let this one go.

"Jacksy's new girlfriend has pink hair. You've got it bad," Beau chimes back in.

"Leave the chirping for the other team. She's not my girlfriend." If only. I like this girl. Like a lot. Like I want more than just friendship and fucks. And that was never part of our agreement. I can't let her know or I'll scare her off faster than if I admitted to liking Star Wars better than Star Trek. I don't, obviously. Judging by the way she went tearing out of my place the other day, I may have already royally fucked it up.

"Hey, man. It's cool, but can you please maintain your focus on the game? None of us need the distractions this year. You too, Fleet." Aspen glares at Sebastian and me in turn, clapping us both on the back as he stands up to give the pregame pep talk. "God, I can't wait to get out of this. I won't have all this stupid shit to deal with in the pros, right?" He's staring up at the ceiling. Good luck on that one, buddy. You think the extra pressure of playing professional hockey tamps down the drama? Unlikely. Dumbass guys will be dumbass guys.

Sebastian was being pissy and started a fight with Cole at practice last week. He seems to have gotten over it, but Cole is still sitting as far away as possible from the rest of the team, glowering at Seb from under his dark brow. I can't blame him. My friend was being a total dick. He's all fucked up too over a girl. I can't let myself get to that place. But my heart is aching to make her mine.

"I've got this, Woodsy." I nod at our captain. Right? I can keep it together whether she's here or not. I really hope she shows up, though.

My eyes are scanning the friends and family section, and it feels like my blades are slashing through my heart when I spot the empty seat I saved for her. I'm still flicking my gaze between it and the action when Seb slides behind the net and shoots the puck to me. I'm open and lined up for the perfect shot and still I miss, leaving the score at one nil in the Phantoms' favor going out of the first period.

"Fuck!" A sharp crack rings out when I take my anger out on my poor stick.

"Vaughan!" Coach's harsh voice cuts through my distraction. Right. It doesn't matter that she didn't show up. I need to be on my A game for myself and, more importantly, my team. They're relying on me to be at my best. Especially Sebastian. He needs the win even more than the rest of us this year, and he's one of my closest friends. I need to show up for him.

"Got it. I'm good." I shake my head at Aspen before he can start up the lecture again. As the fucking alternate captain, I'm supposed to be able to handle my shit and set a good example.

CHAPTER TWENTY-TWO

COCKY BASTARD

TASHA

The competing smells of popcorn, and sugar, and that general stank of humanity that settles in the corners of crowded places are invading my nose. My thighs are burning by the time we make it down the long flight of stairs. Too many squats yesterday. I contemplated not coming, but Emma claimed she was super excited to watch the hockey boys. I don't know what she's talking about. A: she has a boyfriend and B: you can't even see anything under their bulky padding and ridiculously large jerseys.

The marching band is all decked out in purple, black, and gold, moving in a slow L-shaped formation across the ice when we make it to the seats Jacks saved for us. They're right down close to the glass barrier separating us from the ice.

I double check the tickets when we reach our row. "Are these the right seats?" I ask my friend, glancing down at the Lightning jerseys draped over the seatbacks.

"There's a note." Emma picks up the little envelope propped up on one of them and, sure enough, it has my name on it. Well, not my name exactly. "It's for you, Starlight." She smirks at me, handing over the little white envelope with the word scrawled across in distinct bold handwriting. There are little stars inked out beside it.

I sigh, rolling my eyes, wondering exactly how many times this week she'll tease me about this.

Hey, Starlight. These jerseys are for you ladies. Gotta represent. I showed up for you. The least you can do is return the favor. Make It So, Sunny.

Cocky bastard. I debate my options, but upon a quick glance around almost everyone nearby is clad in a jersey or some combination of our school colors. One guy with a bushy red beard and wobbly legs even has his face fully painted in gold and yellow. That's dedication for you.

And Emma has gone all in already, sliding her jersey over her head.

"This would be a cute dress," she says.

"You don't even like hockey?" The shiny fabric is heavy under my fingers and has a faint whiff of coconut clinging to it as I slide it over my head, inhaling the now familiar scent deep into my lungs. He must have had these in his room for a little while. I shift in my seat, a little uneasy with the fact that he's been planning on getting his jersey on me. But he left one for Emma too, so it can't be that much of a big deal, right?

I settle into my seat as the band marches off and scan the bench area, searching for his number. "Hey what number is Jacks?"

She snorts at me, spinning around to show me her back. Vaughan is printed there in bold yellow letters over the number twenty-seven. "You don't know your boyfriend's number?"

"He's not my boyfriend. Why would I need to know his number?"

"Whatever. Keep telling yourself that, but this is the friends and family section. You know where the girl-friends sit. Pro tip. The hockey players call them WAGs."

"What? WAGs? Like dogs?" This is a strange sport.

"Like Wives and Girlfriends. Now I doubt too many of the college guys have wives, but there are definitely girlfriends here."

I scan the surrounding crowd. There are indeed several girls around us, each wearing a different name and number on her back, including the redheaded Jordan.

"Oh." Now I'm a little pissed off. Why would he sit us here?

"I'm sure there are other friends with benefits around. I wouldn't get yourself all worked up about it." She rubs my arm, trying to soothe me.

I finally catch sight of his golden blond hair shining under the arena lights. His hand is swiping through the sweaty mess on his head as he sits on the bench. He spins around in his seat as if he can feel the weight of my gaze on him, locking those impossibly blue eyes with mine.

His infectious smile spreads across his face, and he winks at me before jamming his helmet on. One of his friends is next to him, jostling around and jabbing him with his stick. Fleet. Not sure which one that is. They all look the same with their helmets on.

Lights dance across the ice displaying the team's logo, and music roars over the loudspeaker trying to get the crowd all fired up for the second part of the game. I wasn't sure I'd make it at all when our practice went late, but Emma was excited for reasons known only to herself. She dragged me off as soon as we'd showered and changed out of our derby gear.

I've never been to a live hockey game before or even watched one on tv other than background screens at the bar. Jo and Cherry are pretty into it. I can appreciate the athleticism and skill of any sport when the athletes are at the top of their game. Hockey is extra impressive given the fact they're doing all the usual things. Making passes, scoring goals, and defending their net while balancing on deadly sharp blades. I can respect that.

The crowd goes quiet as the two teams line up on either side of the red line painted down the middle of the arena. Jacks is on the right side, leaning down in a ready position. The whistle blows and the middle players vie for the black puck. It looks so tiny on the vast sheet of white ice. It's pretty incredible they can keep track of it at all.

Jacks is off flying down the ice in a breathtaking display of power and grace. He makes it look so effortless and man is that hot. No wonder he wanted me to come to his game. I'm going to melt like butter for him when its over.

My nipples are already tingling under the jersey and it's not from the cold.

They move toward the other team's net. I glance up at the big score board hanging from the ceiling. We're losing, but only by one point. Pennsylvania. Looks like that's who we need to beat.

I can barely keep track of the puck. It's flying between the players at an incredible speed as they weave in and around each other. My eyes are glued to him, though. He's fast. Faster than the other players. In my not so experienced opinion.

My heart is pounding when he seizes his chance. Instead of shooting it toward the net, he sends it up to Fleet, who tosses it right in. A loud horn blares and a red light spins around in a crazy dance on top of the net as they skate in to chest bump each other. I'm on my feet cheering with what feels like the rest of the school. It must feel incredible to be at the center of all this enthusiastic energy. While get a nice adrenaline boost off our small crowds of derby fans, I can only imagine it's five times as intense for them.

I'm still all caught up in the excitement when Emma tugs at my jersey to pull me down beside her.

After their little celebration, Jacks glides around, turning in our direction and pointing his pink-tipped stick at me.

The game resumes with a pounding rhythm that keeps me leaning forward to watch the action, ready to leap to my feet when our boys score.

We grab some snacks during the second intermission. As we're getting back to our seats with arms full of popcorn and candy, I overhear a conversation between a blonde and a brunette sitting behind us.

"Who is she anyway?"

"I dunno, but it looks like he's off the market. I guess we'll have to settle for a run at Jenson or Marney."

I pause on the stairs behind them.

"It won't last." The deeper voice says.

"Yeah, but she's wearing his actual jersey. Did you see the A on it? I've never seen him give that to another girl.

"Maybe not, but he's not the monogamous type. I bet you could snag him from her tonight if you wore your silver dress."

Ew. Are they talking about trying to steal a guy from another girl? Gross. Where's the sense of sisterhood?

I take one more step forward, my shadow falling over them as I lean down. "You know that's a really shitty thing to say, right? Why would you even want a guy who would ditch another girl for you? Or worse, cheat on her. I think you need to check your priorities and take a look at your lives."

Emma laughs and the two girls just stare at me, red-lipsticked mouths open in matching expressions of shock.

The dark-haired one finally replies. "We weren't..."

I cut her off. "You were. And frankly, I don't personally give a shit. I would never be with a guy who would treat me like that." Or any guy at all in an actual relationship. "But you shouldn't want to be either. Us women have got a good chunk of the male population trying to tear us down. Why on earth do you think it's a good idea to do it to each other?"

A handful of claps ring out around us from the other women nearby. The piercing whistle that Jordan lets out might have caused some temporary hearing loss. "You go, girl!"

Maybe I was talking a little louder than I thought, but who cares? They needed to hear it. Everyone needs to hear it. Us women should be united. It's the only way we're going to overcome the centuries of oppression.

It's hard to sit down after all that. My hands are a little shaky and I wish I could slam someone into the boards to take out my aggression like the players get to do.

"Good job," Emma says. "Did I ever tell you that you're my hero?"

I drape an arm around her shoulder. "Yes, but you usually do it when you're trying to extort a favor from me." I squeeze her tiny frame into my side. It's good to have friends like her that I know will always have my back. Even if she can be a little pushy sometimes with the whole, I'm in a happy relationship, so all my friends need to be too thing.

The girl with the long blonde ponytail sitting in front of us turns around, beaming. "Thanks so much for doing that. It can be so hard dating one of the players some-times. There are always girls waiting to pounce on them after every game. I really appreciate you telling them off. I'm Summer, by the way. Grant is my boyfriend. We've been together since high school. It's nice to see Jacks finally settling down." I haven't got a clue which one Grant is, but I don't want to offend her, so I keep my mouth shut on that point.

"Oh, Jacks isn't my boyfriend. We're just sleeping together."

She's got the laugh of a tiny, happy bird. "Oh, honey, you can be honest with us."

Who is this girl? "I am. We're not dating. No strings attached."

"But you're wearing his jersey." She points a pink painted nail at my chest.

"Uh huh." I look around the arena at the thousands of people wearing Lightning jerseys, many of which have the names of players printed on the back. "And? So are lots of other people."

The wrinkles of confusion between her eyebrows would probably bother her if she saw them. "I mean. It's HIS jersey. Like one he's worn. That actually belongs to him."

I glance down one more time, trying to figure out where this information is coming from. It looks the same as all the other jerseys.

She redirects her long finger to the left side of my chest. I look down, trying to figure out where she's pointing. There's a black letter A there that looks out of place now that I see it. Emma's jersey doesn't have it.

"Are you totally clueless about hockey? He gets the A there because he's the alternate captain of the team."

"Oh. Yeah, I think he mentioned that."

"Anyone can wear a jersey, only girlfriends wear a player's actual jersey."

"Oh."

My brain is processing the new information on the slower side, but I have heard of this rule before. Now that it's sinking in, there's a flame sparking in my guts that has nothing to do with lust and everything to do with anger. Is he fucking with me? Is this some sort of manipulation? What's his game? We had a deal. Sex only. No feelings. And definitely not branding me as a possession with his number on my back.

They're still tied after the second intermission and now I'm sitting here gnawing on my lower lip as the tight game rages on. The puck is flying back and forth from one side of the ice to the other and it's exhilarating to watch. That's the only reason I'm still sitting here. I'm up on my feet cheering when our goalie makes a great save, catching the puck in his gloved hand. Then I'm groaning along with the rest of the crowd when Ellory's shot hits the side of the net, bouncing off the metal bar.

It's getting down to the wire, and the game is getting rough. The sound of a body slamming into the boards in front of us reverberates through my brain, sending my heart into overdrive. I double check to make sure it wasn't Jacks, which is ridiculous. I'm sure he takes hits all the time, and it's nothing I don't experience in the derby, but still, I worry about him.

My worry makes me even edgier, and then it happens. Jacks scoops the puck out of midair, balancing it on his stick, and then flipping it over the goalie's shoulder. That was impressive.

The home crowd loses their minds with the digital clock ticking down the seconds. They keep the puck on their end until a loud horn blasts out, and his teammates are about to swarm him, but he takes off in a flash, skating straight toward us.

He pounds a gloved hand on the glass, ripping his helmet off to make eye contact before the guys descend on him.

The panic and anger come to a head with that display. That feels even more boyfriendy than the jersey. I've got to get out of here. I rip the material over my head, but I don't want to just leave it lying here where anyone can snatch it. I'm pissed, but I'm not that much of an asshole.

My eyes land on Jordan's red curls, shining like a beacon under the bright lights. She catches my look and climbs over a few girls to get to me.

"Want me to take you down to the tunnel to meet him after the game? I know you haven't been here before."

"No. Can you get this back to Jacks, please? I've gotta go."

Her eyes widen, but I turn away before she can say anything and step off onto the sticky stairway to join the growing queue of people making their escape. At least it'll be easy to blend in.

Chapter Twenty-Three

Post Game Funk

Jacks

My knee's bouncing as the second period starts. Get your shit together, Vaughan. I've got to be at the top of my game, especially with the other drama with Kiera still smoldering nearby. If I want to prove to Seattle that I'm worth it, I need to be at my best.

The second line is playing some good defense, keeping the puck out of our net, but their offensive game isn't as tight as it needs to be. The Steel are some of our toughest opponents. We're still losing when I crane my neck one last time before we get called back out for our shift.

The pink hair that inspired my stick tape is brushing the shoulders of the jersey she's wearing. My jersey, of course. Seeing the rich purple fabric that's been on my body draped over hers sends a thrill of possessiveness through me. Instead of the uncomfortable itch that usually takes over when girls try to wear my clothing, I'm content. She's mine. If I could see her in that jersey every day for the rest of my life, I would be all in.

"Our turn." Seb shoves his stick into my ribs. The sharp pain pulls me out of my daze as the marching band heads off the ice in perfect formation.

We tap gloves and hit the ice. He doesn't need to worry about my distraction now. I'm focused as fuck. She's a boss at her sport, so I have this urge to prove I'm worthy of her with a top-notch performance on the ice.

I'm laser focused, waiting for puck drop. The stillness of the arena in those moments is one of my favorite times in a game. The anticipation, the potential for anything to happen.

We immediately gain the advantage, falling back into our practiced rhythm. I throw a shoulder at the D-man who won't get out of my face, ducking around him to catch a pass from Aspen. I skate it forward. The net is calling to me. I'd love to be the one who snags the glory, but Seb's got a much better spot than me, so I toss it to him, putting my trust in my teammate. My legs pump hard as I push forward, getting into position in case I need to snag a rebound.

I breathe a sigh of relief when he flips it in under the goalie's glove, tying us up. We slam into each other as the horn blares.

Fuck yes. This is it. This is the feeling. I glance over to the stands to see Tasha and her blonde friend on their feet, cheering with the rest of the crowd.

She's got the sleeves of my jersey rolled up and it's cinched around her waist with some sort of belt. I can't wait to take her home. She can leave the jersey on while we celebrate.

The roaring of the crowd swells to a skull pounding level and the guys descend on me like a pack of rabid wolves. I push off my blades, skating toward my girl while my chest swells with pride. Being the fastest on the team has its perks, as I keep ahead of the animals long enough to skate up to the glass.

My hair splatters sweaty droplets flying as I rip my helmet off so I can meet those piercing blue eyes while I thump on the glass. Her hands freeze in the middle of a clap, eyes widening when she spots me.

I pound my chest, pointing at her one more time before heavy bodies slam into me from all sides in the post win celly.

My nose wrinkles at my own smell as I'm tearing off my equipment. Skipping the showers to find Tasha would be a terrible idea, but I can't say I'm not tempted.

"Don't do it." The low warning comes from Aspen.

"What?" I ask.

"Don't skip the shower. She won't appreciate it." He's rolling his socks down at a more reasonable pace.

"What are you talking about? I wasn't going to…"

"Yeah, you were, and running out there stinking of game funk isn't going to impress her. Take your shower.

I'll cover the media so you can skip that part and go get your girl."

"I'm not... she's not..." I'm struggling for words to keep up the charade in front of my team, but they're not stupid. They know me too well for that.

"Jackson Vaughan. You're clearly into this girl, and there's nothing wrong with that."

Easy for him to say. He got the girl already. She's a sure thing. I swallow hard. Time to come clean. "Except she's not looking for a relationship." I lean back against my stall.

"Oh, Jacks. Then I guess you're going to have to step up your game to convince her."

He's right. I'd never tell him, but Aspen is always right. He's the stable backbone of the team, and he's in the perfect relationship.

The usual group of girls is lined up, waiting for us to finish our post game clean up. One eager blonde is eyeing me with a hungry gleam in her eyes. Maybe she's looking for me, or maybe it's just because I was the first to emerge.

Blondes and brunettes of varying shades cluster around trying to get a piece of us, but there's no sign of the distinct pink and black bob I'm looking for.

My search gets me nowhere until I spot Jordan. Her curly hair is piled on top of her head in a messy bun and her lips are turned down, brow pinched together in a sympathetic look. I stumble back as if Dev socked me in the gut, acid burning a path down my chest when I see the bundle of fabric piled up in her hands.

My jersey.

Chapter Twenty-Four

Love Language

Jacks

"**F**uck!"

Cole flinches and takes a step back when I hurl my backpack at the wall after my last exam of the semester.

"Sorry, dude." I apologize, running a hand through my hair. "It's not you." It's freaking Tasha. Ever since Jordan handed me my jersey back after our last game before the holiday break, I've been in a rage.

After she left my most recent hilarious text on read, I wanted to hurt someone, but I'm not the loose cannon. I'm the alternate captain. Gotta keep some semblance of cool and control on the ice. If I knew Cole was still here, I wouldn't have come in all hot like this.

"See, this is why dating is a shitty idea," he mumbles. Interesting. He's kept to himself so much since he joined the team this year that I thought I'd never crack his shield, and I have tried. I've pushed and dug with zero results until this moment. Looks like my groundwork is finally paying off.

I'm not one to waste an opportunity. Keeping my tone casual, I pull out my shovel to go digging. "Yeah, girls love to mess with our heads."

"Tell me about it."

"What's your story?" Ok, so casual is not my forte.

He looks up warily again, as if he hadn't realized he was talking to me.

"It's nothing." He shuts down again, but I think I might be able to get in there.

"I had a girlfriend in high school. I thought she was the one. That she loved me for who I was, not my potential earning power after college. Totally off base there." I try so hard not to think about Lena, because it always takes me back to the much more painful moment that led to her breaking up with me. I can't open that vault right now. I'll never dig myself out of it if I do. Even not thinking about it hurts. That ache that never goes away throbs as if it was yesterday.

He looks up, eyes narrowed. "She cheat on you?"

"No. It was worse than that. She ditched me when I needed her the most. I guess it's good I found out then, but it didn't make it hurt any less." This isn't something I talk about with just anyone, but his quiet questioning has me spilling more than I have in a long time.

"Someone cheat on you?" I keep my eyes down, afraid if I make eye contact, he'll shut down again.

His voice goes soft. "Yeah. My ex. With a teammate."

Everything clicks into place with those words. The way he's been so standoffish with us. The mistrust. "Fuck, dude. I'm so sorry. I can't even imagine."

These guys. The Lightning. They're the ones who got me through. Aspen and Seb are the only ones who know my whole story, but the other guys are also solid. We've been there for each other through everything, and the thought of being betrayed by one of them is unthinkable. There's gotta be a level of trust within a hockey team for it to work. And to break that trust in such a brutal way. No wonder he came here.

"Man, that's harsh. You wanna talk about it?"

He shakes his head, looking down at his hands. "I don't even know why I told you."

"I have that effect on people." I flutter my eyelashes and cup my face in my hands. "Most people." The smile vanishes. There's only one person I really want to open up to me and let me in right now and she's ghosted me ever since she came to the game.

"What's the deal? Having issues with Tasha?"

He knows her name. Interesting. Clearly, I have under-estimated Cole's involvement in our house. He might not have been participating, but he's been observing.

"She's ghosting me." I scroll to my last text and flash it at him. "Look. She didn't even reply to my last Picard meme. Sacrilege."

"Picard meme?" he asks.

"It's our love language."

"Love, really." His mouth twists in a bitter line. "Love is a fucking lie."

Whoa. This goes much deeper than I thought. "Maybe you're right." It is what I've thought for years, anyway. Why did I think Tasha was different? Why did I think she'd stay with me through the shit times? People don't stay when life gets hard.

"Shit. I didn't mean for you. I'm sure she'll come through. She probably just needs some space." He uncrosses his arms, smoothing a hand through his trim beard.

Space. That's a hard one for me. It's the Christmas holidays and I'm not even going home. My parents can't face being around their friends and family this time of year. There's too much sympathy and memories, and also not enough. They always go away now this time of year, and they always invite me, but I never go.

I found a hockey camp in Seattle that runs over the holiday break for kids who don't have family to spend time with. It's a great organization and at least I'll be busy and helping other kids who have lost people. There are a couple of members of my future team involved as well, so I can get to know them before I sign my contract to join the Sirens next year. It'll be good.

"Yeah maybe. You heading home for the holidays? Where are you from anyway?" That's one of those basic things I should know about my teammate. But he's been so standoffish, and Seb deciding to take his girl problems out on him sure didn't help. Seb is one of my best friends, but he needs to get his shit together. Abby is a nice girl, and he needs to lock her down. I might not get my happily ever after, but he deserves his after all he's been through with his family.

"Yeah. I'm going home to Miami. It'll be good to see my family again. You?"

"Oh me, no. I'm running this hockey camp thing. My family is travelling." Any more information than that and things will get a little too close to sharing time, and I'm not ready for that.

"Cool."

We slap palms with a little extra oomph, and I pull him in for a shoulder hug and back slap. "I'm glad we talked. And about Seb. Just so you know, he's been going through some shit the last couple of years. It's not personal. Please try to understand that."

Fuck. That three-foot-thick wall he's been hiding behind slams back down. I should have left that alone. I'm not Seb's hype man, but I really hate it when there's a divide between anyone. Especially my teammates. Life is way too short for fear and division. Like the gulf that's opened up between me and my Starlight.

CHAPTER TWENTY-FIVE

BETWEEN A ROCK AND A CUPCAKE DRESS

TASHA

If a fairy princess hired an interior decorator, that's this room. And not the bad ass kind of fairy princess that lives in the forest and learned to fight with a bow and arrow at a young age. I've got nothing against the color pink except when every single surface is drenched in it and accompanied by frills. I flop down on the bed. At least it's comfortable. Honestly, the more time I can spend in bed on this trip home, the better. If nothing else, I can catch up on my sleep.

"Natasha. I've got the dresses. I need you to try them on so I can pick the appropriate one for your sister's shower." Maybe not if my mother has anything to say about it. Ah well. I guess sleep is overrated, anyway.

"Hi, Mom. Nice to see you too. Long drive."

She blows right over my greeting and the hint about maybe needing a little break after my drive.

"There are three. Personally, I like the blue, but I'm not sure if it will clash with your hair." She purses her lips with distaste as she glances at my hair. Pretty sure she'd have a matching frown between her eyes, but the Botox took care of her ability to show emotion years ago.

She lays out three black dress bags that have the name of the store scrolled in gold lettering across them. I'm sure I could purchase my books for a full semester with the cost of each one.

What are the chances there will be a black one? Probably slim to none. After heaving out a sigh, I unzip the first one, pulling out the pale pink fabric. I'm sure it has a fancy name like blush or rosehip. Layers of pink chiffon fall down the length of it. I'm onto her game. This is the decoy. The one she knows I'll despise so it'll make the other two look not so bad.

"Uh no."

She stills my hand when I go to zip the bag back up.

"You must try it on."

"I'm not going to pick this one. We both know this. Why waste our time?"

"Oh well, then I guess my time means nothing to you. I spent hours at Solo choosing the perfect dresses for you. Don't be so ungrateful, Natasha."

Ah yes because shopping at her favorite store is such a hardship. "I never asked you to pick a dress for me." I'm clenching my jaw so hard it's aching.

"I couldn't very well have you representing our family in a dress you picked up off the rack at some department store or ordered from one of your gothic stores."

I shake my head, picking up the awful dress. Not worth the fight.

The thing slides over my skin in a perfect fit, of course, and my mother makes quick work of the zipper up the back. She spins me around like I'm some kind of doll to face the floor-length mirror in the corner.

A laugh is trying to come out, but I hang on to my control by a thread. Everything I do that pisses my mother off is something I'll pay for later. May as well keep the tally low. It's only going to get worse when I have to face my fake-happy sister and her asshole husband, not to mention all their phony friends.

"That's a hard no." I could very well be standing at the top of a silver platter in this one. I look like a cupcake with the pale fabric falling to the floor in tiers as if I've been expertly iced by one of those Instagrammers who post baking videos. Do I get sucked in every time Emma flips one on the television? Maybe, and I'm not ashamed. But even though I might sometimes like to watch cupcakes being made, there's no way I want to be transformed into one.

"Fine. If you're going to be difficult, look at the next one."

I step out of the pink disaster and pick up the next bag. Silvery fabric flows out. Not bad, actually. This one is soft and light on my body, caressing my curves.

The thing I like best is the simplicity. Skinny jeweled straps are the fanciest part of it. The rest of it is a dark silvery color with a neckline that dips in a low curve. It's molded to my body like it was custom made, cut with slits up the side that allow me a little freedom of movement. Still not something I would necessarily pick out for myself, but it looks pretty on me, and is comfortable enough.

"I like this one."

She sighs. Clearly the last one is her favorite, but if I decide on this one, she can't say no since she did pick it out herself.

The third one is ok. It's a pretty pale blue color that highlights my eyes, but it's fitted at the waist with an uncomfortable corset, flaring out in a wide chiffon skirt. Way too Cinderella at the ball. I would never have let some guy who I met once pretend like he was in love with me. That's not how love works. Does love work at all? I glance at my mom, think of my sister. No. Not usually. Love is an illusion, just like this dress. Trying to pretend that I'm a completely different person to impress my parents' friends and their handpicked suitor is not me.

What a surprise. Mom claps her hands together. "This one is perfect. I love this one."

"Sure, if you're looking to marry me off to Prince Charming."

"Well, you never know who you're going to meet at these things. The Conrad boy is home from Harvard for the holidays. He broke up with that awful girl he was seeing. Virginia, Regina? Something like that. Not at his level at all. Sissy said her mother is a waitress."

Of all the snobby things to say. It's so gross to judge someone for the way they make a living. And there's the ulterior motive.

"I like the silver, and... I have a boyfriend." It's a bit of a struggle to get that word out, but it's not a complete lie, and it gives me a good excuse when she starts throwing guys at me. Like with the dresses, she'll probably toss out a decoy or two before she presents me to Chad.

"A boyfriend?" It's almost insulting how surprised she sounds as she grabs the blue dress with her manicured talons. "I'll keep this one anyway, in case there's another event."

"I'm not going to wear it."

"You never know."

This is not the first time we've played this game, so I know I'll never convince her to change her mind, even if it is a colossal waste of money.

"So, you have a boyfriend? Would I know his family?"

"No. He's from Canada." It's a struggle to contain my snort.

My fingers are going a little numb. Delayed reaction to dropping that bomb on her. Now I'm going to be in for a barrage of questions that I don't have the answers to. Particularly since he's not in fact my boyfriend, and I'm not even sure if we're friends with benefits anymore, or if I've successfully squashed that.

"What's his name? What's he taking at school? Is he in business? What do his parents do?"

And that's why I never need to volunteer information. It's guaranteed to be dragged out of me like a school of fish caught in a commercial net.

"His name is Jackson, and he's taking kinesiology. He's on the hockey team, and I haven't got a clue what his parents do." Talking about our parents is not exactly what we spend our time on. One side of my mouth quirks up at the side thinking about the way we spend our time together. I will not be sharing that info with her.

"An athlete." She purses her lips again. I'm surprised they're not permanently stuck in that position. Especially when she's talking to me.

Never mind that he'll probably be making more than Chad when he signs his NHL contract. Money is surprisingly not everything. It also has to come with a side of generational wealth.

"Yup. He's an athlete. He's been drafted by the Seattle Sirens." If nothing else, her disdain kind of makes me proud of him. He's worked so hard at his sport, dedicated so many hours to training and practice, and he's going to make it. Good for him. Living his dream.

"At least college boyfriends are only temporary. You can date him, but when it comes time to pick your partner for life, I hope you'll come to see how important it is to marry into the right family."

"At least you've got Celina. She married Robert. One daughter isn't bad."

Her lips lift in a tight smile. "Yes. There is that. And now she's having a boy. They'll have the perfect family."

Sure they will. If you like stilted conversations and passive aggression. "Is everything all ready for the shower?" If anything will get her off my back and onto a less stressful conversation, it will be talk of the big event she's been planning for months.

"Yes. Now the florist did mess up the color of the table bouquets. The lavender is much too light, so I had her remake those last minute. What a nightmare, but the menu is set and Genevieve at the club is getting the last details in order."

There we go. I let my mother drone on about her precious party planning and zone out. Jacks sent me another meme right before I left for the holidays that made me smile. I'm not quite sure where we're at right now, but I keep reading his texts even if I haven't replied.

He's gone off to volunteer at a hockey camp for kids over the break, so even if I split early from here, he won't be back on campus. Good or bad? Haven't decided. But the thought of him working with a bunch of young kids at a charity run camp during his break brings a smile to my face. I never got a chance to ask why he was going there instead of home to his family. I know his parents are still around, but we haven't exchanged too much information about them.

"Well now. I must see about dinner. Be downstairs at six sharp."

"I will." She insists on serving dinner at six every night. Even if my dad works so late, he rarely makes it in time. Dad's the next hurdle, but at least he doesn't talk as much as mom. He's more of the silent but judgy type.

I flop back on my bed, setting my alarm for five, so I don't miss dinner and shut my eyes, trying to catch a little nap before the ordeal ahead.

The silver shawl Mom insisted on giving me is draped over the crook of my arm, and the silver strappy sandals are pinching my toes with every step. She insisted on the shawl to cover up my tattoos. To be honest, I'm surprised she didn't choose long sleeved, high-necked dresses, but I guess they're not stylish enough.

The Wellington Golf and Country Club looks the same as always. Expensive and musty. Objectively, it's a pretty building made of grey brick with deep green ivy trailing up the sides, but the dark wood door is more threatening than welcoming. Don't come in if you're not among the Michigan elite.

Apparently, I pass muster with my parents by my side as we pass through the massive doors and hand off our coats. The man taking them is dressed in a crimson polo shirt with the Wellington logo embroidered on the left side of his chest. Reminds me of the A on Jacks' jersey and the way I took off on him. Maybe it wasn't fair. He did come to my bout and wore my jersey and cheered me on the entire time. An uncomfortable knot in my throat makes it hard to swallow when I think of how I took off on him. I shouldn't have taken off on him like that. Boyfriend or not.

I should text him. Being stuck here with these people is making me miss him more than I thought I would. His goofy smile and ridiculous comments would make this place so much more bearable. Not sure I'd want to subject him to their scrutiny, though.

"Natasha!" My sister minces over in black heels that look a little high for her to balance on, given the round belly throwing her usually slim figure off balance.

She's still slim. She's got one of those yoga teacher pregnancies going on. Like if you saw her from the back, you wouldn't know she was pregnant. It's all out front.

"Celina. You're looking lovely." It's not a lie. She looks great with her blonde hair swept up in a smooth knot and her French manicured nails held out for a hug.

Her belly presses up against me, and I look down when she pulls away. Obviously not anything I'm ready for, but I'm excited to be an aunt. I'll be the cool aunt for sure.

"How's little Hunter doing?" That was the last name I heard they were going with.

Her smile droops. "He's doing well, but I'm not sure if we're going to go with Hunter. I found at that Kirsten King named her baby Hunter. I can't believe she had the audacity to steal my name."

Yes, I'm sure she stole your baby name just to piss you off. Although knowing the loyalty of her "friends" maybe it was intentional.

Her eyes narrow at me as she pulls away. "Did you have to wear that dress? Do you really think it's appropriate for a shower?" What she's really saying is I look uber hot, and she doesn't like me showing her up. I've got years of experience reading the subtext.

"Our mother chose it for me. Would not have been what I picked out for myself."

"Of course she did." She's making the face a cat makes when it smells something bad. "Please excuse me. I have to greet everyone else. Why don't you head in? You can drop your present at the gift table." Her eyes fall to the small box I'm carrying. I bought something from the register, but I'm sure she'll still find something to complain about.

"Stand up straight, Natasha." Mom grabs the back of my shoulders to emphasize her point and then I know I'm really back in the world I grew up in. I'm stiff as a board and just as awkward.

I can't quite match the huge fake smiles full of perfect white teeth, but I force my lips into a small smile as we mingle in the richly decorated room. High tables with white tablecloths falling to the floor are topped with the bouquets that I assume have the correct color of lavender flowers. No balloons or baby pictures here.

I grab a glass of champagne off the first tray that comes within reach and go off to hide in a corner by the back wall of windows overlooking the golf course. It's still pretty, even covered in a blanket of pristine snow.

"Hey, Natasha. How are you doing?" One of the girls I attended private school with walks up to me, dark hair long and flowing over her shoulders. She rubs at her neck, flashing a huge rock on her ring finger. There's a smug smile on her face that matches the disdain dripping from her greeting.

"I'm good, Callie. How about you?" She was not one of my friends back in the day.

"Oh, I'm engaged. To Patton." Patton Leander. Check. World class asshole. Privileged jerk. Maybe he's changed, but not likely. The trust fund boys rarely grow out of their privilege. Not like Jacks. With that big sunny smile who's right now helping underprivileged kids over the holidays. Stop it. Stop thinking of him.

"Congratulations."

She leans in with a hand over her mouth. "Thank you. I heard something about you."

"Oh, really." Glad to hear I'm already fodder for the rumor mill, not even twenty-four hours after I got home.

"I heard you're dating a hockey player." She's whispering as if it's some sort of scandal. Mom must have told Celina, who told a friend or two and now the entire party knows. Perfect.

"Yes."

"Is he just doing it through college or is he going to the NHL?"

"He's been drafted by Seattle."

"Oh my god." She squeals. "Hockey players are so hot. Is he like amazing in bed?"

I turn to her, brows squinched together. "What?"

"Well, he's an athlete. He must be so strong and flexible."

I turn to her, fixing her with a steely stare. "I'm an athlete too."

"Really? I don't remember you playing a sport in high school."

"I'm in the roller derby."

She laughs. "Oh. That's not exactly the same, is it? That's not a real sport."

This conversation is exhausting. It's not the first time someone has blown off the derby to me, but it's especially grating coming from her after the shitty way she treated me in school.

"It's good you get to have a little fun before you graduate. After that, maybe you'll find a quality man like Patton. I locked him down as soon as I could. A hockey player sounds like a good time in bed, but not classy enough to marry." Her lips are pressed into a thin line as if she ate something sour.

Heat burns through me, and my hands are trembling. How dare she judge him like that? He's one of the sweetest, most thoughtful guys I've ever met. I think of Troy the Tribble sitting in the bottom of my suitcase. I almost left him at home, but he looked so sad sitting on my pillow, so I snatched him up and tossed him in before I could change my mind.

"Jackson is a classier guy than anyone else in this room. How dare you talk about him like that? I can't say it's been a pleasure talking to you, but good luck with Patton." I walk away, fed up with the conversation, with these people. Shaky with adrenaline after that confrontation.

"Natasha. Nice to see you again." Chad Conrad stalks toward me, and that's about the end of my rope. His smile is all smug and arrogant as if he's expecting a warm welcome.

Nope, just nope. "Can't talk, Chad. Gotta go. Lady problems you know." I almost laugh at the disgust that twists his lips down. Jacks and the team have an emergency stash of tampons, and painkillers for their guests. I bet this guy would have his girlfriend sleep in another room if she was on her period.

If only I was back in my apartment or out at a club with my friends. Or in bed with Jacks. My traitor mind pipes in. Maybe I'll make it up with him when I get back. If he'll have me. We did, after all, agree to keep this thing going until the end of the year. It was just a jersey, right? Not an engagement ring. Maybe I overreacted.

CHAPTER TWENTY-SIX

COACH JACKS

JACKS

"Great job, Finn!" I strain my voice, yelling over the excited screams and clash of sticks banging on the ice. Middle school boys are even noisier at celebrating their wins than us college kids, and his hat trick is a great reason for a celly.

I know we're not supposed to have favorites, but I can't help it. Finn has been attending the camp for the last three years, and he's been all in since the first day of camp. He never would have had this chance without the funding from the Kids Skate Seattle program. His yearly fees and equipment are paid for. Not something his aunt and uncle could afford. And because of his dedication, he always gets chosen for the winter and summer camps as well. He's been spending all week catching me up on his past sessions. All the kids benefit from the program, but not all of them have the drive to take it to the top level like Finn does.

He charges over with a huge grin on his face and pumps his stick in the air. "Hey next year when you're with the Sirens, maybe you can help the rest of the year."

"You bet. I can't wait to hang out with you more, buddy." I fist bump his glove.

"You coming for the pizza party?" The eager hope in his eyes outshines the shadows that often lurk there. No surprise after losing both of his parents, but now there's also purpose and excitement. It fills me to the brim, swelling my chest with warmth when I see him like this, because I know how much that kind of loss hurts. The kind that leaves an aching hole as if half your heart is missing. Hockey gives him hope, and I'm so happy I get to be a part of it. Especially at this time of year.

Petterson gives the kids an end of camp pep talk before we head over to Gords for the much-anticipated pizza party. Toronto traded him to the Sirens last year, so this is the first time he's taken on the head coach role here. The guy is one of my all-time hockey idols and I get to work with him and hopefully lace up beside him next year if everything goes as planned.

He's brushing his reddish hair off his forehead when he catches sight of his wife at the side of the arena, and a smile appears under his ginger beard. He skates right over to her, leaning in for a chaste kiss. They've been together since his junior days and are one of hockey's golden couples. Everyone loves Mara. She's been helping a lot with the kids too, and it's been great having her here.

He gives her a wave, skating back over to help me herd the kids off the ice. I do a silent head count to make sure they're all corralled in the dressing room, then flop down on the bench beside him.

"Is it hard?" At first, I was barely able to talk to the guy, and now look at me getting all up in his business.

He turns to me. "Is what hard?"

"Being in a relationship in the NHL. You two have been together your entire career. Is it hard with all the women and the travel and the fame?"

"Of course it's hard. All that time apart. The lies the media likes to print. But you have to decide if it's worth it. You've got to choose each other every damn day. You've got someone in your life?"

"Kind of. Sort of. I don't know. It's complicated." I sigh, rubbing my temples. "But I really like her. She's incredible. Strong, and caring, smart, so fucking smart. She's going to be an engineer. But all that time away. I don't want to be the one who lets her down and doesn't show up for her. I know what that's like. It sucks."

"Well then, it's simple, Vaughan. Don't. Don't let her down. Be honest with her. Share your life with her and be there for her. No matter what. It won't ever be easy, but that's how you know it's worth it. Like hockey. You've spent years working toward your dream. I'm sure you've had setbacks and injuries and struggles. And maybe sometimes you wanted to give up, but you didn't. And now you get to be my teammate next year, so it will all be worth it, yeah?"

He winks at me, and I laugh. He's not wrong. If 12-year-old me had known I'd be on the same team as Petty one day, he would have probably embarrassed himself in public.

"Definitely. Thanks. For being here and for giving me advice. These kids are great, and it's nice to know you don't have to turn into a complete dick when you go pro."

"Gee thanks."

Oh shit. Did I actually say that? To him. Shut the fuck up, Vaughan, before you embarrass yourself further.

I wince. "Sorry about that."

"It's all good. You'll do well, kid. I can tell. I've skated with a lot of guys over the years, so I have a sense for these things. You've got talent, and a good heart, which is sometimes the most important thing."

He gets up to gather the kids again, and I'm still sitting there when Finn barrels into me. "Hey, Coach Jacks. You coming?"

"Of course." I let him drag me off the bench and we head out to celebrate the end of the session.

Two weeks later.

I rip my helmet off, arms out, hugging everyone on the team while thunder rolls through the arena as the fans pounds their feet, chanting Seb's name. We fucking did it. We're in the finals. We're going all the way this year. What a way to end my college career.

"Fleetsy. Where are you going?" I can barely hear Aspen's voice over the din, but I turn to catch Seb flying off the ice like his breezers are on fire.

I go to skate after him, but he turns, giving me a curt nod to catch my attention. His brow is furrowed, eyes laser focused on the exit. Gotcha. He's got places to be.

I turn to look up at the crowd. My parents came out tonight, so I've got someone in the audience cheering me on for a change. They don't get out to too many games anymore because of the distance, but I'm glad they're here to see this one.

A flash of pink and black snags my attention as I'm scanning the packed stands, searching for them. It can't be. Is it? The pink tipped locks are resting on the back of a jersey. My heart gallops when I see my name imprinted there. The thundering roar of the crowd is nothing to the one going on in my head.

I untangle myself from the big old love fest in the middle of the ice, skating closer to the glass. But she's disappeared into the crowd when I get there. If she was even in the crowd to begin with. Maybe I'm hallucinating. I haven't stopped sending her little messages and GIFs to brighten her day, and she still hasn't responded.

My dad gives me a salute, which I return before gliding over to exit the ice.

"You coming to Wright's tonight, Jacks?" Beau asks me.

"No. I've got plans."

"You've always got plans these days," Dev growls. "Where did Seb go?

"It was Abby's showcase tonight." Of course. He went for her.

"Right. You think he's finally got his shit together?" asks Beau.

"I do. I think he's in it for real. Just hope she takes him back. He's been a nightmare since they split up. Besides, I'd like to believe in love." If he can earn it back after everything that happened between him and his girl, maybe there's hope for me with Tash.

Beau looks at me like I'm some sort of alien, freshly landed on the planet. "You? Really? Love? Are you sure you're not confusing love with getting your dick wet?"

I punch him in the shoulder. "I know the difference, asshole, and I've lived up to my promise. No more girls this year."

Beau calls me out. "No, you haven't. You've been with that pink haired chick."

"Tasha," Cole calls out, surprising everyone.

"My revised plan. One girl." Now I've just gotta figure out how to get that one girl back. "Time to stop being an asshole so we can get out of here. Seb's on a mission, and we need to show our support."

It's no surprise that I get pulled for media since Seb bailed, but I get through it as fast as I can and manage to catch the tail end of her showcase.

Chapter Twenty-Seven

Party Crasher

Tasha

"Pretty exciting game last night, wasn't it?" Emma flicks her eyes over to me in the shared mirror, pursing her lips to smooth on some plum-colored lipstick.

"Yeah, it was. I never thought I'd get into hockey, but it's fast-paced, fun, aggressive." Hot.

"I know. I think hockey's my new sport." She smacks her lips together, reaching for my new tube of mascara. "Now be straight with me. Did you drag me along just for the hockey, or was there a certain hockey player you needed to see?"

I glance up at the ceiling to apply some dark liner. "Maybe a little of column A, a little of column B." I haven't been able to shake my thoughts of him since I took off from my first hockey game.

"That's what I thought. Then why'd you drag me out of there when the last puck had barely hit the back of the net?"

"I don't know. It didn't seem like the time and place."

"You chickened out. That is so not like you, Tash. What are doing? You should go help yourself to some of that boy tonight. It's been too long. I can't have you all sex deprived in my house. Wandering around, needing dick."

"Let's make this very clear. I never need dick. I'm quite capable of keeping myself happy. We've been over this. But I wouldn't mind seeing him naked again." But the truth I'm not admitting to my friend is that I like spending time with him just as much when he's fully clothes, and frankly, that is terrifying.

"I knew it. Go over there." She waves her hands at me in a shooing motion. "Go get him."

"We have plans."

"Oh, come on. We're only going to Clash. We go there like twice a week. No one will miss you."

"Gee thanks." I snatch my mascara back from her. Some friend she is.

"You know I didn't mean it like that. Everyone will be delighted that you're going to get railed tonight."

"Delighted?" My eyes fixate on a stray hair when I arch my brow at her, so I grab the tweezers to pluck it out with a vicious yank.

"Yes. Maybe you'll be a little easier on us in practice if you're worn out from the dicking."

I shake my head at her. "Not a chance." I think about it for another moment. "Fine. I'll go over to his place. If he's there, great. If not, I'll see you at Clash."

"Yes! Take that Cherry." There's an evil glint in her eyes as she pumps a tiny fist in the air.

"Em?"

She smirks. "I bet Cherry you wouldn't last the rest of the week. She thought you'd hold out at least until next Friday."

"You've been taking bets on my sex life? Remind me why I'm still friends with you?"

"Well, obviously because I'm adorable and vicious on the track. And you just can't help but love me." She flutters her lashes.

"Uh huh."

I push off the counter, taking one more glance in the mirror. That'll do. I'm looking extra fierce after getting ready to go clubbing. It's good to be back with my friends. It's only taken a couple of weeks to recover from my Christmas vacation at home, but I think I'm good again. Now if I land that internship, I'll be set for the summer, and hopefully the rest of my life, if everything goes as planned.

"Love you." She blows me a kiss. "Now get out of here and get laid."

"See you later." I wave at her over my shoulder, swishing my hips as I go.

What if he's pissed at me for not responding? Nah. It'll be fine. I scroll up to the last message he sent me earlier today.

> I miss Troy. Can I come visit him? Maybe we should talk about joint custody.

There's a Tribble gif under the words. It's not as cute as Troy though.

I pause on my way out the door, spinning around to head back to my bedroom. I snap a pic of the stuffed creature that's been living on my bed since I adopted him.

> We're coming.

I've hit send before I can think too hard about it.

There's an unfamiliar silver car sitting in the driveway of his house. What if he's got a girl over? I'm being ridiculous. He lives with four other guys. It could be anyone. Since when have I been so paranoid?

I sit in my car, drumming my fingers on the wheel for a few minutes to gather up the courage to get out and head up the shoveled walkway.

I pull my coat around myself tighter to stave off the chill, waiting for someone to answer the doorbell.

My mouth drops open when a middle-aged blonde woman opens the door. She's got familiar bright blue eyes that match her fuzzy sweater, and a warm smile.

Did he move?

"Is Jacks here?"

"You're here for Jackson? Come in. I'll get him."

I step through the door into the twilight zone, glancing around. Nope. Place looks the same as before. Other than the man who has stepped up to replace the woman. His hair is dark but shot through with silver streaks and his eyes crinkle in the corners when he smiles. Bright blue eyes that look very familiar. He's wearing a black apron with crossed hockey sticks on it. The tantalizing aroma of roasting meat fills the place with warmth.

"Hi, I'm Ted. Jackson's father." I place my palm in the hand he holds out for a shake.

"Natasha." I go formal, straightening my back, and clasping his hand in a firm hold.

"Are you Jackson's girlfriend? He didn't tell us you were coming over, but it's lovely to meet you."

"Tash?" There's surprise painted all over Jacks' face. "You're here?"

He closes the distance in a few long strides and wraps his hands around my biceps.

"Hi."

"I'm sorry. Am I interrupting something?" Jacks' dad checks in with his mom, who paused on her way to the couch, absorbing the action of a hockey game on the big screen.

"No, you're fine. I'm glad to see you. I kinda didn't think I would ever see you again." His voice drops to a whisper, and I glance over his shoulder at his dad standing there watching us with an affectionate smile.

"I'm sorry. Can we maybe talk alone for a minute?" I'm gnawing on the corner of my lip. Trust me to show up and crash his family time. Way to go.

His face has its usual open, eager expression. No sign of annoyance or anger that I showed up out of nowhere after ghosting him for the last couple of weeks. "Of course. C'mon up to my room."

I hesitate in his doorway, arms crossed over my chest, eyeing the bed and the desk chair in turns. He takes the lead, untwining my arms to lead me over to his bed. He hops up, folding his legs underneath himself and patting the space in front of him. After another moment of hesitation, I jump up, scooching away until my back hits the rail of the headboard, hugging my knees as I pull them up to my chest.

The silence between us is weighty. He parts his lips, lifting his arms then seeming to think better of it and tucking his hands under his legs like a third grader. I've never seen him this patient.

"Okay. Listen. Um." I start and stop a few times, trying to formulate the right words. "That whole jersey thing threw me for a loop, but I must have blown it out of proportion, right? You weren't trying to imply something with it. It's just a jersey."

His face crunches up, and he looks a little sheepish. "I might not have thought it through very well. How the other girls would see it. Jordan told me Summer got to you and scared you off."

"She didn't scare me." I cross my arms over my chest, scowling. "But you weren't trying to imply that this means more than it does. Right?" I wave a hand between the two of us. I'm holding my breath, waiting for his reply.

"No, but I really wanted to see you in my jersey. Like you don't even understand. It's fucking hot. All I could think about the entire game was how I was going to make you keep it on while I sunk so deep inside your pussy that you wouldn't be able to think about anything else the next day." He reaches out, trailing his fingers down my arms until he reaches my fingers clenched tightly around my knees.

Holy shit. I've completely forgotten why I ghosted him. With words like that, I'd have to be crazy to miss out.

He pulls back, his brow pinching together as he runs a hand through that silky golden hair I'm dying to touch. "Listen, Starlight. I'm not being a hundred per cent honest here, and I'm sorry."

My stomach clenches. I knew there had to be something wrong. Did he sleep with someone else while we were apart? The thought of him with anyone else bothers me way more than it should. Way more than just because it would break our rules for this situationship. I swallow hard. "What is it, Jackson?"

"I wanted to see you in my jersey because that's what girlfriends wear. I want this thing between us." He touches his chest, gesturing between us. "To be more. I want to be your boyfriend. I want it more than I can tell you. I want to make you smile every day so I can see that dimple. And I know you're scared. I get it. I'm fucking terrified that I'm going to tell you this and you're going to disappear on me again. But it's the truth, and I owe you the truth. Do you think there is any way we can try? If you have any of the same feelings I do, can we at least give it a shot? Please."

His usual sunny expression is serious, eyes pleading with me to take a chance on him.

I shut my eyes, drag in a long breath through my nose and think about how much I've missed him, how much I want to see his face every day and answer his goofy texts. Watch Star Trek together before falling asleep beside it other. It's a risk, but life is risky, and sometimes the things that are the most dangerous are the most fun. "Okay."

"Really?" He goes completely still, blinking slowly, as if he's afraid he heard me wrong.

I nod, staring straight into his eyes. "Yes. Let's do this. I want to date you, Jackson Vaughan. Will you be my... boyfriend?" The word sounds strange on my lips.

The mattress dips low, toppling me over as he jumps up and off with a thump that should send him crashing through the floor. The world tilts as he yanks me off into his arms, spinning me around until I wrap my legs around his waist.

He kisses that spot just below my jaw that drives me wild, moving on to my cheeks, forehead, and the tip of my nose. "You won't regret this. I promise." Each sentence is punctuated with another kiss. "I'm going to treat you like the queen that you are. I'm never going to let you down."

His lips crash into mine, and I open to him, getting lost in their depths. I've missed this. I've missed him.

"Everything okay up there?" A shout comes from downstairs, and I pull away. His lips twitch in amusement at what I'm sure is a horrified look on my face.

I smack him on the chest, rocking him back on his heels. "Your parents are here," I hiss at him.

"Well, they're not up here. They can't hear us. Dad's cooking and when Mom's watching hockey, you can't peel her away from the screen."

"But still. We should go down. You can't get me all worked up like that when they're waiting for us down-stairs." Worked up in more ways than one. I'm emotionally and physically on fire. Vibrating out of my skin.

His brow stretches up under the hair that's fallen over his forehead. "But it got you worked up?"

"Not the point. You're ridiculous. Has anyone told you that you're completely ridiculous?"

"Of course. On the daily. Wouldn't have it any other way." He smirks at me.

"I guess I should go. I don't want to interrupt this thing you've got going on. Maybe we can hook up tomorrow."

"Uh, no."

"No?"

He shakes his head, stretching an arm up to rest on the door behind me as if he's trying to prevent my escape. "I'm not letting you out of my sight, Starlight. I might never get you back."

"I'm not going to take off again. Let me go. This thing we've got going on. It's way too soon to meet the parents. Right?" I look at him, uncertain. I've never done this be-fore. It's all new to me.

"You've already met them. What difference will it make if you stay for dinner?"

The silence stretches between us while I try to come up with a reason, but I'm coming up blank. His previous words seem to have dimmed my brain power.

"See. You've got nothing. Come on. I was going to help set the table. You can help."

He slides his hand off the door, seizing mine and dragging me off down the stairs to the kitchen.

His dad is humming while he stirs something on top of the stove. The guys here do some cooking, but I'm pretty sure this kitchen hasn't had a full-fledged dinner like this in a long time.

"Where are the rest of the guys?"

"They went out. Since I was away at the camp and my parents were traveling, we're doing a sort of post-holiday dinner thing. We do it every year. The guys figured they'd give me some time with my parents, so they all went out."

The clinking of silverware accompanies his words as he hands me forks and knives to set out on the table.

"See what I mean? Private time with your parents. What am I doing here? I should leave."

"They're happy to have you. They would have been happy to have the team, too. The more the merrier. It was their choice, not my parents."

"Still feels weird."

He shrugs. "Deal with it. You're my girlfriend now." His smile is so wide and open. So him that the word doesn't freak me out as much as I thought it would.

After we've set the table, his dad passes us some dishes to lay out on the table. There're roasted potatoes, a delicious-looking roast beef, green beans, and glazed carrots.

"Tell your mother to peel herself away from the TV, son."

Jacks ducks away to do as his dad asks, leaving me alone.

"Anything else I can do for you, Mr. Vaughan."

"Ted. You can call me Ted. No, we're all set, dear. Have a seat, grab yourself a drink. There's red wine on the counter over there, and white in the fridge."

"No thanks. I'm not much of a wine drinker."

"Really? What's your beverage of choice?"

"Whiskey?"

He smiles, bending down to pull out the tray of rolls he had toasting on the top shelf of the oven. "Excellent. Love that. I'll have my son make you a drink."

"Thanks."

I'm shifting between my feet, clasping my hands in front of me when Jacks slips an arm around my waist. I lean into his back, seeking reassurance. This entire situation has thrown me off balance. I'm not usually one to be uncomfortable in a strange situation. Take charge Tasha, control-the-situation Tasha. Those are sides of myself that are familiar and known. But this isn't like those situations. The warm family love permeating the air is unfamiliar, and I need Jacks as a touch point. To keep me grounded here among his family.

"Yeah. Yeah, I am." I tell him. And now that he's here, it is, which is a strange feeling.

He leads me to the table and pulls out the chair for me. His mom smiles at us. She's got so much warmth in her face, just like her son. But also like him, there's a shadow behind the happiness. Like there's a heavy weight on her heart that she never quite loses. Jacks has it too, but he usually hides it pretty well.

Once we're all settled, his mom holds out her hands. I turn to Jacks and he gives me a sheepish smile, clasping my hand in his. Fine. I guess we're doing this. Mrs. Vaughan's hand is plump and soft, closing around mine with a squeeze.

Jacks leans in. "We've never been huge church goers, but she likes to say grace at meals. Especially since..." His eyes drop to the table and he shakes his head.

"Thank you for my beautiful family and our lovely guest. Please look after the children we left behind in the Dominican. Make sure they have plenty of food and education for years to come. And Jessica. We miss her but know that you're looking after her up there." Her voice cracks on the last sentence, and when she says amen, I look up to find tears shimmering in the corner of her eyes, her lower lip trembling.

I look to Jackson, trying to figure out what I'm missing. Who is Jessica? His eyes are shining too and he's blinking to keep the moisture from spilling out. The haunted look in his eyes leaves my heart aching. All I want to do is reach over, comfort him, tell him everything will be ok, even though that's not always the way life works. I squeeze his hand, twining my fingers with his and bringing it down to rest on my leg. It's the least I can do to let him know I'm here for him.

His father clears his throat a few times, the carving knife shaking in his hand as he picks it up. "Well. Let's get this dinner on the go. How big of a slice would you like, Natasha? Is this good?" He places the knife about a quarter inch in.

"Um. You can call me Tasha. And that's great."

Everyone seems to recover from the moment once the food is served. "Do you go to Lakeview as well, dear?"

"Yeah, I do." I nod.

"It's an excellent school. What are you taking?"

"Engineering." I'm still a little shook, so I'm keeping my replies short and sweet. I really want to ask about Jessica, but don't want to mess with the delicate control that everyone seems to have regained over their composure. I can talk to Jackson about it later.

"Ah, you must be a smart one. Good job, Jackson. He's so smart too, he could have done whatever he wanted, but hockey was all he ever wanted."

I'm expecting the observation to come with some sort of criticism. Like he could have been anything, instead he chose to be an athlete and waste his intelligence. Instead, there's nothing but pride in Ted's voice, and shining from his mom's tentative smile. It's a little less bright than before she said her grace, but still there.

"Yes. I do well in school." The roast beef is cooked to perfection, practically melting in my mouth.

"She's an athlete too," Jacks says. "She's in the roller derby."

The criticism I was expecting doesn't come. Instead, it's more enthusiasm.

"The roller derby! That's so much fun. We've got a team in Hamilton now. Did you know, Jackson?" She turns to her husband. "Ted, we're going to have to go check out the derby. I can't remember the name of the team, but I've seen their posters on the community board at The Grind."

"Yes. We should." He smiles at his wife.

"We're only here for dinner, and then we have to drive back. We're helping at the benefit with the rotary club tomorrow. It's going to be a long day, but I'm glad we made it for our dinner, Jackson. I miss you."

His usual smile is a little sad. "Miss you too, Mom."

"Maybe next time we can plan our visit around one of your derby matches," she says.

Her words set off a ripple of fear, but I turn to Jacks, looking for reassurance. He looks so happy again. These people are genuinely nice. They obviously love each other in a way I never thought people who had been married for years could. There's warmth and love in every word, every gesture. But this must be rare or fake. Maybe they're putting on a show for me? I don't really know what to believe anymore. It's all I lot to process, but I nod and smile.

"It's a bout, Mom, and you know there's only a few months left of school, so it probably won't work out with your schedule. You and dad are always flying all over, helping people."

"I know, but for you and your lovely girlfriend, I'm sure we can find the time."

My back goes stiff, but Jackson's hand slides from my shoulder to rub comforting circles.

"Ok, Mom." He leans back in his chair with a groan. "This was amazing as always, Dad. We'll clean up for you."

"Nonsense." His mom shoots him a look. "I'll look after the cleanup."

He's already pushed up from the table. "Nope. Not a chance. You and Dad relax. We'll look after the rest."

It's like he can tell that the walls are slowly closing in around me and he's offering me an out. "Come on, Starlight." I slice my gaze over to his mom to catch her quiet smile at the nickname that slides off his tongue so easily now. Why have I let him continue to use it? Because I like it. I like the special name just for me.

It's easier to avoid the pointed looks I'm getting from his parents when I keep my hands busy, so I start gathering dishes off the table. I can breathe a little easier when I make it to the kitchen, away from all the looks and smiles.

The kitchen smells like a family show from the fifties. Sugar, and apples, and home-baked goodness. I don't fit in here. This isn't for me.

We move back and forth in an easy rhythm, collecting dishes to deposit in the kitchen. He gives me occasional touches. My shoulder, my back, leaning down to drop a kiss on the top of my head as I work, and it all feels like more. More than I wanted. More than I asked for. But I find myself enjoying it even though I'm worried it's all smoke and mirrors. An illusion of happiness that could vanish at any moment.

"Stop over thinking things, Tash. It's just a dinner." He slides the hair back behind my ear to lean in and whisper the words.

"It's a lot. We just agreed to an actual relationship and immediately jumped into a family dinner. Doesn't that freak you out a little?"

He tilts his head. "Yeah, a little. I haven't brought a girl home to meet them since my high school girlfriend." The creases on his forehead deepen as his lips turn down in a frown. "But I'm so happy that you agreed to this that I'm willing to push past it and enjoy the moment."

Huh. It's as simple as that, is it? There's got to be some kind of strings. Expectations. There always are.

I breathe a sigh of relief when they finally leave, amidst hugs and kind words. I'm on the receiving end of a lot of them.

Jackson pulls me into his chest as they leave. I'm sure he's sad to see them go, and I feel a little guilty that I'm so relieved. I spin around in his arms, burying my head in his chest after the front desk clicks shut. I can make it up to him. Make him feel good, so he'll forget the sadness. My hand slides down his side around the front, inching ever closer to his dick, but he stops me.

"Not right now, Tash. I just need to hold you."

Chapter Twenty-Eight

Unwrapped

Jacks

The guys would never believe it if they saw me re-fusing sex from a willing lady, but that's not what I need right now. My parents coming here. It brought up so many feelings. Feelings I try to keep locked away most of the time. It's not that I haven't dealt with them. I didn't have a choice. I never would have survived if I didn't talk to a therapist after what happened. But it's been years now, and I can't think about it all the time or I'd never be able to do anything, so I keep it under wraps most of the time.

"Come on. Let's go upstairs."

She nods, taking my offered hand and letting me lead her up the stairs. I need to be in control again, but a completely different kind of control than I usually exercise in the bedroom. I need to control the conversation and talk to her.

She turns to me when we settle on the bed. The look of fear in her beautiful icy eyes has eased up a little since my parents left, but there's still a hint of a flight risk in them. Like if I say the wrong word, she'll bolt out of here and I'll never see her again, but there's a soft sympathy too.

"So, Jessica." I pull her in closer and run a hand through my hair. "She was my sister. My only sibling."

"Was." Her voice is soft and pained. "Oh, Jackson. What happened?"

"Fucking cancer." It makes me so mad every time I say it or think about it. It's not fair. It's not fair that she got taken so young. She did nothing wrong. In fact, she was the best of us. It should have been me.

"I'm so sorry." She wraps her arms around my waist in a tight squeeze.

"Yeah. She was diagnosed as a kid, and she fought it off. But then, when we were in high school. I was sixteen, she was fourteen. It came back. And she fought. She fought so fucking hard. So many treatments that destroyed her. It was terrible. Watching her suffer. Watching her waste away. Get thinner and more tired. God, if I could have done anything for her. Given her anything, I would have. Even traded places with her. I would have in a heartbeat."

"But you couldn't do anything. You were there for her, though. I'm sure."

"Yes. But it wasn't enough."

"You know you couldn't have done anything, though? You're not blaming yourself still, are you?" I've heard the words before, but they mean more coming from her. With her sometimes prickly exterior and trouble expressing her emotions.

"I know, but I still sometimes think the thoughts. I can't stop them. And I promised Jess I'd make it to the pros. She didn't get to live the life she had planned out, so I promised her I'd follow my dream. That's the other reason this article thing is eating away at me. I can't go back on the promise I made to my dying sister. Not an option."

She leans in, dropping her head on my chest, and it makes me think of Lena. How she hurt me when I was already down. How she didn't stand by me, and that's scary too. Because if one girl wasn't there for me when I needed it, who's to say another one won't abandon me when I'm at my worst? That's what scares me about Tasha. She's so strong and independent, and so scared to express herself or admit that what we have is special, because it is. Seeing her with my parents. And that step she took. I was brave, and it paid off. She said yes. She said she'd be my girlfriend. That word has me hugging her even tighter, burying my nose in her hair to inhale the sweet scent of her hair. I want to shout it into a microphone, to a packed arena. But it's too soon. She's not ready for that.

"I know. I get it. Not really. I've never experienced anything like what you have. Losing a sibling. So young. But when my grandma died, it felt like the world was ending. My world, at least. My parents never understood me or supported my dreams, so after she passed on, it was all on me. Yours seems nice, though." Her words are getting a little sleepy.

"They are. They've always been there for me. Supporting me. Hockey is so demanding a sport, but they've been there for me every step of the way. Even when it strained their finances, they found a way. They weren't afraid to ask for help when they needed it, and they made sure I was able to get to this level. I'm so glad I'll be able to pay them back for all those years and struggles. Once I get my first big paycheck, it's going straight to them. Although I know they'll try to protest."

"That's nice. It's nice that you'll be in a position to be there for them."

"It is. I'm privileged. I'm so lucky. Now I have to keep my shit together for the rest of the year to make sure I get there."

She twists in my arms. "Are you worried about it? You've been drafted, right?"

"Yes, by Seattle, but they've had a bad run the last few years with a few too many scandals, and they're not looking to add any new team members that will create more drama. That's why this whole thing with Kiera getting printed in the paper was shitty. It makes me look like an asshole player."

"You might be a player, but you're not an asshole."

"Gee thanks." Her soft hair under my hand is making me soft and sleepy. "I'm not interested in that anymore, anyway. Yes, I slept around a lot, but it got old. That's not the life I want. Empty."

Soft snores are rumbling on my chest by now. I don't want to let her go, so I pull the blanket up to cover us, dropping a kiss on her head before laying back. Those words are ringing especially true right now. I don't want to be an all the girls kind of guy anymore. I want to be a one-woman guy, but only if it's this woman. This gorgeous, scared, wild creature.

CHAPTER TWENTY-NINE

SMASH WORTHY

TASHA

J o heaves out a grunt, lifting the bar, and I hover my
hands underneath, ready to catch it if her arms can't
handle the weight. She's really pushing her limits today.

"How did you know Cherry was the one?" I ask when
she drops her hands down to take a break between sets.

"She just worked in my life. That sounds easy, but it
wasn't. I've been hurt before and I really didn't want to
take that chance again, but she kept pushing. Kept trying
to drag me kicking and screaming out of my comfort
zone. You know how persistent she can be." She rolls her
eyes. Oh, I know.

I laugh. Yeah, I know. "But how did you know you could
trust her?"

She swipes a sweaty strand off her forehead. "I don't
know. It was hard. It took time, but she could always see

me. The real me. She could see when I was scared. She knew when to back off and when to push. And we have so much in common. We already shared so much it got harder and harder to resist. She was like the last piece of the puzzle." There's a distant look in her eyes as if she's searching the past, sifting through memories. "High school was hard. My parents were never supportive when I came out to them, but since I got here, to college, things have been good, mostly. You know there are still assholes out there who would prefer I live my life in a way that they approve of, but fuck them. I have enough amazing people in my life. Why are you asking, Tash?"

"I don't know. I met Jackson's family last night."

She lets out a low whistle. "You met his parents? Are they assholes?"

"No. The complete opposite, in fact. It might be easier if they were, but nope, they've gotta be all loving and sweet. I've never spent much time around a family like them. And they've suffered. His sister died when he was in high school, but it didn't tear them apart. That kind of loss. That should destroy, not unite, but it didn't. They're there for each other."

"And you don't think you can have that kind of love?" She lifts a brow at me, gripping the bar to start another set.

"Yes. No. I'm not sure. I've just never seen it before. I don't think I can be a part of that. Love doesn't last. It turns to hate and obligation, and I don't want to do that to him or myself. I don't want to rely on someone else for my happiness. That never works. At least, not in my experience."

Her arms strain, and a vein pops out on her forehead as she lifts. The bar slips as she trembles, but I catch it before it can fall, lifting it back to its resting spot.

"I think you're done for now, Jo."

She grabs the white towel I hold out to swipe her forehead dry, sitting up. "Yeah. Here's the thing, Tash. You're bullshitting yourself. You've been telling yourself all along that love doesn't really exist, and you've done a fantastic job of keeping guys at arm's length. Hell, you keep an entire bus between yourself and any hint of emotion. But this guy snuck in, and you like him. You like him more than you think you should, so you're doing everything in your power to push him away. But you're only going to hurt yourself in the end. You deserve someone to look after you, to love you, and if it's him, that's great. Just let him know I'll break his kneecaps if he hurts you. I'd like to see him try to play hockey then."

I snort. "Ease up, Jo. He hasn't done anything smash worthy yet."

"Depends on what kind of smashing you're talking about."

Cherry comes dancing over from the treadmill. She's only got a soft sheen of sweat on her face after her run, no ugly red face. "Hey, Jo Jo," she sings. "Wanna hit the bags?"

"Me please." I volunteer, needing to take my feelings out on something. It's always a good release to slam the bags around for a while.

My phone rings as I'm walking up the stairs with Em. She pulls her key out to open our door, letting me in first so I can push through the door to answer the call.

My heart picks up, expecting to hear Jacks' voice. "Hello?"

"Good morning. Is this Natasha Deveraux?"

Not Jackson. I scramble to rearrange my professional voice. "This is Cynthia Allen from Everge-En. How are you doing today?"

"I'm great, thanks." Hurry it up with the small talk. I need to hear the news. Good or bad?

"We were very impressed with your application and interviews, and we'd like to offer you the internship at our New York location."

The wild excitement that sets my heart pounding a little harder is a little dampened. Just a little. While I was originally gunning for a place in New York, my wishes have been changing slowly but surely in favor of the Seattle office. Jackson is going to end up there. Crap. Was I planning on rearranging my life around a guy? Never. I've earned this. This is my dream job for my dream company. That's exactly the thing I said I'd never do.

"Amazing. Thank you so much."

"So, is that a yes?" I can hear her smile through the line.

"Yes. Definitely yes. I'm so excited about this opportunity."

"Great. We'll send the paperwork over and if you can get it signed and sent back within seventy-two hours, that would be appreciated."

"Of course. Thank you so much."

My legs are eating up the space in our small apartment as I pace circles around it, trailing my fingers along the wall. "If you have any further questions before you sign, don't hesitate to reach out. You can send them directly to me."

"Will do."

"Congratulations and welcome to the team. Have a great day, Miss Deveraux?"

"You too. Thanks again for the opportunity."

I hang up the phone, squealing. "I got it."

"The internship? Everge-En?" Emma asks.

"Yes! It's mine."

"And well deserved, my friend."

I pull my phone out, flipping it to my celebration play list. "Dance party?"

"Yes, queen!" Emma says, joining in when I blast the tunes and start dancing around the living room.

All the while in the back of my head, I'm a little sad and a little relieved. Maybe this is the sign I was looking for. I'm going to New York City. Hopefully, this internship will turn into a full-time job, and that'll be where I build my life. For the first time, the thought of moving to a new city leaves an ache it my chest.

I'll be leaving behind my friends, who are my chosen family. The ones who have been there since I was a prickly freshman, not so ready to make friends. They didn't give me a choice, though. These ladies took me under their wing and forced me to accept their friendship. I'll always be grateful for my Ladies of the Fight. And hopefully I'll find a new group of like-minded souls in my new city.

The ache is there for them, but I know we'll keep in touch. We'll email, and text, and message every day. But Jackson. He's going off to do big things. I don't think either of us will have the time to keep in contact with our senior fling. And when I think about that. That's when the ache in my heart really throbs.

My head is pounding now, and the euphoria has worn off leaving me fatigued. I think I'll just go lay down. My feet are heavy as I trudge over to my bedroom. Just a little nap.

Chapter Thirty

Hot Doctor

Jacks

I 'm whistling as I walk up to the current house we're working on for the build. It's amazing the difference when you're only here once a week. How fast these places go up. I've got my hockey kids that I love, but I wouldn't mind finding a build to help with in the off season. Mostly because of who I would get to work with.

I can already picture hammering away on a build on a balmy summer day in Seattle. The part that makes me smile the most about the picture in my head is Tasha by my side wearing mouth-wateringly short denim cutoffs and a tool belt. Fuck me. Now is not the time for that. I adjust my hard on in my pants and stretch my neck. *You can't fuck Tash in the habitat for humanity house, you can't fuck Tash in the habitat for humanity house*, I recite to myself a few times to calm down. It doesn't work. I'm just reminded of how she looks stretched out underneath me while I pound into her or her tits jiggling while my girlfriend rides me.

The second-hand boots I bought for the project take me up the stairs and I push through the door. Tasha's car wasn't here, and she hasn't been answering my texts, so I had to drive myself over in my newly repaired car. At this point, Mabel is being held together by duct tape and best wishes, but soon enough, I'll be able to get something new. Nothing fancy. Just something that won't complain every time I ask her to start when the temperature drops below thirty degrees.

"Hockey boy!" Cherry's lips match her name as she blows me a kiss.

I glance around to make sure Jo didn't see the gesture. I'm tough, but I'm pretty sure she could take me in defense of her girlfriend.

"Hey, Cherry. Where's my Tash?"

Her smile slips. "She didn't tell you?"

Panicked thoughts are already racing through my head on a spiral of destruction. Was it too much? Meeting my family, hearing about my sister? Did I scare her off? "Uh no. Talk to me."

"She couldn't make it in today. She's sick."

Sick? My heart races and I spin around. "Sick? What's wrong with her?"

"She's ok. Just a flu thing. She'll be fine. Cranky as fuck, and a little delirious, but she'll live."

Delirious? That doesn't sound ok to me.

"Did she go to see a doctor?" I'm getting agitated now, running my palms up and down the rough denim of my pants. I like Cherry, but without a medical degree her diagnosis of 'she'll be ok' doesn't do it for me.

"Yes, lover boy, she went to the health clinic at the school. It's a virus. They can't do anything about it. Told her to drink lots of fluids, and rest. Nothing else unless her symptoms get worse."

"But she's at home by herself?" I've gotta go. I've got to be there for here. Monitor her. Make sure she goes to the emergency room if things get worse. Because she won't. She's too stubborn.

"Relax. Emma is there with her, and it's just a cold. Ease up."

I'm all ready to tear out of there when Glen walks up to me, chewing on a wad of gum with a clipboard in his hands. "You're with Katie in the back room today, rookie."

I glance at the door and back at Glen. I'm all set to tear out of here, consequences be damned, but I stop and think. That's not what Tasha would want. She'd want me to stay and get shit done. I have to be responsible here. I grab a hammer and hold up the little basket of chocolate bars I brought for her. Mom left me with a huge haul as she always does when they come for a visit, and I made a little gift pack for Tash. Dev complained endlessly after I didn't share any with him, but tough shit. He doesn't look nearly as good naked, so no chocolate for him.

I make sure to ham it up, pushing my lips out in a pout before I take the selfie and send it off with the caption.

Feel better. Glen doesn't look nearly as good in a tool belt as you.

After I hit send, I head off to see what Katie has in store for me to do today.

The minute our shift is done, I'm dropping my hammer in a bin and skidding out the door.

"He's got it bad." I choose to ignore Cherry mocking me to Jo.

My fingers are drumming the wheel as I look down at the chocolate I brought for her. Still a decent gift, but she won't be able to enjoy it while she's sick. I should get her something. Chicken soup? Orange juice? I'll make a quick stop at the pharmacy on my way in to get some supplies.

Emma's hair is sticking crazily out of her pigtails, and she looks a little harried when she opens the door.

"What are you doing here? Tasha's sick."

"I know. That's why I'm here. I brought supplies." Her eyes fall to the overloaded shopping bag I hold up to her face.

"Oh. Cool. You taking a shift? I've gotta head to campus for a group meeting, but I didn't want to leave her by herself. She's a bit... loopy.

Loopy. Sounds interesting. "I'm taking all the shifts."

"Whatever you say." She shakes her head at me and points in the direction of Tash's bedroom. "Good luck."

I kick off my shoes, crossing the room with a couple of big strides, and knocking on the bedroom door.

"Go away, Emma." The voice is deep and raspy, weak. Nothing at all like my usual Starlight.

"I'm handing off to the next shift," Emma calls back.

"Huh?"

I get one more sympathetic look before Emma is gathering up her stuff and disappearing out the front door as if she can't leave fast enough. If it were humanly possible, I think there would be a puff of smoke under her heels.

The door opens a crack into the dimly lit room. There's a Tasha sized lump covered in blankets with a huge pile of Kleenex scattered around it and several empty glasses on her bedside table.

"Starlight. I missed you at the build today."

Some sort of a groan or moan emerges from under the pile of blankets. "Go on... out."

"I'm happy to see you, too."

An empty Kleenex box comes flying at my head and I have to duck to avoid getting a corner to my forehead. That would not be a cool injury at all.

"I'm here to look after you. I brought supplies." Hopefully, I've got something in the bag that will convince her to let me stay and look after her. "Emma had an assignment to work on, so I'm here now."

"Noooo. She's lying. Couldn't stay. I'm her nightmare. Sometimes I have nightmares. The Grinch stole all my chocolate."

"Maybe so, but she still stayed until I got here." I bite back a laugh at her rambling.

"Don't look at me. I'm disgusting." She punctuates the comment with the loud sound of her blowing her nose. It echoes through the small room. Impressive really.

"You could never be disgusting to me." The sound of her repeated nose blow could stop traffic and then she takes up coughing. The harsh barks sound painful. My heart stands still.

I start frantically rooting through the bag of stuff. "I've got some cough medicine. That lemon stuff that tastes like a failed experiment to create sentient lemons, Kleenex." She might need that, given the empty box she just tried to take me out with. "Um, chicken soup, orange juice, some crossword puzzles in case you get bored. Oh, cough drops?"

She takes up hacking again and I'm a little worried a hair ball is going to come out.

"And best of all. I brought the Star Trek, season five special edition DVDs. Did you have something I can play them on? If not, there's a digital version I can get online."

That's the ticket. The black top of her head peeks out from under the covers slowly. I finally get a good look at her as the pink strands emerge. Her nose is red, and her eyes are droopy and bloodshot. She looks sad, but also a little hopeful.

"Star Trek it is. How about some electrolytes to go with it? Do you have a fever?" The glassy eyes and sheen of sweat glistening on her forehead are a pretty good indicator.

"A little. Not as bad as earlier."

Good. That's exactly what I want to hear. That she's getting better. I don't think I could handle the opposite.

"Ok. What would you like? Strawberry, lemon, orange, or wild cherry?"

"Orange please," she says.

"Orange it is." I gather up the assortment of glasses on the bedside table, taking them in to the kitchen. I place them on the counter and grab a fresh one out of the cupboard. After dumping the little packet of powder in the bottom, I fill up the glass from the tap and head back to her room.

She shakes her head at me, but I place the glass in her hands and make her take a sip before she puts it down. She's not getting dehydrated on my watch.

I hop up on the bed beside her and place the cool washcloth on her forehead.

"Why are you being so nice?"

"I'm hoping you let me sleep with you again. Not now, obviously, because you're disgusting. Once you've showered."

Her laugh turns into a cough. "You're a jerk."

"Not the first time I've heard that. Oh, yeah. I almost forgot. You're my girlfriend now. I'm obligated to look after you." I bend down to kiss her clammy forehead.

"Star Trek time?"

She feels hot under my touch when I help her sit up, propping a pillow behind her.

"Yes."

"Drink lots of water. Doctor's orders."

I know she's not quite ready for the emergency when she cranes her neck, glancing around. "Doctor? Where's the doctor? Is he hot?"

"Total smoke show, and she's wearing a really short lab coat. Really, I thought you were more progressive than that. Automatically assuming the doctor is a man." I tease her.

"Not assuming. Hoping."

"Really? Well then, I guess I should get out of here. Leave you alone with your hot doctor. Except... I don't think he's going to watch Star Trek with you."

"Fine. Stay please, Jacks."

The request is music to my ears.

The sound of a rumbling chainsaw startles me awake, and I groan, turning over to find Tasha lying beside me. Her mouth is hanging open, and there's a little trail of drool at the corner of her mouth. The noises coming out of her rival those of a tortured soul in the bowels of hell. And I don't care. As long as she's getting some rest, I'm happy.

I place a cool hand on her forehead, and it's warm but not as hot as earlier. Hopefully, the worst of it is over and she'll be on the mend.

I place the softest of kisses on her forehead, not wanting to wake her up, but she stirs, mumbling something under her breath. It sounds like my name, so I lean in closer.

"Jacks. Please. I need you," she mumbles in her fevered sleep.

"Yes you do, Starlight. And you've got me. For as long as you'll have me, I'm yours. Hopefully that's forever." Her hair is a little sticky when I brush it off her forehead to plant one more kiss there. My lips linger, and I can't help myself from whispering the words I know she wouldn't let me say to her while she's awake. "I love you, Starlight."

"Love you too," she mumbles.

It's like a blow to the heart. Aching need roars to life and everything clicks into place. I know her words mean nothing while she's still sick and feverish, but they still sound so good. They give me hope. That I can make her love me one day. That she'll admit it to herself.

As much as I'd like to stay in bed all day, I get up to clean up the mess in the kitchen. On the way, I pick up all the gross dirty Kleenexes on the way. I wouldn't want her to have to deal with that when she's feeling better.

She loves me. The words fill me up and give me hope I never thought I deserved. But also fear. I'm so scared she's never going to say it out loud. Please let me have this. I can't lose anyone else.

CHAPTER THIRTY-ONE

I'LL ALWAYS CATCH YOU

TASHA

"He's a good one, Tash." Emma skates up behind me, but I swerve away, knowing she's going to try to knock me off my wheels despite her sweet words.

"I know," I say.

"The only time he left was to go to hockey practice and made sure I'd be with you the whole time. He said he wouldn't go, but he's still on thin ice with his NHL team and he can't afford any more mistakes. Plus, his coach said he'd put his balls in a vice if he didn't show."

I swerve around the set of orange cones we lined up along the track. "What use would he be to me, then?"

She catches up and gives me a shove. "A lot. Who would clean up your snotty Kleenexes when you were sick if he wasn't around? Cause I love you, but I draw the line at bodily fluid clean up."

"Thanks. And I can clean up after myself."

Jo, Cherry, and Kat are lined up in a triangle formation we've got to break through to finish the lap.

"Not last weekend you couldn't," she says as we put all our weight into shoving through their blockade.

"What's your point, Emma?"

"Put the poor boy out of his misery. Go out on a date with him."

Am I a jerk for not telling my friends we're dating yet? I'll probably regret this. "He's not miserable. We've both been busy. Honestly, Em, we've been dating. Before I got sick, I agreed to be his girlfriend." I swallow, looking around to make sure no one else heard me.

"Shut up!" She smacks me. "You've been keeping secrets? You're a terrible friend."

I swerve away to avoid a second smack. "It was new, and I knew you'd get all up in my grill. I wasn't ready to spoil it yet."

"Nuh uh. You were just scared. Look. I shouldn't tell you, but he's made plans tomorrow night. It's good. I promise. You won't want to miss it."

"I'll think about it."

I struggle to keep my skates under me when we finally burst through their locked arms. "Yes!" I slap gloved hands with Emma and skate off the track.

After a quick shower in the locker room, I grab a Coffee Crisp out of my bag. When Jacks finally left my house on Sunday night, he left behind a chocolate bar bouquet. All Canadian chocolate bars from the stash his mom brought him on her visit. I smile and pick up my phone.

I'll see you tomorrow

Is that a yes?

It's a yes.

Good girl

Those words never fail to send a shiver up my spine. I can't wait to see where he's going to take me, and it's been way too long since I felt his hands on my body.

He told me to wear my regular clothes, so I threw on a plaid skirt and t-shirt with a roller-skating skeleton on it. Along with the infamous fishnets, of course. I've always loved them, but the way he gets so worked up every time he sees me in them is a bonus.

"Where are we going, Jacks?" I ask him.

"I told you. It's a secret, but we're driving into Detroit."

Well, that doesn't narrow it down at all. "We should have taken my car. What happens if we get stranded when yours breaks down?" I tease, dropping my hand on his leg.

"I thought about it, but then what if yours got stolen? We'd still be stranded, and then who would I get a ride with when Mabel decides she needs her beauty rest?" He pats the dashboard.

"I don't think any amount of sleep will fix this level of ugly."

"Hey. Shhhh. Don't be mean to my baby." The car makes noise somewhere between a rumble and a burp. "See? It's going to be your fault if she takes a break tonight."

"Nothing that happens to this piece of junk is my fault."

A shiver runs through the car. He pumps the gas and jiggles the shifter. I cross my fingers until the shiver levels out.

"Okay. I give. Sorry. I'll never say another bad word about her. Good girl, Mabel." I stroke my side of the door for a minute for good measure.

"Better."

I'm yawning and ready to stretch my legs when he pulls into a public parking lot.

He reaches into the back seat, pulling out a little white paper bag and tossing it into my lap. "Put this on."

My fingers close on a piece of cotton fabric when I reach into the bag, and I pull it out... a t-shirt?

"What's this all about? You told me to wear whatever."

"Look at it," he says, twisting in his seat to watch me with eagerness in his bright blue eyes.

It's a Dream Wife shirt. In fact... "Is this my shirt? Why are you giving me my own shirt?"

"Check the bag again."

This time, my fingers close on a piece of paper. I pull it out to find the barcode for a set of tickets printed out. "Oh my god! You got tickets! Thank you so much."

I wrap my arms around him. "Thank you." It's the perfect gift.

"Don't worry. You can pay me back later, Starlight." He smirks at me, getting all cocky again.

"Don't worry. I will." I reach down to stroke his length under my palm, and it immediately twitches to life under my touch.

"Not now. If you keep touching me like that, we'll never get out of the car and therefore will not make it to the concert."

His face is perfection when I add one more squeeze before I slip out of the car.

"You're going to pay for that later." He smacks my ass, then loops his arm under mine.

The concert was incredible, and he had to keep swatting my hands away on the drive home. There's a party going on in full swing when we get back to his place.

"Jacks!" A happy-looking Seb stumbles up to us as we walk through the front door.

"Seb, man, good to see you."

I know how worried he's been about his friend and how happy he is to see him doing well. A girl with wavy brown hair and a sweet smile is tucked under his arm. The cause of his happiness, I've been told. They had years of struggle to get where they are, but look at them now?

"Hi." She gives me a shy smile that transforms her face. She's gorgeous, but when she smiles, she's mesmerizing.

"Hi, Abby. Good to see you again."

"Jacks. Come hang with us," Beau says.

Jacks looks between me and his friends, but I know he's mine when his eyes fixate on my chest in the tight t-shirt he brought for me to wear to the concert. It's his own fault.

"Not a chance. Some of us have incredible girlfriends to spend time with." He runs a hand up my back, stroking small circles that feel divine.

A loud wolf whistle pierces through the loud music pounding through the house, and Dev walks up. "Yeah you do."

Jacks rolls his eyes, punching his friend on the arm.

He slides his hand around my back and down until he's cupping my ass cheek through the short skirt. His fingers squeeze in a tight, possessive grasp that propels me forward.

"See you tomorrow, guys." I wave at them, and hustle to beat Jacks to the stairs.

He catches up, then stops. "Ladies first." He waves me on, so I bolt up the stairs, only to hear him thundering after me.

He slams into me as we're passing through the door, locking his arms in a tight hold, not letting me fall.

"You can run from me any time, Starlight, but I'll always catch you."

We're both already breathing hard when he kicks the door shut behind him. "Now. Strip and get down on your knees. What's your safe word? You might need it tonight. Although when I'm choking you on my dick, you might not be able to use your words. If that's the case, tap me on my thigh three times."

Holy shit. There's a challenge there, and he knows how much I hate to lose. Those words are enough to have my nipples tingling and my chest heaving.

"Clothes off or I'm ripping them off for you."

Right. I move into action, slipping my skirt off over my hips and shimmying it to the floor. His hands impatiently grip the bottom of my t-shirt, pulling it off over my head to leave me in my bra and fishnets. I reach for my bra, but he smacks my hand away.

"These are mine. I'll do it." His hands slide into the cups, and he squeezes my tits until I'm gasping. He slides out long enough to unsnap the bra and slip the straps down my arms.

He admires for a moment, then leans down to lick each nipple before his hands move down to the fishnets. I hear a tearing sound as he rips them off, panties along with them. I hope he at least left those intact.

"You've got to stop doing that."

"Do you think you're in charge here? If I want to rip those off your gorgeous legs, I will. You don't get to tell me no. Now, what's your safe word?"

"Can I use it to make you stop ripping my fishnets?"

"No. Sassy girl." His palm lands on my now bare ass with a sharp smack. "I think I'm going to have to keep that sassy mouth of yours quiet."

He strips his own clothes off, revealing a body chiseled from stone.

"Hands behind your back," he says when I reach for him, wanting nothing more than to touch that work of art. To run my fingers along the constellations painting his arms, and the unreal ridges of muscle.

He grips his length, sliding it up and down a few times. My mouth watering for a taste. He's more than happy to oblige my hunger. "Knees, now."

I sink to my knees on the plush carpet.

"Now, what's your safe word?" His brows are drawn together as he stares down at me from above. Clearly, he's loving the position of power, and I'm not hating it either.

"Sunshine."

His lips twitch in a smile. "There you go."

Nothing I like better than when my sunshine goes dark, takes control and uses my body like he owns it. There's something about surrendering control to him that makes me so wet.

He takes a step in closer, and I lean forward to lick the tip. "Starlight." He growls out my name in warning, grabbing a fistful of my hair. "Open up."

My mouth falls open obediently, and finally, finally, he slides the tip into my welcoming mouth. His skin is silky smooth, and I lick the salty pre cum off the tip.

Both hands close over my cheeks and he thrusts his hips, forcing his length to the back of my throat, pulling out before I choke on him. He's so fucking big, stretching my mouth and throat to their limits.

I reach forward to grip his thighs when I wobble on my knees, but he says nothing this time. He's too lost in the feeling of thrusting down my throat until tears run down my cheeks.

Heat is building down low, and I need to find my own release, so I push at him when he's between thrusts, tilting my head up to meet his glazed eyes.

"Can I touch myself?"

His lips spread in a smug smile. "Yes you can, Starlight. I want you to come while I'm wrecking your pretty throat. But only because you asked so nicely."

I slide a hand between my thighs until I reach the slick nub at my apex. It's already swollen with desire as I circle it.

Our hips thrust in time with one another. His lower abs touching my nose as he seeks his release down my throat. I'm clenching around nothing as the pleasure builds low in my belly, so slick I'm going to leave a puddle on the floor.

"That's so good, Starlight. You're taking me so well." Of course I am. He's mine, and I'm his. I've never enjoyed giving a guy pleasure like this so much. But his taste, his feel, everything about this feels right. Even when he weaves his fingers into my hair in a firm grip.

He gets a good hold, yanking me off his length with a sting that shoots from the back of my head straight to my center. It's enough to set me off. The pleasure explodes through my body, and I shove my fingers inside, desperate for something to clench around.

As convulsions rack my body, he shoves down deep one more time, holding me there while he groans. He shudders out his release, spurting his hot juice down my throat. Holding me there until he finishes.

By the time he yanks me off him, I'm gasping for breath, shuddering and swaying on my knees.

He scoops me up in one swift move, carries me over to the bed and lays me down tenderly.

I'm barely conscious when he returns with a warm towel to wipe off my face, then between my legs.

I curl around him when his weight dips the bed beside me, and he pulls me in tight.

"I love you, beautiful girl," he whispers, kissing the tip of my nose, each eyelid, and my mouth.

Chapter Thirty-Two

Evasive Maneuvers

Jacks

My body is sore, but my mind is content when I wake up to find my girl still in my bed. I told her I love her, and she didn't run. Maybe I shouldn't have done it. Maybe it was a bad idea, but she's still here and that counts for something, right?

"Morning, Starlight."

Her lips curl in a sleepy smile and she blinks awake, showing me those ice-blue eyes that fill with heat when she looks at me. I love melting that ice a little bit at a time. She can be her strong willed, fierce self and still fall to her knees for me. I love how she lets me take charge of her pleasure. There's so much trust in the act, now if only I can get it to transfer outside of the bedroom.

"Morning." She seems to slip back into her body. "What time is it?"

I glance at the clock on the bedside table. "It's only seven."

She groans, and I pull her curves back into mine when she tries to roll over. "I've got to get up. Get home to change for class."

I do too, but I'd like nothing better than to stay in bed snuggled around her all day.

"Fine. We should change that, though."

"Change what?" She twists around from her position, seated on the side of the bed.

"You should leave some supplies here. A change of clothes. That way, you won't have to rush off in the morning. Think how nice that would be?" A slow smile spreads across my cheeks. "We could have a little morning fun." I reach out, grabbing a handful of that fantastic ass. I've always been a boob man, but I'd hold up the world for this ass.

She's frozen, staring at me. Did I say something wrong?

"I can't keep clothes here," she whispers. "I've gotta go."

She lets me walk her to the door and kiss her goodbye, but something seems off. She's a little stiff, and her goodbye is hurried.

Seb's dark head is lying on his hands on the table when I walk in, and Abby is spinning around the kitchen making breakfast, but the rest of the guys are nowhere to be seen. I caught sight of a handful of randos passed out in the living room on my way in. Some party last night. I don't regret missing a second of it.

"Rough night, Seb." I say, banging a hand on the table next to his head.

He jerks up, moaning. "You're such a dick."

"That's why you love me." The smile falls off my face when I say the words and it hits me like a shoulder in the chest. "Fuck. I told her I loved her." That's why she was acting all strange.

Abby's beautiful singing cuts off, and she turns to me. "You did?" She looks excited. I missed having her around while she and Seb were on the outs.

"Yes. Fuck."

She looks at Seb, but he's useless this morning. His head has fallen back on his hands. "That's great... isn't it?"

"I don't know. She's afraid of the L-word."

Her face falls, sympathy written all over her expressive face. "Why?"

"She doesn't believe in love. She doesn't think she deserves love. I don't know. Her family sucks. But she said it."

"That's good."

"Except she wasn't conscious. I was looking after her when she was sick, and she said it in some delirious fever sleep. So, she doesn't remember."

"It doesn't matter. Or it does, but it means there's hope. You can convince her. Look at me and Bastian." She looks over at her boyfriend, suffering from what is clearly the world's worst hangover. "Today might not be his finest moment, but we were apart for so many years, and he tried to push me away, but we ended up back together, because that's where we needed to be. We needed each other, and you need Tasha, so don't give up."

It's kind of nice having a couple of girls in our group now to get advice from. Her and Jordan are both amazing, but I have to admit I'm jealous. I'm jealous that Seb and Woodsy got their girls. I want mine.

"What should I do? I've been taking it slow with her. We've moved on from the no strings thing to an actual relationship."

"When did you say you loved her?"

"Last night. In bed." I wince.

One of her brow arches into her hairline as she reaches into the cupboard to pull out a couple of mugs for the coffee sputtering on the counter. "Like while you were doing it?"

"No. After. She was starting to fall asleep, so maybe she didn't hear me."

"You need to tell her for real. To her face. In the light of day. And you need to tell her you want more. Be honest. Lay it all out for her. Trust me. Being open about your feelings is the only way to go. Coffee?" She holds up a mug with the team logo on it.

"Yes, please." The mug warms up my chilly fingers when I take it from her. I dump in some cream and sugar, inhaling a noseful of the stuff. "Thanks, Abby. For the coffee and the advice."

"My pleasure. Any time."

She steps over to Seb, running a hand up and down his back. "Want some coffee?"

"No." He's practically growling, but she just laughs and heads back to the fridge, humming under her breath.

It took everything in me to wait until the end of the day. I'm sitting on the steps leading up to her door, shivering in the cold February air. It's almost Valentine's Day. I'd be willing to bet my future NHL career Tasha is not a Valentine's kind of girl, but we could have our own celebration. Anti-Valentine's Day? Throw darts at cupid's face and have nasty sex with fuzzy handcuffs and a heart-shaped vibrator. I'd also be happy to take her out to dinner, but I'm easy. If I can make her mine, I'll do whatever she wants. My heart is hers for the taking, and if she crushes it under the weight of her fears, there's nothing I can do about it. Because it already belongs to her. But the thought is making it hard to breathe.

She finally pulls up at five thirty. I've only been here half an hour. Not that bad. My numb fingers don't agree.

"What are you doing freezing to death out here? Emma's home."

"She is? But she didn't answer the door."

"She should be home." Her fingers fumble in her bag, coming out with a jingle of keys.

The door squeals on its inward swing. "Emma?" No answer. "That's weird. I thought she was supposed to be home." She shrugs. "Maybe she went to Ace's."

"Can I come in?" I ask.

"I will not let you freeze to death out here." Her right eye drops shut in a wink. "Sounds like a lot of paperwork."

"I'm glad to hear you care." But her teasing is promising. She's not being as awkward as this morning.

"Of course."

She tosses her bag on the floor with the thud of weighty books, heading for the kitchen. "Want anything to drink?"

"Got any Klingon blood wine?" A deep chill has stretched all the way to my bones, and I'm worried I'll never be warm again.

"Sorry. All out. How about some tea?"

I'm not much of a tea drinker, but that sounds like an excellent idea, if for no reason but to ease the cold. "Sure. Sounds good."

She busies herself, darting around the kitchen to fill up the kettle and pull a couple of boxes down from the cupboard. I step into her, pressing my body into her chest.

"Listen. I wanted to talk to you. That's why I came over."

"Let me just get this ready." Her laugh is nervous, and I want to rub the tension out of her shoulders. She's trying to avoid this conversation, but I can't let her. Like Abby said, I have to tell her how I feel.

I slide my hands up her sides to grip her shoulders and spin her around to face me. I need to be looking her in the eyes when I say this to her.

"Natasha, look at me."

Using her full name catches her attention, and she tilts her head up to look at me.

"Look. About what I said last night..."

She laughs. "Don't worry about it. You were all sex satisfied. People say things they don't mean when they're in that state. It's totally fine. Forget it ever happened."

"That's the thing, though, Starlight." I grip her arms tighter so she can't escape. "I meant it. I love you. I can't fight this anymore and I don't want to. I love you, and that feeling isn't going anywhere." My fingers lock on her chin when she goes to speak. "Let me finish. I know we said we wouldn't catch feelings, and I wish I'd never agreed to that. It was completely moronic of me to think I could avoid falling for you. My beautiful, perfect girl. I call you Starlight for a reason. You're the light that brightens up the dark side of my soul. That shows me the way to how I want to live my life. With you. I want you in my life. Not just for today or this semester, not as a temporary girlfriend with one foot out the door, but forever. You're the best part of my day. The first thing I think about in the morning are those beautiful moonlit eyes, and the last thing I think about before I go to bed is your gorgeous tits." Her serious look wavers. "I love you, and I think you could love me back if you'd only let yourself."

I know I'm losing her when she closes her eyes, blocking me from looking into their depths. "I can't, Jackson. It's not you. It's me."

I'm vibrating with anger. "You're right. It is you." Her eyes fly open in shock. "For someone with so much love to give, you sure hate the idea of it. I know you haven't had any great examples of it in your home life, but you're surrounded by people in love. You've seen it happen. You've witnessed it all around you. So, it is you. You're going to push me away and lose the best part of your life, all because you're scared."

Her hands slap down on my chest, eyes blazing now. "I'm not scared. I'm fucking terrified. I've seen what love and relationships do to people. They make them give up their selves and their dreams, make themselves smaller, and I'm not willing to do that. Celina had a scholarship to Harvard, but Robert didn't get in, so she gave it up to be with him. She gave up her dreams to become his wife. And now what does she have? A cheating husband and a baby on the way."

"I would never make you give up on your dreams."

"Oh, yeah?" She steps into me, the heat of her body inches away from mine. "I got the internship."

I can't help but wrap my arms around her, pulling her in close. "That's fantastic."

"In New York." Her voice crumbles, and I stumble back, feeling like I've been punched in the gut. New York.

"I thought the company was in Seattle."

"They have offices there, and in New York, and California, and it just so happens that they've offered me a position in New York."

"But can't you..."

"No. See, it's already coming up. Can't you move for me? Can't you rearrange your life for me? And I can't. I won't. This is my dream job. The opportunity I've been waiting my whole life for and I'm taking it. And hopefully they'll offer me a full-time position once the internship is over. You see. It can't work for us. I'll be in New York. You'll be in Seattle." She shakes her head, pulling away from me.

"But we could..."

"No. We're not doing the long-distance thing. We're not going to both suffer until we eventually grow to hate each other. We're going to leave this thing behind us that was never meant to be more and we're going to move on with our lives."

My breath catches in my throat. This can't be happening. "You might be able to just leave all this behind you. To toss me aside like it meant nothing, but I won't. I'm willing to figure out how to make this work. I'd do anything to keep you in my life. You hear that? Anything. If it meant not signing with Seattle and ending the season as a free agent, I'd do it. I've got some bargaining power. I can try to work a deal to end up on the team I want. If that's New York, fine."

She looks terrified. "No. You're not getting it. I don't want you to do that for me. I'm not going to make the sacrifice for me, and I don't want you doing that for me, either. That's what kills love. That's what turns people against each other. So, no. I'm not going to let you do that."

I slide my hands down to clasp hers. "Please, Tasha, I love you. Don't do this to me, to us." Now that I've let the words loose, they're flowing out with ease. But she still won't say them back and it's killing me. "Don't leave me."

Her resolve is weakening. I can see it in her eyes. She wants to stay with me.

"Can we just keep this going? What we've got is good. We're dating and we care about each other. We've got a couple of months left in the school year to figure things out. Don't cut and run now."

I wrap my arms around her, desperate to keep her there, and the stiffness in her body melts.

"Sunny," she says, leaning into my chest.

"Starlight. I've got a date planned for us. Don't bail out. You're going to love it."

"Okay." She tilts her chin up to me, meeting my eyes.

CHAPTER THIRTY-THREE

STEALING HIS LIGHT

TASHA

The pungent smell of yeast and maybe a sour hint of vinegar surrounded us from the minute we walked into Salazar's. The tour guide is pointing out the stacked barrels housing different batches of whiskey.

Jackson snags my hand, pulling me into a shadowed corner. The curved wood of a barrel digs into my back. His hands slide under my ass, hoisting me up until I'm sitting on top of it. His cock is hard, pressing against my core as he leans in for a kiss. A hand trails down and around my side until it brushes the side of my breast. I gasp into his mouth.

"Guys. Come on. The tour's moving." The interruptions bring me back to my senses.

"Fuck off." Jacks mumbles into my mouth.

I shove him off. "I don't want to miss the tour."

"Fine."

I lean into the hand the cups my cheek then brushes an escaped strand of hair behind my ear.

We break apart, giggling as we trot after Aspen to catch up with the group. I would hate to get kicked out and miss the rest of the tour.

"You guys are terrible." Aspen scolds his friend, but there's a smile on his face as if he's actually proud of him.

I thought he'd take us on a solo date, but instead he invited his friends and their girfriends along for the distillery tour. Is he trying to show me an example or something? This is what happy couples look like. Or does he think it's less likely to scare me off if it's not one on one? Regardless, he couldn't have picked a better date. I love whiskey, but I've never been to a distillery. Learning about the technology they've implemented to make the process both more efficient and sustainable also hits me in my nerdy engineering little heart.

We end the tour in a cozy room that has the same tang in the air. There's a long, curved bar that looks like it's been carved out of a tree trunk with matching stools for us to perch on.

We settle in, and the tour guide passes us over to the expert behind the counter. He's got a full dark beard, crinkles around the corner of his rich amber eyes that match the whiskey he's pouring, and a leather apron.

"I'm Hendriks. I hope you enjoyed the tour. Where are you guys coming from tonight?"

"Lakeview," Aspen pipes in, taking the lead as usual.

They chat about the college, and it descends into hockey. Can't help it when you're around these guys, but I don't mind. I'm only just getting to know Abby and Jordan, but I can see us being friends.

In fact, I can see myself fitting so easily into every part of Jack's life. It's the future where I don't see how this can work out. Everything is so uncertain now.

"What's your plan for next year?" I turn to the girls.

Abby's smile genuine smile stretches up to her golden-brown eyes. "I'm moving to LA. I'm a songwriter." She drops her eyes to her hands clasped on the table.

"And a freaking amazing singer," Jordan pipes in.

A blush rises to Abby's cheeks. "Thanks, Jordan."

"You deserve it." Jordan divides her attention between Abby and me equally, and I feel welcome. Accepted by them even though I'm still new to their little group. "Aspen's most likely going to be in Chicago. I'm planning on staying here to help manage the store for the year. Traveling back and forth to visit will be a bit of a pain, but we've known each other for fifteen years. We can handle it. It's not that far."

"And then?" Everything about Abby is a little quieter than Jordan, but the smile she has for her friend is wide and proud.

"I'm scouting locations in Chicago to open a second branch of Top Shelf. Only this one is going to be exclusively romance books. My dream come true."

"That's amazing. I read more sci fi than romance, but I know there's an enormous market for it." I turn back to Abby. "What about Sebastian? Have you guys figured...

sorry I'm prying. Never mind." Heat creeps up the back of my neck. It's been on my mind so much lately that I forgot myself. I don't have a right to ask her about that. We don't know each other that well yet.

I'm pretty sure I spot some actual hearts in her eyes at the mention of her boyfriend. "It's okay, I get it. We're graduating. We've all got things to figure out. He's hoping he'll get signed with the team out there. He was off last year because of an injury.

But what if he doesn't? The question is on the tip of my tongue, but I hold it in.

Her eyes narrow, as if she's reading my mind. "LA might not pick him up. That's a fact of life for these guys. They could end up anywhere, and even if you end up together, they could get traded down the line."

Jordan nods. "Part of the life."

"Doesn't that scare you? How are you going to make it work?"

"We will. I love him enough. We've been through enough together that we'll make it work no matter where we end up."

"Yeah, Aspen and I have been best friends since we were kids. We've been through so much together already. What's a little traveling and moving?"

"But you've got ambitions too? Are you going to just up and abandon your own dreams to follow them around?" Maybe I'm bringing the mood down on our dates, but I really need to know. I need to know these fabulous women aren't going to abandon themselves so their men can live out their dreams. Like my mom did. Like my sister is doing.

"Never. I've worked my ass off for my dream. But that doesn't mean I won't make a compromise here or there, and he will, too. That's what love is all about. Working together and making compromises that work for you both."

It's the compromise thing for me. Somehow it feels like these hockey guys, with their passionate love of the game, are not the ones that are going to end up letting go of pieces of themselves for their girls. It's always on their women.

The chandelier made of whiskey bottles hanging over the smaller table we moved to after the tasting casts a soft glow on Jacks' golden hair. He's just too damn pretty. Keeps sucking me back in with the innocent look in those big blue eyes. I know all too well that he's about as far away from innocent as a college guy can get. But that's fine by me. That's not the problem. The problem is the other look in those eyes. The intense one that hints at longing, and the other L word. It's terrifying.

"What did you think?" He asks me with a smile, clasping my hands under his warmth.

"This was pretty fantastic, Jacks. I have to say for a guy who never dates, you're pretty good at planning the perfect one. Why did you bring your friends along, though?"

My head tilts to the side as I study the sharp lines of his face.

He takes the time to think about his answer, tilting his head to the side. "I thought you might be more comfortable with a group date. It might have been too intense with just the two of us. Plus, this place is amazing. I wanted to share it with my friends."

He's right. This place is full of shadowy corners and intimate lighting. After our blowout yesterday over the L word, I might have been more awkward alone with him.

He squeezes my hands under his, reading me in a way that makes my skin itch.

Why does this big goof ball who takes nothing seriously, have to get all deep on me? When we started this thing, I thought he'd be the perfect fit. Not looking for anything but a one-night stand, but now here we are.

"I guess."

"You know I'm not completely unfamiliar with dating. Before college, I had a girlfriend. For a couple of years."

When I glance up in surprise, he's ducked his head down, shielding his expressive eyes from me. "Really? You never told me that." He's dropped the odd hint that made me wonder, but I've been trying so hard to keep my distance, not dig too deep.

"I try not to think about her."

"Really, why? What happened?"

He sighs. "You know about my sister's illness. It wasn't a quick thing. She was fighting off and on for years, but the last time. The time that finally took her it wasn't good. At home or at school. I was angry, and scared, and I didn't want to talk to anyone about it, so I avoided people. I was busy at home, helping my parents keep everything together. They were so consumed with looking after Jess, and after she died. They were really broken for a while, so I mostly looked after myself, and sometimes them too. Cooking and cleaning. Getting myself to hockey. I didn't have time for her. I think when it came down to it, she was into me when times were good. She liked the glory of dating the star hockey player, but she didn't want to do any of the work reaching out when I wasn't going out to parties every week and doting on her."

I suck in a sharp breath, getting sucked closer to him by the magnetic draw he has over me. "That's terrible, Jacks. I'm sorry she did that to you."

He leans back. "Yeah, I was too, but then I realized I was better off without her. If she hadn't done that to me back then she would have let me down eventually, and that's part of the reason I swore off dating after that. Fucking around, great. Relationships, not so much. Hurts too much when you lose someone you care about. Although now that I think about it, I think it may have been more about the hurt of losing my sister than Lena. So, you see, Tasha, you're not the only one who struggles with trust. But it seemed like when the right person came along, I had to take a chance."

Me. He thinks I'm the right person for him, but I'm not so sure. He's taken me on this perfect date, surrounded me with his friends, and I feel like an imposter. I don't fit in here with this happy group. I'm not willing to give up on my dream, and that dream is likely to take me far away from him soon. The thought of hurting him like his former girlfriend did is crushing. One hit like that he can recover from. Two hits and I'm not so sure. I don't think I want to steal that light out of his eyes.

My mouth slams shut when the waiter steps over to us with a sample of local cheeses and assorted meats on a shiny tray carved out of another tree. I'm barely paying attention as the waiter rambles through the list of cheeses and meats. Even that basket of crispy toasted bread slices isn't capturing my attention right now. I've got one foot out the door already.

"Thanks so much," Jacks says.

I nod and push my lips into a semblance of a smile.

He slices off a piece of white cheese, placing it on the bread and rolls up a slice of cured meat to top it with, but instead of jamming it into his mouth, he offers it to me.

My appetite has vanished, but I reach out a hand to take his offering, taking a couple of nibbles from it. A smoky smell rolls across my palate as I chew, but it tastes like dust in my mouth, getting stuck in my throat on the way down, leaving behind a lump. I drop the slice of bread onto a small plate in front of me.

Jacks moans, eyes rolling back in his head. "This is so good." He looks up from his ecstasy eyes falling to the half-eaten bite in front of me. A frown pulls his brows together. "Not hungry?"

"Not really." I sit back in my seat.

His throats bobs as he swallows the olive he jammed into his mouth. "Is something wrong, Starlight?"

I shut my eyes, steeling myself for the conversation I don't want to have. "It's just. You're such a good guy, Jacks. I never would have known it if we hadn't done this thing, but it's true."

His jaw works hard, as if he's trying to keep his emotions inside. "Uh oh. Is this the it's not you it's me conversation?" His laugh comes out wispy and weak.

"I know how bad that sounds, but it's true. Our lives are moving in different directions, and I'm going to hurt you like she did. It's better if we end this now. Before we implode."

He leans in, his eyes glittering. "That's bullshit, Natasha. You promised me you'd try, but you didn't. Not really. You're going to run scared before this even has a chance. Before we have a chance."

My skin is hot and tight, trying to suffocate me. "This isn't all on me. I told you from the beginning that I didn't want serious. This was only ever supposed to be a sex thing. The only promise I ever made was that I wasn't going to fall for you." But I did, didn't I?

"That's right. You promised that, but you know what? You fucked up because you fell for me. You fell for me, and I fell for you, but turns out I'm the only one brave enough to admit it. I think I fell for you the minute I crashed into you at Roller Park. Took me a little while to admit it to myself, but I wouldn't have kept coming after you if I hadn't."

My eyes are fixed on the chandelier hanging over the next table, not willing to look him in the eyes. "You're right." My lip is trembling. "I fell for you, but I don't think it's enough. Not when our dreams are taking us thousands of miles apart."

"This isn't just some college crush that won't survive after graduation. I love you, and I know you love me back." His knuckles are white now with how hard he's clenching his fists.

"What are you talking about?"

The grin stretching his lips is a little manic as he leans in. "When you were sick when you were asleep. When you weren't standing in your own way. You said it. Those words you're so afraid of. You told me..." His voice breaks on the words. "You told me you love me."

My breath catches in my throat. Did I? I couldn't have.

"That's right. You may not be able to admit it when you're awake, but your subconscious mind knows the truth."

I shake my head, dismissing the claim. "I was feverish. I could have been saying anything."

His head bobs. "You could have, but that's what you said. And stupid me, I thought I could convince you to acknowledge it. But that's not how it works, is it? Your heart is locked down so tight, Danny Ocean couldn't unlock the key."

"I don't know what I said when I was asleep, but in the end, this is for the best. It's better to end it now before we're in too deep."

"Too fucking late. I'm already there, and you could be too if you'd just let yourself. I'm all in. I'd do whatever it takes to keep you by my side, but I can't force you. It has to be on your own terms."

I'm so used to comfortable silences between us that the awkward one feels like we're caught in some kind of time loop. "I... I can't, Jacks. I just can't."

"Fine. You pretend to be so strong, so independent. You say you want to live for yourself and make your own decisions, but you're letting your fear control you, and that's just sad. I hope you figure it out, Tash. I really do because I want nothing more than for you to be happy. And I want to be the guy who makes you happy, but even if I can't be, that's what I want."

He pushes up from the table, walking over to the counter to pay the guy for the uneaten meal.

He's taking up too much space when he strides back over to our table, holding out a hand for me. "Come on. I'll call you an Uber. I can catch a ride with Abby and Seb."

My hands are as icy as my heart, but I know I'm making the right choice. I push up from the table, following him to the door. I say bye to the other two couples without making eye contact.

My hands are wrapped around my chest to keep my limbs warm from the chilly air, and he makes no move to touch me.

When the little blue car pulls up in front of the building, I step forward to get in.

"If you ever let go of your shitty past to embrace a fucking fantastic future, let me know. Maybe I'll still be around. But if I'm not. That's all on you, Starlight."

The look on his face is like a punch in the gut. As if he was used to life in a warm, cozy home and I kicked him out without even a blanket. But his words have me curling in on myself, recoiling from the pain.

"Goodbye, Jacks."

CHAPTER THIRTY-FOUR

NO SHOT

JACKS

The green figures are a blur today. I'm so focused on the puck. I don't see the huge dude coming up hot on my left side, but it doesn't even matter. Dev sweeps in, slamming the guy out of the way before he can make contact.

"Eyes!" Aspen calls out, but I don't need the reminder.

Tonight it's me, the puck and the ice. I'm so focused, and it's paying off. I've already scored two goals tonight and I'm angling for a hat trick. If I can't have her, then all I've got is hockey, so I'm going to give it every ounce of my being. Let the sport drain me dry and chase away the feeling that's lingering in my chest. As if my heart has been crushed in a vice that never lets up. The only relief is the adrenaline pumping as I make a push for the net.

This was always my number one dream anyway. I remember my promise to my sister and push forward. I'm going to do this. I'm going to achieve my dream like I promised her I would. Because she couldn't.

Every game this season has brought us closer together as a team. We're moving like we're sharing one mind. Seb flips the puck to Aspen, who looks for his opening. Beau's got his back. All their defenders are hanging on to the jerseys of the golden trio. I don't know what the team's going to do when we graduate next year. Doesn't matter. I'll be on to bigger and better things.

I slide left and right, weaving through any opening I can find until I'm free and clear with a prime shot on the net.

Aspen is skating it forward and I'm pretty sure he's gonna help me out, but he passes it to Seb instead. Fuck me. I need this goal.

I slam my stick into the ice, skating around the back of the net. Seb's got no shot. It should have been me, and he knows it. What was Woodsy thinking? Now I've got a tail. I race toward Dev, looking for him to help me out again, when the crushing weight of a massive body slams me into the glass. The sound of it rattling reverberates through my skull before I hit the ice.

I'm gasping for breath like a fish, knives ripping through my chest.

The medic comes for me. Fuck no. The game's almost over and I didn't get my hat trick. She ignores me when I shake my head at her, pulling me up and off the ice.

If I could only force the words out, I'd make her let me go back out on the ice, but it's a no go. With me out, Coach switched up the line, anyway. To anyone else on the team, it doesn't really matter. We've got a two-goal lead with not enough time left on the clock for State to catch up. But I wanted this. Off the ice. Away from the thrill and the speed, all I can think about is her. Her soft pink and black hair, hard edges, and glacial eyes.

"I'm fine," I growl at the woman attending to me. Sure, the entire left side of my body is throbbing while the right side is on fire, but I can breathe, and my head is clear.

"You know I have to check you over, Vaughan. Protocol."

She winces at the crack of my fist slamming into the wall beside me but doesn't back down. "Why are you so angry, anyway? You guys pulled off a tidy win." She winds an unnecessary bandage around my ribs. Sure, I'll be bruised and aching tomorrow, but nothing's broken.

"I was almost there. I could have had a hat trick."

"You hockey players. Out of all the athletes I have to tend to, you guys are the worst. You'll play with broken limbs, spit your teeth out on the ice and keep skating. Remember, you're only in college. Save a little of that spirit, and maybe preserve your body for the big leagues."

"Sure."

Her glossy lips are pursed as she studies me with a healthy amount of well-deserved skepticism.

The horn blares and I can hear the celebrations of the crowd from back here. I want to be there, inhaling the energy. Dragging it in deep to chase away the emotions I swore I'd never let myself feel again.

Stella is objectively cute. She's a few years older than us, brown hair pulled back in a tight ponytail and strong hands.

I let my lips slide into the smirk I haven't used in a while, running my eyes up and down her body. She's got some curves underneath the black jacket zipped up to her chin.

"Watcha up to later, Stella?"

Her expression is amused. Am I losing my touch? Has all this one-woman bullshit messed with my game?

"I'm going home to my boyfriend after my shift is done, Vaughan."

That was a solid shut down. Doesn't touch me at all. I'm sure I can find one or two other someones who would be happy to help me forget.

CHAPTER THIRTY-FIVE

HALL OR NOTHING

TASHA

Max comes barreling at me the minute the front door opens, leaping up to plant his massive paws on my chest. I laugh, stumbling backward as a long wet tongue swipes up the side of my face, leaving a slobbery trail behind.

"Max. Get down!" Nora rushes in, grabs his collar, and yanks the big dog down before he can get to the other side of my face. "I'm so sorry Natasha. You're going to want to turn around and walk right out the door at this rate. This place is a madhouse."

As if to prove her point, the twins come racing into the room screaming at each other.

"Mom! Braden touched my horses."

"Well, she told me I did my homework wrong. I didn't."

"Kids. Enough. Natasha is here. Did you want her to stay or would you rather she walk right back out that door? Because I'm not leaving the house if you two are going to act like a pair of feral dogs."

My lips are twitching up that the corners, but I stifle the laugh that's threatening to bubble out. I know better than to encourage them.

"Tash!" Bethany races up to me, throwing her small arms around my leg, and I smile. This is exactly what I needed. To get out of my place. Every day after school, I've gone home to an empty house more often than not, and the evidence of him surrounds me. The bouquet of chocolate bars taunted me from the front hall table until I finally tucked it away into the top shelf of my closet and buried it under a fleece blanket. I thought about throwing it away, but that would be sacrilegious. Only crappy chocolate belongs in the garbage. Even the rink holds memories now. He and his giant teammates stuffed into purple tank tops to cheer us on. Ugh. It was a good decision. The smart thing to do. We couldn't have made it work.

But my chest feels a little empty whenever I think of him.

I run a hand through Max's silky ears and turn to Nora. She's smoothing her hands down her hips over the black dress that's hugging her curves. It's good to see her dressed up like this. I'm glad I agreed to babysit. She deserves the break. Plus, Braden and Bethany are pretty fun when they're not trying to commit fratricide. Is that the right word?

"Ok. You know the drill. Emergency numbers are on the fridge. Only call me if someone requires stitches or the house is literally burning down, and have fun.

Adam walks in, letting out a wolf whistle when he spots his wife. "Looking beautiful, honey."

A thousand-watt smile brightens her face, minimizing the tired lines around her eyes. "You don't look too bad yourself, darling." Her eyes rake down his body from the blue button up to the crisply ironed black slacks.

They've been married for a dozen years or so and they still look at each other like they haven't seen each other at their worst.

An uncomfortable pinch in my gut has me shifting on my feet. One case proves nothing. I've seen more than enough unhappy marriages to prove my point.

"We'll be fine. Right, guys?" I turn to the twins with one brow arched in a question that's more of a command.

They seem to get the point. Nodding and smiling gap-toothed grins at their parents. The only thing missing are miniature halos floating over their golden heads.

"Have a good time. Don't worry about a thing. Just enjoy yourselves."

Nora hesitates for one more second before sliding her arms into the black wool coat her husband is holding out for her. "Thank you again. Remember, bedtime is at 7. Don't let them try to convince you otherwise. One story each and then straight to bed." She and her husband give each of their kids a hug in turn, before heading for the door.

"Got it." This isn't the first time I've looked after our little neighbors downstairs.

Two sets of big blue eyes turn to me as soon as the door clicks shut behind their parents.

"Can we bake cookies?" Braden asks, hopefully.

"Can we play roller derby?" This request comes from Bethany, my little future derby star. She thinks I'm some kind of celebrity or something and it's adorable.

"No to the cookies, but we'll order pizza for dinner, and maybe I'll add on the cinnamon sticks. But only if you behave, sir." I boop him on the tiny nose, and he nods eagerly.

"And yes, we can play roller derby, but only in the hall. I don't want you knocking any glasses off the table like last time."

"But it's more fun if we can use the entire house."

"Hey. That's the deal. Hall or nothing."

"Fine," she huffs. That girl is going to be a force to be reckoned with one day.

I collapse on the big grey couch after I've finally gotten the two kids to stay in their beds. It sucks me in like a hug and I drop my head onto the pillow that has Max's goofy face on it, complete with lolling pink tongue.

As if he's jealous of the pillow, he chooses that moment to bound up to me, licking my hand. I push him down when he tries to jump on the couch but stroke the soft top of his head when he obeys.

The twins kept me busy and exhausted, but now that I'm alone, I've got a little too much time with my thoughts. I pick up my phone to check my messages one more time, and there's nothing new. My fingers automatically slide to his name like they have been way too many times a day since I walked out on him. He's still listed as Horny Student. I never got around to changing it. Instead of making me laugh, though, seeing it there has me blinking away tears.

Still waiting is the last text he sent this morning. I ignored it, but I didn't delete it. I should just get it over with. But when my thumb swipes the message to the side, I can't quite hit the delete button.

I resist the urge to check the score of the game they're playing tonight, instead picking up the remote to surf the channels idly. Of course, all the romance movies pop up first. It is almost Valentine's day. What a stupid holiday. Very few people are actually happy on the day. They're either worried because they're spending way too much money on a mediocre dinner, or they're alone.

I'm browsing the sci fi recommendations when Star Trek pops up. The ache in my heart intensifies. No way. No way has he ruined my favorite show. I click on it, probably to prove to myself that I can handle it.

The swooshing noise of a door opening is not coming from the screen and the first thing I think is that it's him. My ring tone.

Nope. My heart sinks. It's my sister. Should I answer? No, but she is my sister, raging bitch or not, and she rarely calls, so I hit accept and press the phone to my ear, curling my legs under me on the couch.

"Hello?"

A sniffle is the first noise to greet me.

"Natasha?"

My family refuses to call me Tash or Tasha, no matter how many times I ask.

I sigh. "Yes."

"Robert's gone."

I sit up in my seat, immediately alert. "Gone? Gone where?" Knowing my sister's flare for the melodramatic, it could be to the corner store.

"He left us."

"What happened?" I drop my voice to a soothing tone.

"He cheated on me."

Am I a bad person for rolling my eyes? I know he cheated on her. She knows he cheated on her. Everyone within our family's inner circle knows he cheated on her. But she's been pretending it never happened for so long I didn't think she'd ever admit it.

"I'm sorry."

"What are you sorry for?" Her sharp tone lashes out at me through the speaker. "You didn't do anything, did you? Did you sleep with him too?"

Ew gross. "No, of course not."

"Well, Melinda did, and now he's leaving me for her."

Disgusting. Melinda is her best friend. How could he do that to his pregnant wife?

"Oh. That's terrible. I'm so sorry. What are you going to do?"

She sobs. "I'm moving back in with Mom and Dad. At least until the baby comes. Then we'll see."

This tracks. She's never lived alone for a day in her life. She wouldn't know what to do with herself all alone, with a baby. I'm sad, but I'm angry too. That she let herself get to that place. Where she can't even look after herself. I would never let myself be so reliant on a man that I had to go running home if he left me. Guilt scrapes at me under my skin, though, for the judgy thoughts. I'm not being fair. We both had to grow up in that loveless house, and we both delt with it differently. She let our parents quash her artistic aspirations, choosing to attend business school instead. She followed the guy who never treated her right to school and clung to him as if he might be able to provide the things she really needed. What did I do? I went the opposite way, but all this has done for me is to leave me hollow and empty. Alone with my ambition and an ache in my chest that won't go away.

"Well, that's good. At least you'll have them. If you need anything, please let me know. I'll do whatever I can."

"What are you going to do, Tasha? It's not like you live close enough to babysit. There's nothing you can do to help."

Even when I'm trying to help her, she's digging at me. She's hurting, I remind myself.

"If you need to talk. Let me know. I know I'm too far away to help much, but I love you, and I'm so sorry. I can swing down and stab him in a dark alley if that would help?"

A quavery laugh breaks through her tears. "I don't think that would be the best idea, as delightful as it sounds. My baby should still have a father, even if he's a sleazy cheating piece of shit."

There it is. The side of my sister she tries to hide under her perfect image. She's got a little of the bad ass in her too, hidden underneath all the designer clothes and expensive handbags.

"I guess. But let me know if you need help to come up with a less violent revenge plan. I've got more than a few ideas socked away for a rainy day."

"Thank you."

I hear Mom's voice in the background. God, I can't imagine having to move home after my taste of freedom. Never.

"I've gotta go."

"Ok, sis. You look after yourself and the little nugget."

"I will. Thanks for listening."

"Anytime."

"Bye."

"Bye."

My hand falls to the couch after I hang up the phone. What an absolute shit show.

All the reasons I left Jacks in the first place come rushing back. I can't believe I was wavering at all. This ache in my chest will go away. It's way better than the complete shattering collapse my sister is going through right now. She's got nothing left. Her dreams are long gone, and now her life is going to be consumed with being a mom. And there's a simple solution. Don't get too close.

CHAPTER THIRTY-SIX

BURNING BRIDGES

JACKS

There's a tiny construction crew drilling away on my skull from the inside. My fuzzy brain tries to trace the words to the thought that's trying to break through. Construction crew. Right Habitat. I was supposed to help on the site today. This will be the second week I've missed if I don't show up. What the fuck time is it? I roll over and open my eyes into tiny slits to check out the angry red numbers on my clock. The pounding triples or quadruples in intensity from the sliver of sunshine streaming through the gap in my curtains despite my effort to keep out as much light as possible.

What did I drink last night? My stomach flips when I roll over, leaving behind a queasy feeling that has my ears ringing while I swallow back the moisture that's gathering in my mouth.

"Oh, god." What the fuck was I thinking?

Right. A trail of tiny confetti hearts leads to the way to Seb's room, where I hear a feminine giggle. Valentine's Day. I went to a frat party to drink away the emptiness of a Valentine's Day spent alone. It's never bothered me before. In fact. Before Tasha, Valentine's Day was prime pickings. Lonely single girls are always looking for a guy to fuck away the tears.

The girls weren't any different this year. But I was. I couldn't do it. My mind was fixed on her. I checked out the tits and asses they were waving in my face. I even looked at the pretty faces to see if anyone appealed to me, but they didn't. No one really reminded me of my Starlight, but there were pieces of her everywhere I looked. A pale substitute. Pink hair, sculpted muscles emerging from tiny straps, blue eyes. None of them tempted me, though. Not in the least.

I feel like a bag of shit for not showing up for the build today though. Great excuse, Vaughan. I was too hungover because I can't deal with my own feelings. But the thought of being that close to her without being allowed to touch causes an ache far worse than the massive self-induced headache.

There's a faint smell of coffee wafting up from downstairs, so I make that my mission. Coffee first.

Cole is the only one in the kitchen today. Seb and Aspen of course spent the night with their girlfriends, Dev and Beau probably went to train. I'm the only one who wasted away the morning wallowing.

"Cole."

"Hey," he says, not looking up from the paper he's got his nose stuck in at the table. He's got to be the only college student at Lakeview who reads a physical copy of the paper.

I glare at Cole when he doesn't look after the piercing shriek of his phone.

"You gonna get that?"

His dark eyes pop up over the top of the paper. "Are you going to get it?"

Oh shit. I changed my ring tone. Right. I grab the offending thing off the kitchen counter, where I must have tossed it in my drunken stupor when I stumbled home last night.

"What!" I bark into the phone. Literally willing to do anything to make it stop.

My trembling hand flies to my stomach to hold everything in when a tidal wave swells at the sound of the voice on the other line.

"Vaughan."

"Dan. Hi." I swipe my hand across the back of my mouth and smooth down my hair as if my agent can see me on the other end of the line.

"We've got a problem. Seattle caught wind of some photos of you making the rounds on campus and they're not impressed. There's talk about cutting you loose."

"What?" It's an entirely different tone from the harsh one I answered the phone with. "What pictures?"

"Drinking, girls, partying. Everything you swore you'd lay off of after the last incident."

"Oh, God. I didn't do anything with any girls." Didn't want to. No one compares to her.

"Mmm hmm." Doubt is heavy in his words. "But you're not denying the rest of the charges?"

I can't. It would be an obvious lie.

"Look, man. It's been a rough couple of weeks."

"I don't give a shit about your excuses. You're on the verge of a professional career. If you can't act like a professional, then I haven't got the time of day for you."

He's bluffing, right? He's not going to drop me over a handful of pictures doing regular college things.

"Your coach also messaged me you didn't show up for your volunteer shift last week. Is that true?"

"Yes, but I can't go back there. I'll find somewhere else to volunteer." Sin had an entire list of opportunities. None of them sounded appealing, but it's gotta be better than suffering there.

"What did you do to burn that bridge, Jackson?"

"I didn't do anything. It wasn't me. There was this girl." It's not right. Not right to describe her that way. My heart. And why am I even discussing this with the shark of an agent I barely know?

His bitter little snickers slice straight to my core. "There it is. A girl. You promised you were done with the man whoring for the year. What did you do?"

"I was done with it." I have to defend myself. "It wasn't girls. It was one girl, and I didn't do anything. She broke up with me."

"One girl? You've been dating one girl? For how long?"

He doesn't need the exact terms of our relationship. That probably wouldn't do me any favors.

"Since November, but she broke up with me a couple of weeks ago."

"A girlfriend. I can work with that. I can spin that in your favor. You've been at the top of your game on the ice and things have been quiet enough for the last couple of months. I think we can make this work, but you'll need to make some sort of public declaration. A media statement after your next game talking about how in love you are, and you can't wait to bring her along on your future career. That should repair the damage. They'll skip over the drinking and partying if you're in a stable relationship." Acid burns the back of my throat.

"But I'm not. Like I said. She broke up with me."

"Well, fix it. Fix whatever you did and mention her after the next game. The media will be happy to latch on to that story. I'm glad that's cleared up. I'll call you if I need anything else from you. Bye."

The line goes dead, and I pull the phone away from my ear, staring at it in disbelief. Now I have to pretend like I'm happy and in love? That won't bite me in the ass or anything. I'm completely disgusted with his slimy suggestion, but I'm also a little desperate.

"What was that all about?" Cole asks, snapping the paper in his hands as he flips pages.

"My agent's a dick."

"Aren't they all?"

Now I've got to come up with a plan to pull this shit off. Even thinking about it makes me uneasy. Maybe I should look for a new agent.

CHAPTER THIRTY-SEVEN

FRAUDULENT THOUGHTS

TASHA

"Tasha, this is getting old." Emma gathers a pile of tiny wrappers that are scattered around me on the couch and spilling over on to the floor. Then she has the audacity to swipe my phone right out of my hand.

"Really, Natasha? Are you really doom scrolling the Lightning fan sites on Insta? You've sunk to a new low."

"No, I haven't." The protest falls flat when her pointed gaze lands on the bag of mini Matcha Kit Kats I've been mainlining, while I punish myself with pictures of Jackson partying it up while I'm at home sulking.

She shakes my phone in my face. "I have eyes, you know. I can see exactly what you're doing?"

"What do you care?"

"I'm your freaking best friend. Of course I care if you're being a flipping idiot and grinding your own happiness under your heels."

I snort. "He's the one out there partying it up. Didn't take him any time to move on, did it?"

I snatch the phone back, scrolling to one particularly incriminating picture. It's clearly the shaggy back of his golden hair standing way too close to a girl who has her red talons resting on his arm.

Emma snickers.

"You think that's funny?"

"Oooh, a picture of him standing next to a girl. How incriminating."

"Well then, what about the interview we saw last night? You can't make excuses for that one. He's moved on. He's got a new girlfriend."

Emma wanted to watch the game last night, and I couldn't make myself go there, but I snuck a peek at the local coverage afterward where he declared his love for some girl. He went on about how happy he was and how she was the one he wanted to spend the rest of his life with.

She rolls her eyes at me. "He was talking about you."

"Obviously not. We're not together." I made sure of that, doing my level best to push him away for good.

"Natasha. You are a very intelligent woman. He was talking about you. Did you hear the words he used? Fierce, strong, independent. The smartest girl he's ever met. You're going to graduate in the top one percent of your engineering class. He was talking about you."

"Why would he lie about that, though? We're not together."

She taps her foot on the floor, her little button nose scrunching up. "I don't know why he would do it, but I'm sure he had a good reason. Hmmm. If only there was some way to find out why? I feel like there's some way to talk to people when they're in a different location. What could it be? Telegraph, nah. Fax? That's not right. Oh yeah. That thing in your hand you've been torturing yourself with for the last two weeks. Ah. Yes. A phone. That's it. Get your head out of your ass and call him."

"I can't."

"Yeah, you can. Although personally at this point. I don't think a phone call is adequate after what you put that boy through. You need to show up and tell him how you feel. Maybe grovel a little and beg for him to take you back."

"I don't grovel." It's almost a growl.

"There she is. That's my girl. I knew you were still buried down there beneath the sugar high, the greasy hair, and the moping."

"Thanks. Such kind words."

Her lips quirk up at the corners. "You're welcome. That's what best friends are for. Truth bombs. Now get your ass up. We've got our last session for this round of Foundations today. You're coming. No excuses."

"Fine."

"Good girl," she says and a weak flame flares up when I think of those words on another set of lips. I shiver.

My under used muscles stretch as I glide around the obstacles, leading our Foundations group in a last obstacle run around a brand-new track we set up for them. I feel like myself when I'm out here. I can't believe I let my melancholy drag me under so far that I've missed some of our practice sessions recently. That's not who I am. Out here, on the track, I feel powerful. In control.

We finish the run, slamming into each other for a round of hugs and high fives.

"Ok, ladies. Dance party time."

Jo takes my cue, cranking up the music with a crackle of the aging PA system. Music quality is not the point. We shake our booties and wiggle our hips to the beats, skating backward and forward with varying levels of skill to celebrate a successful end to the session. Every one of these women showed up, handled some falls, and learned to get back up on their skates. I always learn from them as well.

Emma skates out in her signature inflatable pink flamingo costume, and everyone laughs.

My skates clatter as I race over to the microphone.

"Hey, everyone. Eyes on me."

The din quiets down as they zero in on me.

"I want to thank you all for coming out to hang with the Ladies of the Fight." I pause as a cheer swells the room accompanied by the stomping of skates and a handful of whistles that could take out your eardrums.

"It's been a fantastic session. You've all done amazing, and you know what that means? Chocolate!" I toss bars at them. "Some of you have been invited to move on to the Intermediate Derby class. The rest of you are welcome to do the Foundations lessons again. Join us for some Learner Scrimmages or just enjoy the new skills you've learned on your own."

More cheers.

"You've all embraced something that's new and a little scary, and I hope you've enjoyed your time here, learned lots and you're going to take all this newfound confidence out into the world and fucking rock it!"

The cheers get louder at this one.

"Congratulations, my rebel ladies. Be brave, stay true to yourself, and roll on!"

The rest of the team skates in tight, Jo and Cherry flanking me, while Emma continues to do loops in her ridiculous costume. And I love it. I love these ladies, and I'm so proud of them, but an unsettling feeling wells up inside me. I feel like a bit of a fraud. Here I am telling them to take chances and live their best lives. All while I've been cowering at home, because I wasn't brave enough to accept the love that was offered to me wholeheartedly. I am a coward. Jackson was right.

I pass the mic to Cherry, and push off, bending into a crouch to increase my speed as I skate for the change room.

Flamingo Emma skates up behind me. "Where are you in such a hurry to get to?"

"I've gotta figure something out. I'll probably need your help, but I'll let you know.

My phone is in my hand before I've unlaced my skates and I make the first of a few important phone calls.

"Hi, Abby, it's Tasha. Can I ask you for a favor?"

CHAPTER THIRTY-EIGHT

HOME TURF

JACKS

My eyes stray to the stands way too many times, as they always do these days. Ever hopeful she'll be there, but as usual, there's no sign of her. I'm deluding myself at this point.

I drop a gloved hand onto my jiggling knee, attempting to still it. It's hard watching the end of the game from the bench. We're playing our last exhibition game before the semis, and with a handful of our strongest players graduating at the end of the year, Coach has been trying to give some of the second line players more ice time where he can. My eyes have been glued to the puck, watching every steal, every goal, every missed pass. Cole is on fire out there. He'll definitely be the top player on the team next year. Honestly, if it weren't for Seb, Aspen, and I, he would have been on the first line this year, but we're the golden trio. I'm going to miss them.

I jump to my feet with the rest of the crowd when he backhands the puck into the net, pulling us ahead by one.

Seb keeps giving me weird looks.

"The fuck is wrong with you, dude. Don't you already have a girlfriend?" I think I'm only being crusty with him because I'm jealous. It hurt so much to say all that bullshit in my interview. All the bullshit I wish was true.

"Nothing," he says with a smile.

We step out onto the ice to celebrate our win with the rest of the team when the horn blares, then do a little victory lap. Aspen throws an arm out to stop me when I make my move to skate off.

"The fuck, dude."

"Hang in here for a minute. They're doing some special presentation."

"What?" I don't have time for this. I'm sweaty, and tired and irritable. All I want is to shower and head back to our place to binge some Trek. I know. I'm a glutton for punishment.

My heart stops, then restarts double time, pounding in my ears when I spot the familiar faces on the ice. It's her. On a pair of ice skates for a change. Here she is on my turf. Fuck me. If I thought she couldn't get any hotter, I was wrong. She's a goddess on the ice. A goddess in fishnets, black shorts that form a second skin on her ass, and a purple jersey. Not mine. Her derby jersey fits her curves to perfection. Why is she here?

I barely notice her friends, spread around the edges of the ice, riling up the crowd.

"Good evening, my fellow fans. We're here tonight to celebrate the amazing season our Lightning are having." Her confident voice rings out through the stands. She's no stranger to speaking in front of a crowd, so she's holding them and me in thrall. "Come on, give them a hand."

Thundering stomps echo across the ice, but they ease up when she gestures with her palms. They're eating out of her hands. Like I did every minute I was privileged to spend with her.

"I'm also here to represent another team you might not have heard of. Thanks for giving me this time." She nods toward the sidelines where Coach is standing. "I'm Natasha, also known as Tasha Scar, and these are the Ladies of the Fight."

She spins around gracefully on the skates, pointing to the rest of the team before lifting the mic back to her mouth.

"We're part of the local roller derby league. Anyone ever seen a derby bout live?"

A smattering of applause rings out.

"Well, for those of you who haven't, let me tell you, you're missing out. You think these guys are brutal? You should see us ladies jamming."

Whoops, hollers, and catcalls ring out.

"If any of you are interested in joining, we'll have our next Foundations session coming up in a couple of weeks. You can find us at Lakeview Ladies of the Fight dot com.

You can also check out our upcoming schedule there if you want to come see what we're all about. Watch us put these hockey guys to shame."

More laughs and cheers.

"That takes care of the business side of things, but I had an ulterior motive when I came out here tonight." Her voice has been strong and steady throughout her speech. Until now. Now her voice is wobbling a little, and I the mic is shaking in her hands.

"This is a little more personal, so I hope you'll bear with me."

"You see, I've always prided myself on being strong. Standing up for what I believe in, following my dreams. That's how I ended up here. I love the derby life. But I've discovered recently that I've been a coward at the same time. You can be both things at the same time. Brave and cowardly. Who knew?"

She pauses, struggling to get her voice under control. Where is she going with this? It can't be what I'm thinking, right? It's not about me.

"Anyway, a few months ago I met this really great guy, and we had this thing. It was amazing. Best... everything I've ever had, but I pushed him away because I was terrified. I was terrified he'd break my heart, hurt me, control me, take my dreams and ambition away from me. Don't get me started on why I thought that. You'd need several sessions and a psychology degree to get to the bottom of that."

My vision has tunneled to her. I can't see or hear anything else. The roars of the crowd have faded away.

My teammates beside me don't exist. Everything comes down to her.

"But I need to let go of that. I've been teaching all these women to be brave while I've been hiding from my own feelings. Enough of that." She hands the mic to Emma, standing tall at her side, and pulls something out of the bag she brought out with her. The purple fabric unfurls from her fingertips, and she drops it over her head. Need, want, love. All the feelings swell up in my chest at the sight of my name and number emblazoned across her back. The jersey's so big it falls almost to her knees, covering her hands, but it looks better on her than the sexiest lingerie.

She grabs the mic back, spins around and skates straight for me. She's slower on the ice than she is on wheels, and the anticipation is killing me.

My heart is pounding faster than it does in double overtime. I can hardly breathe when she reaches me, one hand falling to my padded shoulder, the other holding the microphone between us.

"Jackson Vaughan, I love you. Will you be my boyfriend?" She looks vulnerable, scared of the rejection I could never give her.

I toss my gloves on the ice, grab the back of her head and seal my lips to hers, making every promise I can without words.

She leans into me for a minute, sliding her tongue in to meet mine, tangling her fingers in the sweaty post game mess of my hair, then pulls away and lifts the mic back up with a shudder.

"What do you think, everyone? Was that a yes?"

The arena explodes. I'm a little jealous. I don't think I've ever heard them this worked up.

"Fuck yes! A million times, yes," I say into the mic before peeling her chilled fingers off of it and handing it to Aspen.

The next words are for her alone.

"I will go anywhere for you. I will follow you around the world. Learn to love punk rock. Take you to every Star Trek convention we can find. But most important, I will never stop loving you. You stole my heart the first time I opened my eyes to see the stars in yours. And I will spend the rest of my life proving to you that you're my equal in every way, and every decision we make will be a team effort. I love you so fucking much, Starlight."

CHAPTER THIRTY-NINE

PORTABLE SUNSHINE

TASHA

I 'm on my feet almost the entire game. I've tried sitting down, but it never lasts. Every time someone slams into Jacks, I can feel it reverberating through my side, and every time he gets a shot on goal, I'm chewing on my lip. At this rate, I'm going to nibble all the lipstick off before the game is over.

"Is it always like this?" I turn to my right and ask Jordan. She's been to lots of these games over the years with how long she's known Aspen.

Her lower lip pushes out in a pout. "Always, but a big game like this is the next level. I'm so glad I got to come this year."

They've made it to the third period with one goal apiece, and it's killing me. I've never been this nervous about one of my own bouts. But this is a big one. The finals. This is the make-or-break game. If they take it, that's it. They're the champions. Ending their college hockey careers on a high note before moving on to the big leagues.

Beau skates in front of a defender from the other team, letting Aspen pull ahead to snag the pass Seb tossed at him. I'm tucked in between Abby and Jordan, who are competing to see which ear they can steal my hearing from first.

Jacks is trying to get away from his shadow and failing, and I squeeze my eyes for the briefest of moments before opening them again. I don't want to miss the action.

Our side of the crowd gasps when Aspen shoots it forward before it gets stolen, but one of the other team's D-men steals it before it can reach Jacks. His reaction is immediate. He slips forward, snags the puck from between his opponent's legs and flips it into the net over the goalie's glove. That was freaking incredible.

The crowd agrees, taking down the house with their cheers. What a move.

The rest of the game is a nail biter. We're fighting for every inch. The puck is back and forth across the ice so fast my eyes hurt from tracking it, but after a nail-biting final half of the last period, it's over. We're on our feet cheering our boys on. I'm jumping up and down.

Our boys are out on the ice, arms wrapped around each other while they accept the trophy, get their pictures taken. It's going to be a helluva celebration tonight.

An eternity passes while we wait for them to shower and change, and talk to the press, but I've got my girls with me. I'll miss them next year as much as I'll miss my derby girls, but there's so many good things to look forward to that the heaviness in my chest can't sink me.

The minute I let go of my fear, I called Emerge-En and asked if I might be able to serve my internship in Seattle, and they said yes. New York was a dream, and maybe I'll still get to live there one day, but I've learned that sometimes compromising one dream is worth it when the reward is so intense.

So I get my dream job and my dream guy. And we're moving to Seattle, which will be a crazy amazing adventure we get to experience together. It may rain a lot there, but I've got my own personal sunshine to keep me warm. Speaking of...

They come walking toward us, shadowed at first, but as soon as his eyes land on me, he's all I can see. He looks delicious in his grey suit, hair damp from the shower, and I want to be by his side all night while he celebrates the big win. But first I want nothing more than to get him back to the hotel room, so I can strip that suit off piece by piece.

The heat in his eyes as he stares at me in his jersey lets me know he feels exactly the same. He can't close the distance between us fast enough, arms slipping around me to lift me up in his arms and spin me around.

My heart's soaring when I close the gap between us.

"Congratulations," I whisper into his ear, before his large hand closes around the back of my neck, turning me to meet his lips.

My legs wrap around his hips, and I can feel his hard length against my throbbing core. We can't take this back to our room fast enough.

He pulls away long enough to say, "You look so fucking hot in my jersey."

"Not as hot as you look in mine." I nibble on his ear, laughing.

Soon we'll have a new home, new jerseys, and a new life, but as long as we're sharing it, I know everything will work out just fine.

CHAPTER FORTY

CHAPTER 40

TWO MONTHS LATER

The past month has been incredible. My stomach is fluttering with nerves now that I'm headed to training camp with my new team tomorrow. Tasha has settled in perfectly at her internship. When it comes right down to it, I think she's actually braver than I am.

The door of our apartment swings open, and she bursts through looking hot in her black pencil skirt and blouse. She's stayed true to herself, though. Her fancy work blouse has a subtle skull print pattern scattered across it.

"I've gotten assigned to a new project, and it's perfect." She stops. "Wait, are those cookies? Did you bake for me?"

I walk out in nothing but my red apron, wielding a spatula with a swagger in my step. "I was stress baking. Smartie cookies. You want a taste?"

Her eyes trace my bare arms, the hint of chest peeking out from the top of the apron, and then I spin to give her the full show.

She laughs, racing up to me to smack my ass as I walk back into the kitchen.

"Was that a rhetorical question? I always want a taste."

I keep walking, swearing, when I snag a cookie fresh from the oven off the tray. She swats my hand away when I offer it to her over my shoulder and her hand slips under the front of my apron.

"Maybe once I start training, you can return the favor," I say to her in a voice gone husky with need.

"We'll see if you earn it."

CHAPTER FORTY-ONE

EPILOGUE

TWO YEARS LATER

"**I**'m so glad you ladies are here tonight." I wrap one arm around Cherry and one around Jo after we pile out of Emma's car.

"Hey, don't forget about me." Em slips under my arm to shove herself in the middle of our group hug.

I squeeze her tight. "I could never forget about you. Since you're basically a stalker, and you followed me to Seattle." After Ace turned out not to be the perfect guy, she packed up her life and moved out here. It's been great having her back for the last few months.

"Shut up." Her sharp elbow slams me in the gut. Nothing I didn't deserve.

"Aw, Baby Slice. You know I love you. Enough of this love fest. Let's get in there." My stomach hasn't stopped churning all day, and now that we're here, I'm feeling a little lightheaded. Got to pull myself together.

We break apart, heading for the back door of the abandoned box store. The metal bar creaks a little as we push through.

Cherry and Jo return my fist bump.

"Wish you could lace up with us, but it's nice to have you here, anyway. You can totally come to practice on Saturday before you fly out." I've grown to love Seattle. Its energy is fantastic, the people are amazing, and my job couldn't be better. It would be great to have these two out here as well, but it's a bonus that I always have a place to crash in their tiny apartment in NYC. I like to travel there to hang out with them sometimes when Jacks is at away games.

My heart's pounding so hard I'm worried it's going to burst through my chest by the time we hit the track. There's a decent turnout tonight, but I've only got eyes for one person. My man is sitting right up front, wearing a Rain City Rippers shirt with my name on it. The fluttering wings in my stomach temporarily still when I lock my eyes with those bright blue ones of his. He's beaming at me from under the overgrown golden bangs falling over his brow, and a warm glow starts in my chest, spreading through my numb limbs.

Aspen and Seb wave at me from their seats beside him. I wish I could have seen his face when he got home from practice to find them waiting for him. Those idiots better have taken that video I asked them to. The other guys couldn't make it out, but the fact that these two showed up is a testament to their friendship. Our own little mini Lakeview reunion.

"Tasha Scar. Get your shit together." Mackenzie barks at me. She's our team leader, and I know better than to piss her off.

"I'm good, Mack." I nod to her.

"You better be." Her words are harsh, but her eyes are soft with understanding. "You bring all those cocky hockey boys into our house we've got to be at one hundred percent."

She doesn't need to tell me. Watching how successful Jacks has been on his new team sparks that competitive flame like nothing else. They made it to the playoffs last year but lost in the second round of their conference. We won our derby regional championships, but the state championship slipped through our fingertips. This year we're both going all the way.

"Go, Rippers!"

The bout flies by in a blur. I don't even realize we've won until the announcer calls us for a victory lap. "Congratulations to your winners, The Rain City Rippers led by Mack Sabbath!"

My legs pump, getting me around the track one last time before Emma's little hands shove me toward the announcer's stand. Right. I drag down a huge breath, grabbing the mic, and skate out to the middle of the track, spinning around to face the crowd. My eyes land on my sister and niece. I'm so glad she made it out. Wait, is that ... Mom? She's got my mother with her. I don't even know what to think about that. Sure, she's been reaching out a little more since Dad got sick. He's getting treatment and doing better, but they both seem to have realized that life is short and are making a bit more of an effort to stay in touch. Our relationship is tentatively better than before, but I never expected her to come out for this.

My hands are a little shaky on the mic when I turn back to Jacks.

"Hey everyone." I give a little wave, clearing my throat. "I'm going to borrow your time for a moment longer."

"For those of you who don't know me, I'm Tasha Scar." Cheers rattle the sky-high windows.

"Thanks. I'd like to invite someone up here with me. You might know him as Jackson Vaughan, star rookie for our very own Seattle Sirens. Or you might not, because who keeps up with hockey around here?"

Laughter is competing with the cheers.

"Anyway, to me he's just Sunny. Come on up, Jacks, don't be shy."

His eyes are wide, and he's mouthing, "What the fuck?" At me while his friends shove him.

Once he pulls himself together, he stands up, sweeping his arms in the air and bending in a few deep bows. Of course. Big show-off that he is, can't resist playing it up for the crowd.

I keep my eyes locked on him as he makes his way over to me, rubbing a hand down my fishnet covered thigh before grabbing his. It closes over mine in a comforting squeeze.

"Sunny."

"What's going on, Starlight?" His words are too quiet for the mic to pick up clearly.

"You know I love you. I wouldn't be here in this amazing city with this fantastic group of ladies if you hadn't come crashing into my life. Literally." Scattered applause rings out. Since Jacks has about zero filter and a huge media presence, all of Seattle probably knows the story of how we met.

His laugh has a nervous edge to it.

"We might not seem like a perfect match from the outside, but somehow, we work. You make every single day a little lighter, a little more fun, and you drive me freaking insane sometimes." He smirks. "But I love how you challenge me to be a better person. You make me whole. And so...." I scrabble in the waist pouch Jo passed to me after the bout. "Will you drive me crazy for the rest of our lives? Will you marry me, Jackson?" The bright overhead lights glint off the golden ring in my palm.

His mouth is hanging open, and I can't read his expression. The twisting of my stomach intensifies. Is he annoyed with me?

He leans into the mic. "Are you kidding me, Starlight? Way to steal my thunder."

"What?" I pull back.

He reaches into the pocket of his jeans. "I was going to propose to you. I've been carrying this around for weeks. It was all planned out." He pulls out a small grey velvet box.

My chest shudders with laughter. "You always were too slow to keep up with me. Better get your skate coach to work on your speed."

He leans, brushing aside a stray lock of hair to whisper in my ear. "You like it when I take my time." Tingles break out over my entire body at his words, and now I can't wait to get him home.

"Wait. So, is that a yes?" I shove at him to get a little distance. It's entirely possible I could self combust if he doesn't give me a bit of space.

"No."

I gasp as he drops to one knee.

"Starlight. You're my world. That day I knocked you over at that shitty roller rink was the best day of my life. I say was, because every day I've gotten to have you in my life has been a little better, and the day I get to slide my ring on your finger to make it permanent. I can't wait for that. So, Tasha Scar, will you marry me?"

My smile spreads all the way up my face, his eyes falling to the dimple I've grown to appreciate. "Fine. But just remember. I asked first."

The crowd goes bananas, cheering and stomping, calling out our names. And I hold out my hand. The dark metal ring is cool and smooth, sliding onto my ring finger as if it belongs. It's got a deep purple stone instead of a diamond. Perfect. I never thought I'd be the marrying type, but I've never been more certain of anything in my life. I want to spend the rest of my life with this ridiculous man.

He pops to his feet, holding his left hand out to me. I make my claim on him, liking how my ring looks on his finger almost as much as I like seeing him with my name on his back.

We crash together to seal the deal. His lips are soft under mine. Familiar and new at the same time. Our first kiss as an engaged couple. He fists my sweaty ponytail, dragging me in closer until we're welded together. I slide a hand around his waist, inching toward that fantastic ass. His back muscles flex under my palm.

"Break it up. You're in public." A teasing voice breaks through my trance.

I tangle my fingers in his soft golden hair, tugging him to me for one more searching kiss before pulling away.

The audience is losing their shit. My friends and family surrounded us while we were lost in each other's arms.

"Sorry about that. Got a little carried away." I say into the mic still clutched in my hand.

"Congratulations." Emma rolls over for a hug.

We get swarmed with affection. Hugs and congratulations from all of our friends. We're surrounded by so much love it almost hurts.

"Congratulations, Tasha." My sister walks over to me once the crowd eases up a bit.

"Thanks, sis. And you too, Greyson." I grab my nephew's tiny foot and he kicks it out, giggling with that wide smile of his. I don't get to see him in person enough, but I've watched him grow up over Facetime. Celina went back to school this year. She's figuring out who she is on her own for the first time, and with a new baby by her side. I'm so happy for her.

"Natasha. Jackson. Congratulations." Mom walks over, giving me a brief hug.

"Thanks for being here, Mom. We're going to head out for dinner. You coming?" The thought of her in our favorite local restaurant is kind of funny. It's got amazing local food, but the atmosphere is far from the five-star dining she's used to.

"Yes. I'll join you."

I turn to my sister, and she gives me a small nod.

"Great. I've got to get changed, but I'll meet you all at the Lion."

Jacks won't let go of my hand, following me down the hall to our change room in the back.

"You know you can't go in there with me, right?" I glance down at our joined hands.

He leans in, crowding me until my back hits the cool surface of the wall. One arm is propped above my head, caging me in when he dips down, hovering above my lips.

"One more kiss."

I comply, capturing his full lower lip between my teeth and biting down. He slips his tongue to slide against mine. One hand slides up under my shirt until he grazes the skin just below my breast.

Skates clatter down the hall toward us and we break apart.

"Go on." I flick my eyes up to meet his. They're clouded over with lust.

"I'm going to wait right here for you, so make it snappy."

"What about your friends?"

"They can wait. I'm here for you, Starlight. Future Mrs. Vaughan."

"How do you know I'm going to take your name?"

He tilts his chin up, Adam's apple bobbing. "You're right. Maybe I should be Mr. Deveraux?"

I shake my head. "Nah. You're my family now. I'd rather share your name any day."

"Good. Because you're mine. I think you were always been meant to be mine. My friend, my lover, my girlfriend, and pretty soon you'll be my wife."

Wife. I like the sound of those words way more than I should.

"Make it so."

***

Cole's story is coming soon in **The Game**. If you're curious about his story and you love a fake dating romance, preorder The Game here.

Two Friends. Two Days. One Bed. What could possibly go wrong? - If you haven't read Aspen and Jordan's story yet you can get it for free when you sign up for my newsletter, along with bonus content (maybe some more Tasha and Jacks scenes), contests, and all my latest writing shenanigans. Author Nikki Jewell

Thank you for reading my book. I hope you enjoyed getting to know Jacks, Tasha and all their friends. I've got lots of plans ahead for these characters and I really look forward to sharing the rest of their stories with you.

If you enjoyed this book, share the love. Reviews are the best way to get a book in the hands of other like-minded readers.

If you'd like to keep up with all the latest steamy shenanigans you can follow me on Instagram, Threads, and TikTok @nikkijewell_books or check out my Facebook Page.

instagram.com/nikkijewell_books

tiktok.com/@nikkijewell_books

ACKNOWLEDGEMENTS

It's never easy to write a book, but Jacks and Tasha were so much fun. I'm going to miss them when I move on to the next in series. So first of all thanks to them for being such colorful characters. The mouth on you, Jacks...

I couldn't have published this book or any without the support of my husband, who has been by my side every step of the way. Every time I have to hole up in my writing cave for hours on end to meet a deadline, you're there for me. I love you always. To my amazing children. As always you're my inspiration to live my best life. Kisses, hugs, and all the love. PS maybe don't read these books.

As always, shout out to Steph, girl boss extraordinaire, and my bestest friend. I hope your like Tasha. Her strength, attitude, and STEM aspirations remind me of you.

This book would not be what it is without my editor Susan. You helped bring this up to the next level. Your insights were so spot on, you made me laugh, and cry, and your enthusiasm for my characters was fantastic. I'm looking forward to finding out your thoughts on Cole.

To my cover designers. Taylor at Sweet 15 Designs LLC. Sorry for making you look for sexy men that day, but it paid off. These hockey dudes are hot. You're the best and thanks for supporting the indie author community. Hope Brown at Nerd Sisters Designs looked after the discreet paperback cover and it is fire. Those colors. Stunning. I'll definitely be back for the rest of the series and to grab some awesome swag for my hockey boys.

And to Meg at Literary Inspired. Thanks for taking charge of my ARC team. You've been fantastic, and I'm looking forward to working with you more throughout the year.

The authors of the Write 10K in a Day group have been so inspiring and I'm going to get that half a mill this year. It's happening.

20Booksto50K. This group has been an incredible help on my publishing journey. I had the privilege of attending the Vegas conference in 2023 and it was life changing. Thank you so much to all the authors and service providers I met there for selflessly sharing their knowledge and experience. 2024 is my year to level up.

My Mastermind Goddesses, you ladies are amazing, and I'm looking to achieving amazing things with you this year.

And to the people I met in Vegas, thank you. In particular, Alby, my conference bestie. I made the right choice when I sat down next to you the first morning of 20Books. Our daily check ins have been so helpful. Sorry I fell of the boat the week before my publishing deadline. I'm the problem. It's me. And my chaotic brain. But you inspire me to keep writing and achieving my goals, and I can't wait to eat under the mushroom with you when we're 6 figure authors.

ABOUT THE AUTHOR

Nikki Jewell is the queen of steamy romance and sipping coffee like it's her lifeblood, and she's always up for a new book boyfriend. Whether it's one she wrote or someone else's creation. She has a coffee addiction so legendary that she's even convinced her coffee beans to write her a thank-you note.

When she's not mainlining caffeine, Nikki is busy crafting tales of passion, love, and swoon-worthy heroes. She's especially fond of athletes, celebrities, and rock stars, so you'll find lots of those in her books. Her steamy romance books have been known to raise temperatures, set hearts aflutter, and make readers swoon in public.

When she's not writing, she escapes the confines of her writing cave to wander the great outdoors, communing with trees, birds, and squirrels that judge her for drinking coffee in the wilderness.

Nikki's secret identity as a romance writer is so well-guarded that her twin children don't know about her double life. But let's face it, what kid wants to read about their mom's romantic escapades? Probably none. Her husband is in on the secret and he's the real-life hero who keeps the inspiration flowing, even when her characters refuse to cooperate.

So, if you're in need of a fictional escape filled with passion, laughter, and maybe a few coffee stains, Nikki Jewell is your go-to romance guru. Just be sure to have a fresh brew on hand and monitor your heart rate—her stories have a tendency to make it race!

The Red Line is the second book in the five book Lakeview Lightning College Hockey Romance series. You can follow her on Instagram, Threads, and TikTok @nikkijewell_books to keep up with her latest shenanigans. She's got a new Facebook page that she doesn't know what to do with as well.

instagram.com/nikkijewell_books

tiktok.com/@nikkijewell_books

Made in the USA
Coppell, TX
26 February 2025

46427469R00215